CHRISTMAS WITH THE KNIGHTS

HANNAH LANGDON

Storm

Ebook ISBN: 978-1-80508-399-3
Paperback ISBN: 978-1-80508-401-3

Cover design: Rose Cooper
Cover images: Shutterstock

Published by Storm Publishing.
For further information, visit:
www.stormpublishing.co

For Rose
Love you more!

ONE

The party sparkled with Christmas magic, even this early in the season, and I looked around with satisfaction at the results of our hard – sometimes gruelling – work over the past few weeks. Although there were some big events still to come for my company, this was the biggest, held in the opulent Dome of the Victoria and Albert Museum and attended by major influencers as well as stars of fashion and TV. Even my mother was there, although of course she had been far too busy being fabulous to spare the time to speak to me, the lowly events organiser. But there was nothing lowly about this event. The space was staggeringly beautiful, with its high ceiling, gallery and marble floor and columns, not to mention the extravagant glass Chihuly chandelier which hung centrally. The people holding the event, a television and film production company, had given us a brief which was wide open and creative: my favourite kind.

'We want something fabulous, obviously,' said China, the woman who had hired us. 'It has to *scream* Christmas but absolutely no kitsch, unless it's heavily ironic.'

Sam, my business partner, glanced over at me and grinned. We were used to these sorts of demands, and it was part of our job to interpret them and deliver exactly what our clients wanted, and often what they didn't know they wanted.

'Got it,' I said, scribbling notes in my book. 'Any particular colour scheme or theme?'

China regarded me through narrowed eyes.

'Well, *obviously* we don't want any sort of over-the-top Christmas theme – no, oh, I don't know, reindeer or elves or anything.'

'Understood.'

'But given the new TV show, there must be a nod to fashion, without it taking over the party.'

I wrote all this down. The show she mentioned was in the popular mould of taking a group of people – in this case, skilled clothes designers – and culling them week by week by judging them on various tasks, then eliminating them until one exhausted soul was finally crowned the winner.

'So,' I said, glancing up at China's immaculately made-up face – how long *did* it take her to get ready in the morning? 'Fabulous, Christmassy but not tacky or themed, fashion. We'll get some ideas to you by the end of the week.'

And now, as I stood and ran my eye over the finished space where the guests milled around screeching at each other, their minds only on who would be most useful to talk to, I thought we had done an excellent job. We had decided to use the space itself as our theme, particularly that stunning chandelier, decorating enormous real Christmas trees with specially commissioned sparkling glass decorations. Vastly oversized wreaths created with hundreds of matt emerald green and gold baubles hung from the gallery, and Sam and I had spent hours wrapping empty boxes in shiny paper and tying them with huge ribbons to place in enormous piles under the trees. As the space was called 'The Dome', we had turned over ideas relating to this for a week. Eventually, we had decided to hire enormous glass domes, underneath which were displayed iterations of famous dresses, in tasteful Christmas colours. One held a royal wedding dress in emerald-green silk with gold accents, under another was enclosed a recreation of Marilyn Monroe's *Seven Year Itch* dress, but green rather than white. Its reimagining was gorgeous, and I would have loved to try it on, but firmly under the dome it stayed, and I had to look elsewhere for a suitable dress. There was even a nod to Björk's swan, which had been created with a peacock instead. We had mined the museum's archives for more flamboyant representations of peacocks, then given our favourite of these, a glorious wallpaper by Walter Crane, to an artist who had used it to inspire an extravagant design for the invitations, menus and place setting cards. A four-piece band played jazz versions of Christmas songs and carols and guests were being offered a special cocktail that a mixologist had created for the occasion; made with Green Chartreuse and shimmering with gold lustre, it was proving very popular.

'It's a triumph,' said a voice beside me, and I turned to see Sam. 'You've pulled it off again.'

'Thank you. China told me she was *satisfied*, which is probably the most gushing she ever gets.'

'I saw your mother and she was very complimentary – she said it was one of the most elegant Christmas parties she'd ever been to. Have you seen her?'

I laughed drily.

'No, of course I haven't. She wouldn't want to hobnob with the staff – except you, of course. And she may well tell *you* that, but she'd never dream of saying it to me.'

Sam nodded sympathetically. He and I had known each other for years, and although he got on well with Mum, he was under no illusions about how tricky our relationship could be.

'Look, Fallon, why don't you go home? Talitha and I can look after everything from here. You've barely slept over the past month; I'm worried about you.'

Truth be told, I was worried about myself, but I shook my head stubbornly.

'Thanks, but no. The clients expect me to stay until the end, and I will.'

'I think you need a break, darling. And not just tonight – a proper break from work.'

I shrugged. 'But I can't take one, because there are too many jobs coming up.'

'Jobs that you've already done all the work for. Talitha and I can easily oversee them while you take some time.'

'And what would I do? Where would I go?'

'Anywhere you can get some time to yourself? I'm deadly serious, Fallon. At least agree to think about it.'

'All right, I will think about it,' I said, not for a second intending to. 'But for now, I'm going to go and make sure the waiting staff know which wine to serve with each course.'

I marched off, determined to do my job thoroughly and see the night out, even as the balls of my feet screamed in pain, my eyes longed to close, and my head buzzed with everything that had to go right.

The party finished at two a.m., and I didn't leave until nearly half past three, having overseen the clearing up and made sure that everything was left immaculate. We often worked with prestigious venues like this one and wanted to be sure we would be welcomed back. I thanked the taxi gods as an orange 'for hire' light appeared almost as soon as I left the building. I fell in gratefully, glad to be out of the cold night air, gave the driver my address and slumped back to stare out of the window for the short journey home. Once inside, I greeted my sleepy little dog, Runcible, kicked off my shoes and slipped out of the glamorous dress I had worn, putting it carefully on a hanger to return to Marcella, the designer I had rented it from.

It was about the only thing in my flat that *was* in the right place: my exacting standards at work sadly did not extend to home and the place was a disaster. There were unwashed clothes spilling out of the hamper, clean ones waiting to be put away, books and magazines strewn everywhere, and several used mugs dotted around. The bathroom looked all right if you only gave it a cursory glance, but I didn't dare move too many of the myriad bottles as I was sure the hidden corners were manky. I pretended to myself that I maintained an acceptable level of hygiene in the kitchen, but the truth was that there was a light layer of greasy grime on everything, and so much clutter on the small work surfaces that it made getting through to clean them seem like a Herculean task. I hated living in squalor, but the task of sorting it all out felt overwhelming, given how drained I already was. I had started, once or twice, but quickly felt panicky and despairing, so I just did the bare minimum and promised myself I would take some time when work slowed down. Which it never did.

Now, I stood in the bedroom, in my underwear, suddenly wholly unable to make the simple decision about what I should do next: have a shower, eat something, go straight to bed? My mind pinged between these basic possibilities as if they were life or death decisions, and I could feel my heart begin to race as my breathing became shallow. The more I tried to force a decision, the more I panicked, until eventually I collapsed onto the bed and started crying, great tearing sobs wrenching through my body, my throat aching with the gasping effort. All my attentions were on trying to calm myself down, so it was a moment before the urgent knocking on my front door registered.

'Fallon! Fallon! Please open up!'

It was Sam's voice. I dragged myself to my feet, yanked open the front door and fell into his arms.

'Oh, my darling, my poor darling,' he said, hugging me to

him as he kicked the door shut, then helped me to the sofa. 'Come on, breathe, that's it, in and out.'

As he coached me, rubbing my back, his soothing voice eventually had an effect and the gasps turned to gulps and then calmed altogether as my chest released slightly and I began to relax.

'Sorry,' I said, sniffing, and reached for a tissue. 'I'm okay, just a bit tired.'

'Fallon,' he said sternly, wiping my eyes like I was five years old. 'You are not okay. I knew that tonight, which is why I came over. If you were okay, you would not be sitting here sobbing in your underwear at four o'clock in the morning.'

That made me laugh, even as tears still dripped down my face.

'Sorry about the underwear, too, not that you care,' I said. 'To be fair, I wasn't expecting you. I'll go and put something on – I'm cold.'

I ran to the bedroom and grabbed a dressing gown, avoiding the mirror as I was sure I looked beyond terrible. When I returned, Sam was in the kitchenette, making tea.

'I assume you don't want anything stronger?' he asked.

'Definitely not, although maybe I'll need it, if you're about to lecture me.'

'I'm only lecturing you for your own good. You've done an amazing job with the business, but you've been working too hard. You cannot carry on like this, and as your friend as well as your business partner, I cannot let you.'

'But I can't possibly bail out at this time of year – it's too busy.'

'I disagree. As I said before, everything is in motion, and Talitha and I can handle it. In a way, it's the *best* time of year to take some time off, before all the new bookings pour in. You're on the verge of burning out, darling, and if you push it too far, you'll end up having to take even more time. What about those headaches you keep having?'

'I can get on top of them with painkillers,' I said sulkily, knowing he was right.

'Well, I'm staging an intervention,' he replied. 'You must take some time off. Starting tomorrow.'

'But I'm seeing my mother for lunch tomorrow,' I protested. 'I'll need to do some work either side of that for the mental health benefits.'

He pulled a face.

'Ha ha. Monday, then.'

'Monday's the last day to finalise everything for that law firm's Christmas do. I promise – *promise* – that I will take some time after that. I know I need to.'

Sam smiled.

'Great. A nice, relaxing break over Christmas will do you the world of good.'

If only we had known then how my 'nice, relaxing break' would end up, he might have been less confident.

TWO

FIVE DAYS LATER

For many people, being alone in a car with my mother for four hours would be a dream; it was my idea of a nightmare. But nevertheless, here we were, hurtling up the motorway and probably both glad of the fact that the back of the chauffeur-driven car Douglas had sent for us came equipped with a couple of bottles of champagne.

'Your suitcase is very small – are you sure you've brought enough clothes for the time we'll be there?'

Twenty minutes of silent sipping since our last conversation about why I couldn't get some highlights – as my greys were sure to be coming through soon, given what my mother considers to be my advanced years – and this is how she breaks it. Funny how I seem to be catching her up in age, rather than the gap between us remaining the same, but that is just one of many mysteries my mother is fond of nursing close to her ample bosom. Others include my father's identity and exactly what goes into her morning 'vitamin mix'.

I sighed, wishing I was tucked up on my sofa at home watching daytime TV, stroked Runcible's head, with its random sprouts of hair, and replied:

'I'm sure it'll be fine. After all, I'm going to relax and recuperate, not much else, so hopefully all I'll need are pyjamas and fleecy leggings.'

As I had slightly intended, my mother almost choked on her champagne.

'*Leggings?*' she hissed. 'Fallon, I didn't bring you up to wear *leggings*. Please tell me you have *something* presentable with you, or we'll have to go shopping as soon as we arrive. It is Christmas, after all – you'll need some sparkle.'

And, as she had fully intended, I instantly capitulated.

'No, of course I do, there's no need for that.'

'And what about the James Bond cocktail party Douglas has arranged to welcome us? Have you got something for that? Please don't tell me there is just a can of gold spray paint in that suitcase?'

I snorted with laughter.

'Now *there's* an idea! Why didn't I think of that? No, I'm having something delivered tomorrow – you'll like it.'

'It's not about *me*, darling. I've told you how into Bond Douglas is, he'll be very disappointed if you don't make an effort.'

'Why *does* he love it so much? I'm a bit surprised, I thought it would be a bit... I don't know, clichéd, I suppose?'

'It is – unexpected,' admitted Mum, 'but it's just something he's loved ever since he first picked up one of the books. Apparently, he's got quite a collection of memorabilia at the house in Yorkshire. I've seen his Aston Martin, of course, but not much else. Anyway, if he wasn't such a fan, we never would have met, so it was obviously meant to be.'

That was true: my mother and Douglas had met at a Bond convention. He had attended as a superfan and she was there because she had had a very small part – blink and you'd miss it – in *Octopussy* and, coupled with her fame as a soap actress now, was hugely in demand for these occasions. She would be in her element at this themed welcome party; I was dreading it and could only bear going because I liked Douglas and he was, after all, hosting me for Christmas.

'What are you going to wear?' I asked, nervous of any mention of a white bikini. She smirked.

'Wait and see. Just please make sure your outfit is suitable – and *fun*, darling. It wouldn't kill you.'

'So, not Oddjob, then?'

She glowered at me but didn't reply and we fell into silence again. I gazed out of the window as the scenery flashed past. I am so used to frustrating and disappointing my mother by not being anything like her that I tend to weaponize it now, mainly to push home the message that there is no point in her even trying. She would so love a glamorous, charismatic daughter to show off and share her clothes with, but, while I am perfectly acceptable-looking and even enjoy a good pair of heels when the wind's behind me, I am somewhat lower-key than she is, and she has never forgiven me for it. My mother is called Jacqueline Honeywood, although of course that isn't her given name. That was Jackie Woodcock and is one of the few of her many secrets that I know. She changed it when she got her first acting job, and it has served her well in her stellar career as a soap actor, looking good as it does splashed across magazine covers and newspaper gossip columns. If you ever want to upset my mother, the quickest way is to abbreviate her name; she has worked hard to distance herself from what she describes as her 'common roots'. I told her once that she shouldn't use the word 'common', but she was typically unrepentant. 'That's what we were, darling, and I'm glad we're not anymore. I'd rather be a snob, if anything – some people do care which way you hang the loo paper, darling, even if you don't.' And I really don't. She named me after her favourite character in the 1980s' American soap opera *Dynasty*, and I can only feel that I got off lightly because I didn't end up being called Krystle or Sammy Jo.

Fallon Honeywood is memorable, which is useful when you run an events company, but not so silly that people don't take you seriously.

I was roused from my thoughts by Runcible waking suddenly from her sleep with a quiet yip. I stroked her head fondly, ignoring my mother's delicately wrinkled nose.

'I don't know why you insist on keeping that... creature. If you must have a dog, I don't see why it couldn't at least be something pretty.'

'Well, I think Runcible is beautiful, and she's beautiful on the inside as well.'

It is true that my beloved dog hasn't been blessed with conventional good looks. She is small with long, thin grey fur that tufts up at random over her body, neglects to grow at all on her chest but forms a lavish beard on her chin. She has skinny legs, huge sticking up ears, a small but plumy tail and a protruding bottom jaw, due to an injury as a puppy, before I got her. When I saw her at the rescue centre, the only remaining member of a litter unwanted by the mother dog's owner, I knew we were meant for each other. Mum wishes I had the same reaction to men, or babies, that I do Runcible, but my heart has never melted quite enough over those I've met so far. I named her Runcible after the spoon in *The Owl and the Pussycat* because no one knows exactly what it means, and it's impossible to know my little dog's heritage; a bit of Chinese Crested, for sure, some Yorkshire Terrier maybe, perhaps a bit of Chihuahua? Anyway, it doesn't matter – I love her, even if other people tend to shrink away and whisper about gremlins.

'I don't know what Douglas is going to make of her, let alone his son and grandson. The nobility are used to proper dogs, particularly in Yorkshire. They'll probably think she's some sort of lure.'

I hugged Runcible to me, and she snuggled into my neck.

'Don't be horrible. Douglas seemed nice the one time I met

him, and I'm sure his family will be too. Anyway, if they're as noble as you say they are, they should be too polite to comment.'

'It's not just what *I* say, darling, they're bona fide titled, and so will I be soon.'

I tried to stop my eyebrow flickering heavenwards. My mother never misses an opportunity to drop in the fact that if Douglas proposes, as is fully expected, she will be Lady Knight, and her happiness in life complete. Apart from her only daughter's dowdy spinsterdom, of course. Feeling too tired to needle her about it, I decided to change the subject.

'Have you met his son or grandson? What are they like?'

'No, I haven't. They rarely come down to London, and although Douglas is often up there helping with the boy – Theo, his name is – this is the first time I've had a long enough break in filming to be able to go with him. His son, Alexander, has had a hard time of it, and Douglas is nothing short of a saint the way he steps in.'

'If you do get married, won't he expect you to go to Yorkshire with him?'

'Not at all. Douglas, for all his pedigree' – she shot another scowl at poor Runcible – 'is a very modern man. He knows that I have to work and understands that *Mayfair Mews* can't keep giving its star long periods of time off. My fans wouldn't allow it.'

This much was true. Mum had worked on the soap about upmarket Londoners for over twenty years and was much-loved by millions of people. She had steered the role of Ophelia Cromwell from little more than a walk-on part to being the central character: the classic soap matriarch who presided over her extended family and ran the neighbourhood, yet still had time for a dramatic love life. I was glad when she found someone who had never heard of her or seen the programme, yet fully supported and respected her work. She was a formidable woman who had achieved a great amount and, complicated though our relationship was, I did admire her. I poured us both some more champagne, hoping it might perk me up.

'So, why has Alexander had a hard time?'

'Well, his wife left him and his son about four years ago when the child was only little – about five – and went off with an Italian banker. But then she was killed in a car accident a year or so later.'

'How awful.'

'Yes, isn't it? But it's not just that. Alexander was a wildly successful heart surgeon, but before she left – maybe part of *why* she left – he had an accident of some sort himself and damaged his hand, so had to give up surgery.'

'Sounds a bit like a storyline from *Mayfair Mews*,' I said, sipping my champagne and wishing I felt uplifted by it, rather than even more tired.

'Doesn't it? Although there's not been much of a happy ending for him. He's teaching at the university and has started some sort of drinks business on the side, but he'll never regain the status – or the salary – of a surgeon.'

'Must have been so hard, though, being a surgeon. Imagine the pressure and the weight of expectation – quite literally holding people's lives in your hands.'

'Maybe, darling, but plenty of people cope with pressure better than you do.'

And there it was. Just as we were having a pleasant conversation, out shot the barb. Tears stung behind my eyes, and I tried to take some deep breaths, as I had been told by my doctor to do. The problem with my mother is that if you spend too long trying to compose yourself before replying to her, she has a tendency to carry on the attack. For about the millionth time, I deeply regretted agreeing to come away with her this Christmas; she was exhausting at the best of times, but I felt too fragile to cope with it all right now. I could see her gearing up again, so I spoke quickly, but as calmly as I could:

'I *am* able to cope with pressure, and I think I've proven that, Mum. I built my business from scratch and it's very successful.'

'But—'

I carried on, sounding more determined than I felt.

'However, I made a mistake in taking on too much work and not enough help. I am driven to produce excellence for my clients, and these things combined led to complete exhaustion but not, thankfully, a complete breakdown.' I was talking like a mental health manual now, but it was the best way to get my point across without letting emotion in. That only succeeds in irritating Mum and stopping me from thinking clearly. I continued, 'I do need some recovery time, as you know, but I will return to the business in the new year *better* equipped to deal with the pressure than I was previously – and with more under-standing of and sympathy for how people can be affected when life becomes overwhelming.'

My mother's lips tightened, a rare occurrence which is usually quickly corrected, due to her terror of how it might accelerate the forming of fine lines. I decided it was a prudent move to return the conversation to her favourite subject: her.

'Anyway, Mum, you haven't told me how you managed to get a month off *Mayfair Mews* over Christmas. I can't remember the last time you had such a long break.'

Her mouth relaxed into its familiar pillowy smile, and she topped up our glasses.

'True, true. Being the axis of the whole show does come with some penalties – uneasy lies the head that wears a crown and so on, darling.'

I debated with myself whether a bit of idle provocation along the lines of 'well then, don't you think it's time to retire?' might be an enjoyable way to pass a few minutes but decided to save that for another day, when more serious distraction tactics might need to be employed. She continued.

'But I said to them that Douglas was simply *pining* for more time with me. The festive season spent at his family seat, getting to know them all, was the perfect opportunity, especially seeing as the big Christmas episodes are filmed weeks in advance.'

I hid a smile in my glass. I suspected that Douglas and his family might not have warranted quite so much of her company if the visit had interfered with the seasonal ratings war between all the big soaps, which *Mayfair Mews* had won for seven years straight.

'Have you got a juicy storyline again this year? I liked last year's brush with death at the hands of that deranged doctor.'

She shot me a sideways look.

'I'm sure you did, darling, but – and I'm sorry to disappoint you – this year we decided to go for something equally dramatic but more feel-good. I'm at the heart of the story...'

Naturally.

'...naturally, but it also features Margot leaving Dirk when she hears the news about him and the online account.'

'Margot leaves Dirk? But I thought they were one of the Soap's most solid couples?'

'Well, yes, but the producers seemed to think that Lucinda was pushing for too much screen time and have decided to edge her out. I'm devasted, of course, such a wonderful actor and a dear friend, but I'm sure they know exactly what they're doing.'

And I'm sure you know exactly what you're doing, too, I thought. The producers – yeah, right. This had Jacqueline Honeywood written all over it. Poor Lucinda: she'd been playing the popular part of Margot for five years, but it didn't look as if she'd make it to six. Mum could be ruthless, but it was part of the reason she'd made such a success of herself, as I know full well as her daughter. Although she brushes any memories I have of growing up with her aside as if I were making it all up, my recollections of my childhood are clear. When I was little, I was often left with random friends of hers when she needed to go away for work or to socialise, and there never was any sense of stability. She often wasn't there, and when she was, she would spend much of her time telling me not to get used to it because she would be going away again soon. When I was six or seven years old, a teacher at school once asked my class to write about their families and all I could come up with was: 'My mummy is the lady in the Martini advertisement on telly. My daddy has gone away.' I found the exercise book it was written in not long ago and such a pang of sorrow shot through me for that child. I remembered how alone I felt. But my mother's success became mine too. Her status and salary rose stratospherically, and I was sent to a fancy boarding school in Devon aged eleven. I absolutely loved no longer being alone all the time and I was blissfully happy for seven years. After university, I got a few work placements and finally a job in a small events company whose main customer base was discreet millionaires who wanted fabulous parties for themselves, their children and even their dogs. I appreciated their high standards, which I not only reached but usually surpassed, and when the woman who owned the company decided to retire, I took over, at first as a salaried manager then eventually buying her out. I have resisted letting the business grow too big, holding on to our niche and very exclusive status and sticking with only two other permanent members of staff – Sam, who our customers worship, and Talitha, as sharp and organised a PA as anyone could hope for. Despite all this, I worked so hard, with so few breaks, that my stress, exhaustion and inability to sleep all eventually caught up with me. It was Sam who had given me the final push I needed to take a break, that night after the party at the V & A. After agreeing to take some time off, I had been looking forward to Christmas spent largely at home doing some long-overdue reading, cleaning and general pottering but then foolishly mentioned this to my mother.

'Oh, don't be ridiculous, darling, you can't spend Christmas mouldering away in that little place all by yourself.'

'But I'd quite like to moulder – I think it will be restful.'

'Nonsense. You'll only end up checking your work emails and worrying about the gas bill. A change is as good as a rest, so you'll have to come up to Yorkshire to spend the season with Douglas and me. There's heaps of room – it's a manor house, you know – and it's only his son and grandson otherwise. I insist.'

Surprise at my mother's unexpected desire to spend any time at all with me, let alone an extended period of several weeks, led me to agree. It was only later, mulling it over with Sam and a bottle of wine, that I suspected she was probably just throwing herself into the new role she hoped for as lady of the manor (despite the fact that Douglas spent most of the year in his Kensington home) and a simply marvellous relationship with her only daughter fitted the picture better than the strained, twice-a-year lunch style relationship we had in reality. By then it was too late to change my mind, and anyway, the thoughts of getting away from London and maybe even healing the fractured relationship with my mother were appealing.

A sharp rapping broke into my thoughts, and my eyes, which had started to droop shut, sprang open; it was Mum, tapping her long nail on the glass barrier between us and the driver. I saw him touch a button and it slid smoothly to one side.

'Madam?'

'How much longer?'

'Only another minute or two now, madam.'

'Thank you.'

The glass slid shut again and I smiled tentatively, a little flock of butterflies taking a stroll around my stomach.

'Why are you looking so tragic?' said my mother, taking out

a small compact mirror and starting to dab at her already-immaculate face and hair. 'It's going to be a good Christmas. I'm the one who should be worrying, I have to pass muster with his bloody son and God knows how many more family members.'

As she took out a golden tube of lipstick, I saw her hand trembling; for the first time in a long time Jacqueline Honeywood was nervous, and I reached out to squeeze her knee. Our eyes met with a flicker of unprecedented mutual understanding, and I would have spoken had the car tyres not crunched to a gravelly stop and the sepulchral tones of the driver come through the speaker:

'We have arrived.'

THREE

We stepped out of the car and, as the driver removed our luggage and my mother walked up to the front door, I took Runcible into the slightly overgrown grass to the side of the driveway. This gave me a good opportunity to look at the house in which I would be living for the next few weeks. Now, I'm a typical Londoner, used to displaying a certain calculated disinterest when presented with anything impressive, from a soufflé to a film star, but even I stood open-mouthed at the building that rose up before me. It was perfectly symmetrical, with two rows of five huge windows across its grey stone frontage. The middle double window was above the imposing wooden front door, and above it were two smaller, arched windows. These were side by side and set into a triangle, the point of which rose high up into the leaden afternoon sky and was flanked by four gigantic, hexagonal chimneys, two on each side. Smoke puffed cheerily out of two of them, and I hoped that meant that the house would be warm, which it didn't appear to be from outside. It was all a bit too *Wuthering Heights* for me, with the wind slipping its icy fingers up my sleeves and down my neck and the uncompromising landscape stretching out beyond. It certainly didn't scream Christmas cheer. Once again, the image of my cosy, if messy, place in London flashed into my mind and I felt resentment spike in my heart. Or maybe it was nerves. But here I was, so I had better get on with it. Looking down, I saw that poor little Runcible had finished her wee and was shivering violently. I scooped her up and tucked her inside my coat, as the front door opened. I had half expected a uniformed butler to appear, complete with silver salver, but it was Douglas who emerged. A tall man with thick greying hair and kind blue eyes, he gathered my mother into a warm hug, and they kissed before he waved at me.

'Fallon, welcome! Come on in, quickly, before we all freeze!'

I scuttled over gladly, and he hugged me as well, provoking a small squeak from Runcible.

'Is this your little dog?' He tugged gently at the collar of my coat to see her better, then recoiled slightly, a reaction I'm used to. 'Oh! She's very, er, small. She must be cold too. Come on, we've got a fire going in the Hall, and it must be about time for tea.'

I followed him in, thinking that the hallway was an odd place to sit and have tea; indeed, I could see no fire there, although it was twice the size of my living room at home and had a magnificent, sweeping oak staircase which rose up to a galleried landing. There were also several of what I assumed were Bond-related items on display that I didn't manage more than a glance at: a briefcase with a strip of coins protruding from the side, a golden gun in a case with a single gold bullet and some vintage-looking posters. It was only when Douglas led us through a door to the left of the staircase (past a suit of armour, of course) that I realised by 'hall' he meant Great Hall. We were standing in an enormous room with a stone floor covered in faded rugs. The timber vaulted ceiling soared above us, and a welcoming fire was indeed blazing in the cavernous stone fireplace.

'Ah, Alexander, there you are. And Annabel. This is Jacqueline and her daughter, Fallon. Are you joining us for tea?'

It was only when Douglas spoke that I noticed there were two people already in the room: a dark-haired man with blue eyes and a tight-lipped expression, undoubtedly Douglas's son, and a reed-slim blonde woman dressed in a high-necked, ditsy print floral dress and a chunky beige cardigan, clutching a lidded orange cooking pot. She issued us all with a gracious smile and opened her mouth to speak when Alexander barked:

'No! That is, I'm going to go and find Theo, and Annabel is heading home.'

It seemed that Annabel did not agree. She perched on the arm of a sofa, and I thought she was more daring than her flowery appearance suggested; not only was she clearly being shown the door, but the sofa also looked about a hundred years old and in a slightly shaky state of repair. I wouldn't have put *my* bodyweight on the arm, but then mine was probably twice hers.

'I'm sure Theo will love this casserole, Alex darling, so why don't I just wait until you fetch him, and I can show him?'

Alexander, now glowering, started towards the door.

'Thank you all the same, Annabel, but we can't accept it. Theo is experimenting with vegetarianism anyway, and we wouldn't want it to go to waste. I must go and find him and welcome our guests.'

The uncharitable thought crossed my mind that what I could really do with was being given a peaceful bedroom and left alone, rather than welcomed by anyone, especially this haughty man, but I stood patiently, hoping things would move on quickly.

Luckily for me, even the tenacious Annabel couldn't ignore the door being held open for her and, simpering at us, left with a dignity I'm not sure I could have mustered in the circumstances, wafting by in a cloud of lily of the valley.

'Maybe I'll make a lovely bean dish next time!' I could hear her trilling, but she received no reply other than the front door being closed firmly behind her. Alexander came back into the room, his face saturnine and his blue eyes shadowed.

'Right, not much of a welcome. Hello, Jacqueline, it's lovely to meet you. And welcome to Blakeney Hall. Hello, Fallon.' We all shook hands and murmured greetings in return as he continued, clearly still irritated by his unwanted guest. 'Annabel can be somewhat... adhesive, and if it's not her, then I'm infested with her clones, all seeming to think that just because a man and his son live alone, we somehow need looking after. We're perfectly fine, and now she's taken up yet another half an hour I can sorely spare. I'm going to go and find Theo.'

He stamped across the room – his father patting him warmly on the shoulder as he passed – and left by another door on the far side. I rather hoped he might get lost in the bowels of the vast house and not reappear; I already had my mother to contend with, the last thing I needed was to have to be polite to Douglas's ill-tempered son. Given how rude he had just been to the woman who had brought him a casserole, I didn't think I would fare much better when all I had to offer was my little dog and my current exhausted state.

'I'm sorry about that,' said Douglas, waving us to sit down on the enormous sofas that flanked a table which looked like a slab of tree trunk on legs and were angled perfectly to catch the warmth of the fire. 'Since his own accident and then what happened to Holly, he's been determined to prove that he can have a career and bring up Theo, but I'm not sure who he's trying to prove it to. I know he's more than capable, and there isn't anyone else who matters.'

'When you've been hurt that badly, it can take a long time to heal,' said my mother, in never-before-heard sympathetic tones. 'From what you've said, he's wonderfully good at everything, and so handsome, which never hurts. He'll be fine.'

Douglas reached over and squeezed her hand.

'Thank you, my darling, I knew you'd understand,' he said, gazing at her. 'You have such insight into people – I suppose it must come from being an actress and inhabiting different characters.' He turned to me. 'Your mother has opened my eyes to so many things in life.'

I refrained from comment. One thing she *was* right about, though, and that was true-to-form for her to mention, was that Alexander was ridiculously good-looking, even – or maybe especially – when he was throwing out women bringing him casseroles. I started to imagine what he looked like when he smiled, but shut that thought down instantly when my mother finally finished simpering at Douglas and turned to me.

'Didn't you think so, Fallon? That Alexander is frightfully handsome?'

I could hardly say 'no' when his father was standing there, and it would have been an outright lie anyway, but to admit that I thought he was gorgeous could open a door with my mother that I wanted to stay decisively shut: her involvement in my love life. Besides, good-looking he may be, but it hardly made up for his grumpy personality. Thankfully, I was saved from answering her by the return of Alexander himself, holding hands with a small boy who continued the family resemblance as if he had been the next one plucked out of a stack of Russian dolls: thick, dark hair, cobalt eyes and strong bone structure. He was also smiling, shyly, and I couldn't help but smile back. I didn't know any small boys – or small girls, come to think of it – but this one struck me as particularly nice. Maybe he took after his mother.

'Everyone,' said Alexander. 'This is my son, Theo.'

The boy gave a little wave, and I lifted Runcible's paw and had her wave in return.

'Is that your dog?' Theo asked, his smile growing.

'Oh, I didn't notice it before,' said Alexander, peering at her. 'It's, er, very unusual-looking.'

I suppose that's an aristocratic way of saying 'ugly'. I forced a smile. 'Yes, this is Runcible. She's a bit of a mix of breeds and very sweet. Do you like dogs, Theo?'

'I *love* them. Can I stroke her?'

'Of course you can, she loves being stroked and cuddled.' He came and sat next to me, and I put Runcible on his lap. She gave his hand a tiny lick and settled down to be petted. 'I think the two of you are going to be best friends.'

He beamed at me, and I grinned back, then glanced up to see a matching smile on Alexander's face. Dear God, now he had knocked 'handsome' right out of the park; he looked positively beautiful. I looked away again quickly.

'Thank you,' he said. 'Theo loves all animals – he was so happy when he heard that a dog was coming to stay. Now, who would like tea?'

Feeling dehydrated from the journey and champagne, I was a fan of this idea, but Mum was quicker.

'Yes! Why don't you help Alexander fetch it, Fallon, darling? It doesn't look like Runcible needs you for a bit.'

I could feel my lips tighten, and I quickly smoothed them out. I didn't care about the wrinkles, but I didn't want to get off to a bad start with the Knights, especially having seen how rude Alexander could be.

'Of course,' I said. 'Which way?'

Runcible had now closed her eyes and was snoring gently, with Theo looking on adoringly.

'Oh, er... thank you, Fallon,' said Alexander, looking doubtful. 'The kitchen's through here.'

I followed him out, ignoring my mother's smirking face.

.   .   .

'Wow,' I said, as I followed him through two doorways, along a gloomy passage and past a narrow flight of servants' stairs before we emerged into the kitchen. 'The tea will be cold by the time we get it back!'

'That's one of the problems with living in a huge house like this: everything's always likely to be cold unless you're right in front of a fire. Luckily, we have an assortment of hideous tea cosies, so that solves the tea problem.'

'Thank goodness for that,' I replied gravely, as he opened a drawer to show me about five tea cosies, each one uglier and more lumpy than the last. 'Ha – and you had the nerve to look askance at my dog! Who knitted them for you – your army of female admirers?'

He had the decency to look ashamed.

'Look, I'm sorry about that. I must have looked like an arrogant so-and-so. I just try to fit a lot into the day and Annabel does take up a great deal of time if you let her. She'd interrupted me right in the middle of a piece of work that was already taking me away from Theo and his reading homework. She's an old family friend, though, so I should have been more patient, I suppose. And I'm sorry for not being more enthusiastic about your dog. She's sweet, and Theo is besotted.'

I hoped he wasn't going to keep up this new charming yet self-effacing behaviour. Combined with his looks, he was already making it extremely difficult not to fancy him, and there was no way I was going down that path. I had a hard and fast rule in my dating life, which was that men with children, or who wanted children, were a no-no. I was terrified by the thought of inflicting myself on some poor child, given the chance I might follow in my own mother's footsteps – and anyway, I wasn't giving my mother a front row seat to my love life this Christmas. No, this holiday was to be strictly R and R so that I could get back to my business and life in London. I returned my attention to the tea cosies, passion killers if ever I'd seen one.

'Thanks. Theo seems a lovely boy. Right, I'm going to choose the worst of these, just to see the look on my mother's face.'

Alexander busied himself with kettle, mugs and a tray.

'Does she have high standards then, your mother?'

I snorted. 'Oh yes, the highest. Higher than our recently departed queen at times.' Then I remembered that she was in a relationship with his father and added hurriedly, 'But she's mellowed as she's got older and more successful – I think she doesn't feel she has so much to prove anymore.'

He nodded. 'I can relate to that.'

My eyes flicked to his right hand. I could see the end of a scar between his thumb and forefinger, which ran through to his palm – how bad was it? He was using the hand without any difficultly that I could see, except perhaps for a slight stiffness as he grasped the handle of the kettle.

'It's healed quite well,' he said calmly, as he poured water into the teapot.

'Oh, I'm so sorry, I didn't mean to stare. Mum mentioned you'd been injured.'

'A while ago now. Have you chosen one of the monstrosities yet?'

I hurriedly plucked an orange and green tea cosy with purple pompoms out of the drawer and handed it to him, glad of the change of subject.

'Do you have a range of matching hats? Or a special festive tea cosy with snowmen cavorting round it?'

'Ha ha. Sadly not. Biscuits?'

'I never say no to a biscuit.'

'Sensible woman.'

He handed me a tin, picked up the tray and led the way back to the hall.

. . .

As Alexander poured the tea, I found a dog biscuit for Runcible.

'Put her down,' I said to Theo, 'and give her this – you'll love what she does.'

He placed her gently on the rug in front of the fire and offered the treat, which she took delicately from his fingers. Then she lay down and, as she always did, propped the biscuit up neatly between her two front paws and started nibbling.

'Oh, she's so sweet!' said Theo, lying down next to her and watching her, enchanted.

Alexander smiled over at me, and I dared to glance at my mother who, for once, looked slightly flustered. I don't think she could decide where to focus her attention: the disgusting tea cosy, my scrap of a dog or the fact that Alexander and I seemed to be getting along. So, in true Jacqueline Honeywood style, she swung it right back to herself.

'Douglas, darling, can we go into York tomorrow? There's a restaurant there everyone says I *must* try – La Cosita – and I must keep my Instagram exciting for my fans.'

I stared hard into my cup of tea to prevent my eyes from rolling. My mother's Instagram account is another whole world of madness, to which she is slavishly devoted, but with more than a million followers, who can blame her? It's brought her in a tidy sum from advertising, and the adoring comments help her while away many an idle moment.

'Of course we can, my love,' said Douglas, 'but I've heard of that place, and it's booked weeks in advance.'

Mum waved an airy hand.

'Don't give that another thought. I'll have Acanthe make the booking; I'm *never* refused tables.'

Theo suddenly sat up.

'But Dad...' He trailed off and then looked uncomfortably at my mother.

'What is it, Theo?' asked Alexander.

'Well, it's just that I thought Grandpa was looking after me tomorrow so that you could work, and we could go to the cinema in the afternoon to see that new Santa Claus film. That's all.'

'Can't you go to the cinema another day?' asked Mum, looking up from her phone, where she'd been tapping away. 'I've emailed Acanthe now.'

'My fault entirely,' said Douglas. 'Theo and I do love a Christmas movie; maybe we could go to lunch the day after, Jacqueline?'

She pouted.

'That would be very disappointing on my second day here.'

A small silence ensued, before Alexander spoke.

'Look, it's fine. I'll get some fayre work done this evening and squeeze a bit more in tomorrow – Hetty will be able to help too – and we can still go to the cinema after while Grandpa and Jacqueline can go to lunch. Everyone will be a winner, okay?'

Theo nodded, smiling, and resumed his observation of Runcible, who had now stretched out luxuriously to her full length of about thirty centimetres and was toasting her bald tummy in front of the fire.

'Well navigated,' said Douglas. 'Thank you. I bet you wish poor old Annabel was so easily dealt with.'

Father and son exchanged matching amused eye rolls.

'Yes, it's very gracious of you, Alexander,' said Mum, smiling. As if she had ever expected any outcome other than getting exactly what she wanted. I looked at Alexander, recognising the pull he must have been feeling to fit everything in and make everyone happy.

'What's the fayre?' I asked.

'It's a local Christmas event,' replied Alexander. 'Lots of

stalls for presents and food and so on. It will be my first big event for the artisan gin company I'm launching, so it's a big deal for me.' He spoke calmly, but I could hear the stress in his voice. 'There's still a lot to do, but I've got time – just – and the help of Hetty, who's a part-time PA.'

An artisan gin launch was exactly the sort of job I do all the time, and I opened my mouth to offer some help, then closed it again quickly. I had come to Yorkshire to recuperate, not to take on yet another pressured piece of work. No, this Christmas I was going to have the break I needed.

FOUR

Once we were all suitably refreshed, Douglas showed us upstairs to our rooms. I must say, I could have lingered for some time just admiring the elegant staircase, which was like something out of *Downton Abbey*. It was oak, worn and polished over the years to a glorious, chocolatey shine that urged you to run your hand along the smooth, solid handrail and enjoy the clunk as your foot hit each wide step. My mind flicked to the narrow, concrete staircase with iron railings that led to my flat in London; utilitarian and fit for the job, but a poor cousin to this magnificent affair. I imagined generations of small Knight children sliding down its inviting banisters and felt a tug of temptation to do the same myself. At the top, from the galleried landing, carpeted in worn but still luxurious red wool, you could peer over the hallway – grand but homely with its leather Chesterfield sofa and muddle of coats, shoes and bags. Only my mother's camel coat had made it to a hanger; everything else was draped on the sofa or, with a nonchalance that only the aristocratic would ever dare have, flung over the exquisitely carved finial at the bottom of the stairs.

I could see my suitcases outside a door down a corridor leading to the left.

'That must be my room?'

Douglas nodded. 'It is. Would you like a rest after your journey? We don't meet for supper until about seven thirty.'

Thank goodness that Douglas was such a thoughtful man and must have realised that I could do with some time to myself.

I smiled at him. 'Thank you, that would be amazing. I'll see you later.'

'Of course, just shout if you need anything – we're down this way, third on the right.'

I pushed open the door with relief. The journey and meeting new people had tired me, and I was reminded how scant my resources currently were. An hour or so to myself would set me up for the evening, whatever that may hold.

I was so busy gathering my things together and ushering Runcible through the door that it was only once I was inside the room that I looked up. I gasped aloud. Having lost my bearings inside the house, I hadn't worked out that this would be a corner room. Two of its walls were taken up with huge wooden-framed floor to ceiling windows, with long blue and cream patterned curtains hooked back to allow in the light which, although wintery and fading as the afternoon ebbed away, was still uplifting. Leaving my cases, I ran over to look out at the view, which was so staggering that tears sprang to my eyes. Beyond the large garden and some outbuildings, stretched the Yorkshire moors, as bleak as one might hope for at this time of year with their coarse, uncompromising greyness, dotted with moss and stubborn, wiry little trees. But the undulating landscape was so vast that it made me feel comforted. It had a timeless quality, and a calming sense of stolidity that helped me breathe more deeply. I rested my forehead on the cool glass and let my eyes drift across the miles, picking out details as I did so: some ridiculously fluffy sheep grazing, a quaint stone building, a small river twinkling with frost. The view from my home in London was one which I spent little time looking at, just a city street with a newsagent and chain bakery opposite, and a charity shop below. Awestruck now, I suddenly wondered how I could have lived so long that way, and how I could ever go back. Then I gave myself a little shake. Of course I would go back! I wasn't normally given to such romantic flights of fancy; it must be the stress talking. I had been advised by the doctor to let worrying thoughts float by, and that is what I would do now. Briskly, I crossed the room back to my luggage and hoisted it all up onto the bed, a heavily built four poster that must have been created for this room maybe four hundred years ago. I couldn't imagine that you could disassemble it and take it somewhere else; flat pack this was not. Runcible had finished sniffing around in the corners of the room, so I popped her up, too, sure that nobody would mind her being on the bed and, to be honest, not caring if they did. She always slept with me, snuggled into my stomach. I quickly put away my clothes and placed my toiletries on the mirrored dressing table. Nearly finished, and sure that I had got on top of my sudden urge never to return to London, I went to draw the curtains; the light had faded quickly, and the dark stretch of the moors was now less enticing. As I turned away, I spotted a curtain on the opposite wall: surely not more windows? I lifted it to one side and hooked it up and, to my astonishment, revealed a small archway, with a twisting set of stone stairs beyond. Thank goodness for whichever Knight had thought about mod cons, because there was also a light switch, which I flicked.

Consumed with excitement and curiosity, I descended the short flight and found myself in a bathroom unlike any I had ever seen before. Built from stone, with no rendering or tiles, it was small and semi-circular, rather like I would suppose a turret room to be. I hadn't noticed any turrets from the front, but a glance out of the small, deep-set window showed me that this looked over the side of the house. It was hard to see much in the gloaming, but I managed to pick out further lawns, trees and what looked like a lake or large pond; I would look forward to exploring those tomorrow. Turning back into the room, I walked slowly around it, running my hand along the large, square art deco sink with its slightly corroded chunky chrome taps and elegantly bevelled mirror above. The bath looked Victorian, but I had never seen anything like it. It was in the shape of an 'L' lying on its back, with a tall domed open cubicle at one end which housed a shower head and a strange array of enamel knobs and little holes, which presumably squirted out water at different heights. It reminded me of the sort of rainforest experience showers you find at fancy spas, but this wasn't modern. I couldn't wait to have a go in it. Next, I reached out a hand to touch the sturdy metal towel rail, which was deliciously warm. Somebody had – at some point in the house's history – gone to a great deal of effort to make the bathroom comfortable, even encased as it was in stone, but it couldn't have been touched for decades. Reluctantly, I returned to the stairs, resolving to ask Douglas about the bathroom's history and, indeed, that of the entire house. I re-emerged through the arch and let down the curtain, ready to sit quietly with a book for a while, when a tap on the door was quickly followed by the appearance of my mother.

'Hello, darling, settling in all right? Isn't it the most marvellous house? Mind you, Douglas's place in London is just as grand and more up to date.'

I decided not to mention the wonderful bathroom – one look at it and she'd have been making noises about tile cladding and a power shower. Mum has no truck whatsoever with history, she likes things to be sharp and modern, like herself – no hint of the past.

'Yes, it's gorgeous, and the views are amazing.'

Mum sat down in an ivory armchair and tucked her crossed ankles to one side, just as she had seen Joan Collins do.

'The views inside the house are splendid, too, don't you think? Alexander is absolutely *divine*. I mean, I'd seen pictures of him, but they didn't do him justice one little bit. Oh, come on, don't say you didn't notice, you were positively flirting with him.'

'I *wasn't*! For goodness' sake, we were just talking.'

'Whatever. But don't you think he's the handsomest man you've ever seen?'

'Not particularly, no. I mean, he's perfectly nice-looking, I suppose.'

I trailed off. Nobody could deny that Alexander Knight was an absolute knockout, and my mother knew it. She snorted.

'A little too much protesting, darling. He's an utter hunk. You could have a lovely Christmas present to unwrap if you play your cards right.'

'Well, I don't want to. Apart from the fact that that's not what I've come here for, what about Theo? I don't want to be a mother.'

Well, I thought, *I don't want to be a mother like you were, and that surely amounts to the same thing...*

'Oh, don't be ridiculous, darling. For a start, I was only suggesting a little festive dalliance, not setting up home together. And what's this about not wanting to be a mother?'

'It doesn't matter.'

'It *does* matter. It's the first I've heard of it. Are you intent on focusing on your career? You know I'm all for that, but the two don't have to be mutually exclusive, as I've demonstrated.'

She gave a satisfied smile and I glared at her, feeling the heat rising in my face.

'Because *you* handled it so marvellously, you mean?'

She laughed.

'What *are* you implying, Fallon? I suppose you resent me

for leaving you with people because I had to work? Plenty of mothers do that, and without your father on the scene, I didn't have much choice.'

'No, Mum, I know that you had to work, of course I understand that. What I have a harder time with is the way you left me with strangers so you could party several nights a week. You made it abundantly clear that I was a nuisance.'

Her mouth tightened. 'You're being a nuisance now, to be honest.'

I fell silent. I should have known better than to challenge her. The moment my mother believed herself to be cornered, she went on the attack. I braced myself.

'You *never* understood that aspect of my job, Fallon – that I had to *socialise* in order to meet people who would help me in my career. I still have to do it now. Maybe you still resent me not washing your hockey kit, or whatever the equivalent is at your age. For what it's worth, I think you'd make a wonderful mother, but then I think I did too.'

My eyebrows nearly hit the ceiling, but her imperious gaze made it clear that the conversation was over. Oh, what was the point in trying anyway? She would never even try to understand. It wasn't that I didn't like children, but I was terrified of the responsibility – of making mistakes with them that might last a lifetime. How on earth people were brave enough to embark on parenthood was beyond me.

'Anyway,' I said, 'from what we saw when we first arrived, it seems very clear that Alexander isn't remotely interested in finding anyone, let alone a mother for Theo.'

'Well, there you are then, darling, we're back exactly where I started.' I almost expected her to punch the air in triumph. 'Have a lovely Christmas fling with him, no hard feelings and so on. Enjoy yourself!'

'I fully intend to enjoy myself, but not in that way. Just drop it, Mum. I don't want a fling, with Alexander or anyone else, just some peace and quiet!'

Even my mother was thwarted by this argument, although I feared only temporarily – I had no doubt that she would rise again to matchmake another day. She finally stood up.

'Well, enjoy your chaste Christmas, darling, more "miserable-toe" than mistletoe, but it's up to you, I suppose. I think love is good for keeping one young and desirable, but maybe that doesn't worry you. I still think Alexander is gorgeous.'

'I don't care how bloody gorgeous Alexander is, I am *not* having an affair with him!'

This, of course, as the door opened and the man himself walked in.

'Sorry, have I missed something?'

FIVE

I could do nothing more than gape in total mortification at Alexander as he stood in the doorway. My mother, however, brazen in these situations, burst out laughing.

'Oh, hello, what *marvellous* timing! I was just saying to Fallon how handsome you are, but she wasn't having any of it. Mind you, she always flatly refuses to discuss her sex life with me, so who knows *what* she's really thinking.'

What I was thinking was that I wanted to howl with embarrassment, then immediately return to London, but I rallied.

'The only thing that I'm thinking right now, Mum, is that I'd like some rest. Why don't you go and find Douglas?'

'Very well!' she trilled, squeezing Alexander's shoulder as she passed him, then saying in a stage whisper, 'Don't give up hope, darling!'

I had no idea who that last comment was directed at, but I chose to ignore it, and instead looked imploringly at Alexander.

'I'm so sorry about that. Mum can be a bit...' *Intrusive? Pushy? Rude?* '...*giddy* sometimes, and I get impatient with her. Please don't be offended.'

'Offended? By being talked about like an object behind my

back? I can't imagine why you think I might be. Anyway, I just
came to say that we normally have drinks before dinner at
seven, so we'll meet in the Hall then.'

I started to say thank you, but he had already left, closing
the door behind him with a sharp click. I threw myself down on
the bed flat on my stomach and moaned into the pillow. Could
there have *been* a more cringe-making start to my stay here?

'Fallon?'

I lifted my head from the bed to see Alexander standing in
the doorway once again.

'Are you all right?'

'Yes, yes, just, er...' I tailed off miserably and tried surreptitiously to wipe away a small dribble of drool from the corner of
my mouth, which had escaped during my smothered wails.

'Right. Well, I forgot to say that we don't bother dressing for
dinner, just in case you were wondering.'

I nodded, still prone on the bed, and he left the room again.
I may well have cried, had a gentle, soft muzzle not pushed
itself into my hand, and a warm, scraggly body pressed against
my leg.

'Oh, Runcible,' I said with a sigh, 'thank goodness you're
here.'

Tightly wound though I was, I managed to fall asleep for an
hour, and woke feeling better. All right, so things hadn't got off
to a brilliant start, but there was plenty of time to redeem myself
as the perfect house guest. Alexander had said that they didn't
'dress for dinner', something that hadn't even crossed my mind
as a possibility, but nonetheless I could do with freshening up
after the long car journey and nap. I gave Runcible her supper –
boring-looking dry food, which the vet had recommended and
she always gobbled up – then went to the amazing bathroom
and had a quick shower, gazing out into the darkness through

the deep-set window. I got dressed in a pair of soft trousers and a cosy cashmere jumper, scooped up Runcible and entered the Hall just as the large clock on the mantelpiece struck seven, with a tasteful tinkling of bells. Punctual I may have been, but I was the only person there. I popped my little dog down, then wandered about marvelling at what I suppose an estate agent would describe as 'original features' but anyone else would consider museum pieces. I had come in through a sort of ante-room, with an ornately carved wooden wall separating it from the main room. Above this I could see a minstrels' gallery. There was a second doorway in the wooden wall, covered by a curtain, and I poked my head around this to see some very old wooden stairs leading up. I was just debating whether or not to give them a go, when a voice behind me made me jump.

'You can go up if you like.'

I turned around to see Alexander and Theo standing behind me, with matching amused smiles on their faces. I felt my cheeks flush pink and wished I'd been a few minutes later to come down.

'Caught in the act of snooping. I'm sorry, it's just so intriguing. I think the last time I saw a minstrels' gallery was at Hampton Court. In my defence, part of my job is looking at amazing venues, so really, it's work, kind of...'

'It's fine,' said Alexander. 'It is a wonderful house; we're very lucky to live here – and we discover new things all the time, don't we?' He turned to his son, who had crouched down to pet Runcible, the dog bustling over to greet her new friend.

'Yes, we do,' Theo answered eagerly. 'In the summer we found a weird little stone dish thing hidden behind a panel on the wall.'

'That's right,' said his father. 'It was an in-built holy water stoup that we think was hidden during the English Reformation. I'll show it to you at some point, if you're interested?'

I was about to reply when a quick clicking of heels announced my mother's arrival, followed by Douglas. She had clearly decided to ignore the instruction not to dress for dinner and was wearing a burgundy silk tea dress with a cream mohair cardigan which was begging to be stroked, it looked so soft and cloudlike. It wasn't my mother's usual style, but she looked stunning. Maybe, I thought, glancing down at my own outfit, she *hadn't* dressed for dinner, but, in fact, this was considered normal clothing, and it was I who needed to up my game? *Eurgh.* I shook the thought away and instead paid attention to Douglas, who was asking everyone what they wanted to drink. Given my exhausted state, I had decided alcohol was to be strictly limited, but as I saw Mum's eyes raking my poorly dressed body, I cravenly asked for a gin and tonic and promised myself I'd try again tomorrow. *Oh no, wait.* Tomorrow was that blasted James Bond-themed welcome party. I wasn't getting through that on mineral water. I'd try again... when I could. After a few minutes, Alexander and Theo disappeared.

'They're making the dinner tonight,' said Douglas. 'We usually have help in the house with cooking and cleaning and so on – a wonderful married couple who look after us all marvellously – but their daughter has just had her first baby, so they've gone on a sort of grandparental leave for a few weeks and we're fending for ourselves.'

'So generous of you, Dougie,' said Mum, simpering at him in a way I had never seen before.

'It was Alexander who suggested it,' he replied. 'He's here all of the time so misses Stephen and Chrissie's cooking the most, but he believes that family should come first for everyone, and it's not like we can't manage – we just lower our standards dramatically.' He smiled self-deprecatingly and I thought again how very nice he was. 'We normally take it in turns to cook when they're away,' he continued. 'So, prepare yourselves for my unrivalled pasta pesto on repeat.'

Oh God, if that was his signature, what on earth was I supposed to make? I didn't want to make anything, actually, and felt a pang of longing to be at home and not having to make an effort to impress anyone.

I summoned up a smile, though, as Douglas was so well-meaning. 'Sounds good to me, but you've stolen the main dish in my repertoire. I'll have to Google something else. Or maybe I'll just buy some Christmas puddings and dish those up – they're usually filling enough not to need another course. What about you, Mum?' I asked, naughtily, as I know my mother can't make toast. To my surprise, she pulled what I can only describe as a comical face, and answered grandly:

'Darlings, I shall do what all sensible people do. Order in!'

Douglas roared with laughter.

'Now that, my darling, you are exceptionally good at!'

Self-deprecation had never been one of Mum's acts; maybe Douglas would be good for her. She certainly seemed different around him – softer, I suppose. I was about to ask him about some of his Bond memorabilia, when Theo came back in, glee-fully whacked the huge gong that stood at one end of the hall and announced:

'Dinner is served!'

We followed him through to a strange, windowless room at the other end of the hall from the minstrels' gallery and sat down at a large, simply laid table.

'Welcome to your first meal at Blakeney Hall,' said Alexander. 'In case you're wondering why we're eating in a prison cell, this is the Buttery – the room where the butler would have kept the provisions, wine and so on.'

Theo took over from him.

'In the past they would have eaten in the Great Hall, but that's more of a sitting room for us as you've seen, so we use this because it's nearer the kitchen. It is a bit weird with no windows, but you get used to it.'

'Exactly,' said Alexander, smiling at his son. 'Right, we've made our favourite – baked potatoes with a selection of toppings – so please just dig in.'

The food was delicious, and I began to relax as we ate and the conversation flowed. The talk turned to Christmas.

'When do rehearsals start for the Nativity?' Alexander asked his father, adding some more cheese to his potato.

'This week,' replied Douglas. 'Theo and I are raring to go, aren't we?'

'Yes! We're innkeepers this year, *so* much more exciting than boring old shepherds like last time.'

'And no sheep to misbehave either,' said Douglas wryly. He turned to me. 'I should explain, Fallon. Each year the village holds a live Nativity performance which winds its way through the streets – well, street, since Lingfoss is a tiny place – with anyone who wants one taking a part and the vicar narrating the whole thing. It's been done for centuries and it's fun to be part of. Last year, as Theo says, we were shepherds, and we had the stubbornest sheep in Yorkshire as our companion. That blighter *would not move!*'

'I'll look forward to seeing it,' I said. 'Are you going to do it too?' I looked at Alexander.

He shook his head.

'No. I have done in the past, but I'm getting my new business up and running this year, so I'm way too busy. I did wonder if Jacqueline might take a turn, though – I'm sure the village would love it.'

I hardly dared look at Mum. If it doesn't go through her agent six times, she doesn't do it: that's pretty much the rule to get her out of bed. But, to her credit, she forced a smile.

'Now then, I don't think Nativity is my *métier*, darling. And from what I've seen of the photos, it requires wearing a woollen robe, no matter what part you have.' She gave that smile which makes you question whether she's joking or not. 'My fans would never forgive me; I think I'll resign myself to a supporting role.' She smiled soppily at Douglas, who reached over to stroke her face, and I hid my smirk in my wine glass. My mother has never ceded the limelight to anyone; I wouldn't put it past her to appear in a surprise star turn as an angel in some Dior gold silk number. Alexander saw my face and grinned.

'How about you, Fallon? I'm sure there's still time to sign up?'

Over my dead body.

I raised an eyebrow at him.

'No, thank you, I'll leave the theatrics to everyone else.'

He wasn't going to stop teasing me, though.

'Oh, what a shame, don't you like dressing up? I'm sure they could find you some lovely old wool cloak that's been sported by various members of the village over the past hundred years.'

Theo pulled a face.

'Yuck. It's not that bad, Dad. Mine was only a bit itchy last year.'

'Absolutely, you should consider it, Fallon!' chimed in Douglas. 'The authentic scents increase as the wool warms up and really add to the atmosphere.'

I dropped my head into my hands and laughed.

'I'll pass! I'm dressing up for the party tomorrow night, so I think that's going to be the beginning and the end of costumes for me.'

No doubt Alexander would have carried on ribbing me, had his phone not rung.

'Oh, sorry, I'd better get this. Won't be long.' He answered the call: 'Finally, Hetty!' and left the room. When he returned, he was as white as a sheet and sat down heavily in his chair.

'What's happened?' asked Douglas, looking concerned. 'Bad news?'

Alexander had a long drink of water and refilled his glass. I thought he was going to cry.

'It's Hetty,' he whispered. 'She's had to go up to Scotland –
her mother has been in an accident and has to have surgery. I'm
awfully sorry for her, but what on earth am I going to do about
the Christmas Fayre?'

A sympathetic silence fell. It was Douglas who broke it.

'Oh, Alexander, that is a setback. Can I help in any way?
How much is there left to do?'

Alexander sighed deeply and raked his hands through his
thick hair.

'Too much, far too much for me to manage without Hetty.
The actual product is fine, I've distilled and bottled that, but I
still need to do the publicity, labelling, setting up a stall... I'll
have to manage somehow, but it won't be the launch I had in
mind, and it was such a golden opportunity.'

I stared bleakly at my plate as the conversation continued
around me – Douglas, Mum and even Theo trying to suggest
ideas. I already had about five I could action quickly and that
would be successful; this was my job, after all. But with visions
of the last six months of stress whirling around my exhausted
brain, I couldn't organise my mouth to speak the words I should:
I'll help. Instead, I just sat silently, uselessly, praying that
someone else would come up with a proper solution. Then, my
mother piped up:

'This is ridiculous, none of us has the first idea about any of
this. Fallon will help, of course. She knows what she's doing
with this sort of thing.'

I used to write down compliments my mum had given me in
my diary, treasuring each one as they were so scarce. But as I
grew up, they became basically non-existent, the diary was lost
during a house move and I learned to rely on my own inner
voice to give myself credit where it was due (and sometimes
where it wasn't). So, when my head snapped up, it was more in
surprise at my mum's approval than in horror at the suggestion I
should help. Alexander didn't see it that way.

'Absolutely not. Fallon is here as a guest and to get some rest. I won't hear of it.'

'Nonsense,' said Mum, in a voice that meant business. 'Of course she'll help, won't you?'

I was wishing vehemently now that I hadn't had that gin and tonic. My head started buzzing and there was a telltale pinprick of pain behind my left eye, foretelling one of the crushing headaches that had been hounding me over the last year. I opened my mouth to speak, but was stopped by Alexander who had not, to be fair to him, ever had experience of arguing with my mother.

'No. It's fine. It's not the end of the world. I'll probably just drop it for now and then find somewhere else to take it when Hetty's back...'

'But Christmas was the perfect...' started Douglas, tailing off when he saw the look on his son's face and laying a hand over Mum's. Silence fell again. I was desperate now to get some of my pain medication before I was stuck with a bad headache, but through the fuzziness I knew what else I had to do.

'Look, it's fine, of course I'll help. I really, really don't mind. Maybe it will do me good, keep me ticking over or something. It sounds like you're already well on the way, and it's not like some investment bank do at the National Gallery. Much more manageable—'

'Right, then that's settled,' said Mum. 'It was obviously the best idea.'

'It's a super idea,' said Douglas. 'As long as you're sure, Fallon?'

A scimitar stroke of pain shot through my head, and I clenched my teeth.

'I would be hugely grateful,' said Alexander stiffly. 'This company does mean a great deal to me.'

'I'm absolutely sure,' I said, not really caring, now, one way or the other. 'Christmas events are my favourites. I'll be glad to get started tomorrow. Er, would you all excuse me? I just need to pop upstairs.'

I pushed my chair back and moved as smoothly and quickly as I could up to my bedroom, Runcible trotting after me, where I took some painkillers and pressed my head against one of the cold windows, staring out into the darkness. A tear of exhaustion and pain ran down my cheek. I hoped I hadn't made a colossal mistake.

SIX

I slept deeply that night and when I woke up, the headache had all but gone, although I still had that unpleasant, foggy feeling I get left with. The best thing for it was a blast of fresh air, and, looking out of the window at the steely moors, I could imagine that fresh was what it would be. I pulled on several layers of warm clothing and went down the huge oak staircase. Douglas was in the large entrance hallway with the door open, collecting some newspapers that had been left on the step.

'Good morning, Fallon, I hope you slept well? You must think me terribly old-fashioned still having my papers delivered, but I can't seem to shake the habit. Alexander thinks I'm mad – he reads everything on his tablet.'

'I totally get it. I always buy magazines rather than reading them online. It's fairly harmless, as vices go.'

He smiled.

'Well, quite. Are you coming to get breakfast?'

'Actually, I was wondering whether I could get something in the village? I could do with a walk.'

'Yes, absolutely. Lingfoss is surprisingly well-resourced for such a tiny place. There's a little café which will be open at this time and won't mind the dog, just head out of here, turn right and keep going, you can't miss it.'

I nodded my thanks and reached for my coat.

'Fallon, I also want to thank you for offering to help Alexander with the Christmas Fayre. It was a tremendous blow to him, Hetty going away like that. I don't know how much Jacqueline has told you, but he's not had an easy time of it over the past few years. This new venture is doing him good already, but if the launch goes well, it could be the start of a desperately needed new chapter.'

'I'm glad to help. I'm sorry I was lukewarm last night; I was brewing a headache. I'm sure it will all go well.'

We bade each other goodbye, and I set off to the village, Runcible tucked into my coat. There was a delicious smell of woodsmoke in the air, but the wind was biting, and although my top half stayed reasonably warm, by the time I got there, my legs were tingling with cold and my ears painful; I would need some warmer clothes if I was going to be outside much while I was here. As Douglas had said I would, I spotted the café easily, a charming, whitewashed cottage with a tiled roof and two fat bay windows with wooden frames and small panes of glass, some with round 'bullseyes' in them. Both were abundantly decorated with fat swags of holly and ivy, which were hung with dozens of red and gold baubles and had twinkling fairy lights strung through them. They flanked a deep porch with a paned wooden door; when I pushed it open, I was gratified by the light 'ting' of the bell above me and the baking-scented steamy warmth that enveloped me. The inside of the café was as beautifully decorated as the windows, with a tall tree in one corner, smothered in decorations, a pile of wrapped presents beneath it and more greenery, tinsel and fairy lights hanging from the walls and above the doors. Even in my fragile state I felt the warmth of Christmas cheer wash over me. A tall, slender, smiling woman in a pale-yellow apron came round from behind the counter.

'Morning,' she said. 'Welcome to Meg's. Breakfast, is it?'

'Yes, please.'

'Sit down, I'll be over.'

There were a couple of people already there, but I was glad to see that there was a free table in one of the bays and I went to sit down, divesting myself of a couple of layers of clothing as I did so and settling Runcible onto my lap. I picked up the menu and ordered a full English breakfast and a pot of tea, the latter of which materialised almost immediately. I had been expecting a small metal pot with a single tagged bag, but instead was presented with a large Brown Betty and a strainer.

'Just what I needed,' I said to the woman, who grinned.

'We know how to do proper tea up here,' she said. 'I'm Meg, by the way.'

'Fallon. I'm staying up the road with Douglas and Alexander Knight. My mother is dating his father,' I added quickly, in case she thought there was any intrigue. I was aware of the speed at which news travels in a small village.

'Oh aye, we've been expecting you. No doubt we'll see you and your mam around a bit.'

I was doubtful whether my mother would be visiting the village much, and, when my breakfast arrived, delicious and headache-relieving though it looked, I wasn't sure it was the kind of fare her Instagram wellness followers would approve of. I tucked in greedily and was just cutting into a particularly golden and crispy hash brown when a small green bus pulled up at the stop opposite. I watched idly as it disgorged a few passengers. The last person off was not someone I expected to see in a sleepy Yorkshire village: a tall, beautiful girl in, I guessed, her mid-twenties, with waist-length, silvery lilac hair. She was wearing a fabulous pair of purple patent Doc Marten boots and a long tapestry coat and carrying a huge backpack. I looked hurriedly down at my plate as she pushed open the door of the café, setting the bell ringing. I didn't want to be caught staring, but she was striking and with such a sense of *life* about her – a sort of energy, I suppose, that I hadn't had myself for a long time. I surveyed my reflection in a spoon; could I carry off hair that colour?

'Meg!' the girl shrieked, and threw her arms around the proprietor, who hugged her delightedly.

'Coco! What are you doing here? I didn't think we were going to see you again for a while.'

'No, well, you weren't meant to, but I couldn't have stayed another second at that restaurant. Fancy it may have been, but the head chef spent more time trying to grope my bottom than doing any work, while I got stuck on peeling onions for weeks at a time to make me learn my place.'

'It sounds terrible, duck. Come on, let me get you a coffee.'

'Meg, you're an angel. I've been on a coach half the night, followed by that bus and I've got to go and face Daddy and Alexander now. They'll be *furious* – or, worse, just deeply disapproving – that I've ditched the job, but honestly, I couldn't have put up with that sexist pig a moment longer.'

As she turned to find a table, I stood up quickly.

'Excuse me? Are you going up to Blakeney Hall?'

Coco smiled at me warmly. 'Yes, that's right.'

'I'm staying there myself, do come and sit with me,' I said, surprised at my own daring.

She shot over and took the seat opposite.

'That breakfast looks delicious. You don't always expect to get such good food in a little village, but this is definitely more Meg's than Greggs.' I laughed at her cheeky grin, and she continued, 'Meg! Please can I have whatever – sorry, I don't know your name?'

'Fallon,' I supplied.

'Whatever Fallon is having?' She turned back to me. 'I'm

going to need to keep my strength up. Why are you staying at the Hall? Are you a friend of Alexander's?'

I laughed at the open curiosity in her face.

'No, sorry, nothing like that.'

'Oh, that *is* a shame. He needs to meet someone nice, and it might have distracted him from my latest woes and given us all a happier Christmas.'

'I'm Jacqueline's daughter – Douglas's... erm, girlfriend?'

'Oh, how wonderful! Then if they get married, we'll be sisters!'

I raised an eyebrow.

'Oh, sorry! Douglas is my father and Alexander is my half-brother. Dad married again after Alexander's mother died – a long time after – and I was the result. Mum and Dad divorced when I was tiny, and I lived between them growing up. Mum's not far from here, she'll probably pop in at some point – knowing her, she'll probably stay for a month, since she loves Christmas and she'll be dying to meet Jacqueline.'

I couldn't imagine that Mum would be dying to meet *her*, but I refrained from saying so.

'I think Mum mentioned that Douglas had a daughter. The job you had sounded awful – sorry, I couldn't help hearing what you were saying to Meg. I'm sure they won't be cross with you for chucking it in.'

She sighed.

'I hope not. It's not what I want to do, anyway, work in a restaurant, but Dad thought it would teach me stuff. He's probably right, but I've done it in various places for a couple of years and now I'm ready to set up on my own.'

'Sounds great – a catering business, you mean?'

'That's right. I want to specialise in private parties and show everyone how delicious local produce is. There's a lot of work to do, though, getting flyers and a website and working out menus and stuff. I'm hoping I can stay at the Hall and get working on it.'

'It sounds like a brilliant idea,' I said warmly, then added impulsively, 'I'm in PR – I can help you get started while I'm up here, if you like?'

'Would you? That would be amazing.'

I wasn't doing very well with my relaxation plan – that was two jobs I'd taken on now in the space of twenty-four hours, but I just couldn't help myself. It couldn't be as bad as London, and maybe a sort of cooldown would be better for me than going cold turkey? I do love work, just not the headaches and sense of existential dread that have gone with it recently. We finished breakfast, chatting nonstop, and paid Meg. I lifted Runcible up from where she had been snuggling on my lap.

'Time to face the music, I suppose,' sighed Coco, hoisting her bag onto her back. 'Oh! Is that a dog?'

She stroked Runcible's little head gently and I introduced them.

'If you don't mind being delayed by a few minutes, I have to pick up a parcel from the Post Office,' I said. 'I wasn't sure about having things delivered to the house, so I had it sent there.'

'The more delay the better, as far as I'm concerned,' said Coco, grinning.

'Thanks. Oh, I should tell you about what's happening. The parcel is a dress that a friend of mine made me for the party tonight – Douglas is having a James Bond-themed party to welcome Mum to Yorkshire. You'll need to find something to wear!'

Coco waved her hand breezily.

'Don't worry, I'll put something together. I'm used to Dad and his bonkers Bond thing – I've probably got something in my bedroom I've worn before, since he can't resist theming whenever he can. What are you wearing?'

'It's the long black dress with the diamanté neckline that

Barbara Bach wore in *The Spy Who Loved Me*. I wanted some-thing simple and forgiving, neither of which are words that usually come to mind when you think of women in Bond films.'

Coco laughed.

'It sounds divine – I'm sure you'll look fabulous. I can help you with your hair and make-up, if you like? I trained in that before I went to catering school.'

'A woman of many talents!'

'A woman who can't make up her mind, more like!'

'Well, I'd love you to help me, thank you.'

I felt sorry for Coco when we got back to Blakeney Hall. I'm sure she had been hoping to slip in and deal with her brother and father – and, eventually, my mother who would probably soon be her stepmother – separately, but, as luck would have it, everyone was right there when we opened the front door.

'Coco!' shrieked Theo, the first to notice her. He ran over and gave her a huge hug, which she returned. 'Auntie Coco, it's so good to see you! Are you staying for Christmas? Oh, *please* say you'll stay for Christmas! The nicest dog has come to stay, her name is Runcible, and she is so funny – she holds her biscuits between her front paws!' He suddenly noticed me and looked guilty. 'Fallon and Jacqueline are staying as well, and they're nice too.'

I burst out laughing.

'Don't worry, Theo, I'm more than happy for Runcible to steal the limelight and,' I added naughtily, 'I'm sure that Mum feels exactly the same.'

I'm sure only I noticed the momentary thinning of her lips, but, to her credit, my mother managed to summon up a slightly bilious-sounding laugh as well.

'I suppose if I *must* be upstaged, then I'm glad it's Runcible,' she said. I refrained from further comment.

'Well, I'm thrilled to see you, Theo, and I've already met your doggy friend,' said Coco. 'As well as Fallon, down in the village; glad to meet you, too, Jacqueline.'

She gave Mum a little wave, and received the most gracious of smiles in return, then hugged Alexander.

'Well, this is all very cosy,' said Alexander, no doubt wondering who all these mad people were who had invaded his house, 'but what are you doing here? I thought you were working at that restaurant in Manchester?'

Coco glanced at me, and I gave her an encouraging look.

'I was, but I couldn't stay. The chef...' She broke off and looked at Theo. I helped her out.

'The chef wasn't a suitable colleague. I'm sure Coco can fill you in later.'

'Yes,' she said, with relief in her voice. 'Can I do that? Alexander, Dad, I was hoping I *could* stay over Christmas? You said that Stephen and Chrissie are away... I'll do all the cooking...'

Nobody needed anything further to be said as the relief-o-meter zoomed to the top. A chorus of voices agreed warmly, only dying down when Alexander cleared his throat.

'That is a very kind offer, Coco,' he said, his face serious but a telltale smile touching his lips, 'but are you *sure* you shouldn't be at work? Maybe you should ring them, offer to finish your contract or something? And besides, as you can imagine, we're all *very happy* sharing the cooking, we don't need to be rescued from ourselves. Maybe we should take some time to think about it...'

Nobody spoke, all desperately hoping, I'm sure, that the time he needed was about three seconds.

'Okay, I've thought about it. Oh, come on everyone, stop looking so desperate! Of *course* you can stay, Coco, this is your home as well as ours, you don't even need to ask! And we'll be bloody grateful to have you cook, although' – he looked round at us all – 'everyone was very polite about the prospect of takeout and pesto for the next month and God only knows what would have happened to Christmas lunch.'

Now it was Coco's turn to fling her arms around him. I could have done the same myself, and not just because I'd been saved from hell's kitchen. He was looking particularly dishy in the cold morning light and a freshly laundered shirt, and since poor Annabel's banishment, he seemed to have lightened up considerably.

'Thank you!' she cried. 'I'll look after you all brilliantly, I promise. Have you had breakfast?' Everyone nodded disappointedly. 'Cereal and toast, I imagine. Well, if I can borrow the car, I'll go shopping. You won't be sorry I turned up.'

'Never that,' said Douglas, taking his turn to hug his daughter. 'It's always lovely to see you, darling. You haven't got your mother in tow, have you?' he added.

'Not yet,' she replied, grinning. 'Not yet.'

'Might she come here, do you think?' asked Mum, ever so casually. I wasn't fooled, but I *was* interested to see her look slightly worried. *She must really like Douglas*, I thought.

'Oh, probably!' said Coco. 'She's a total homebody but does like to pop by every so often.'

'She never liked this house,' said Douglas. 'Always said it was too big and cold. But, as Coco says, she comes and stays every so often anyway.'

Mum's lips tightened, just a fraction.

'And is she given to staying for long...?'

'She always says it will be a flying visit,' said Coco. 'But I'm afraid it does usually turn into a few days. Her husband comes with her, though,' she added, and I saw Mum's face relax.

'Well, I'll be delighted to meet them, if they do come. Douglas has told me so little about her, just that she is very interested in baking.'

I saw a lightning glance flash between Coco, Douglas and

Alexander – what was going on there? Nobody explained, Douglas merely smiled weakly and said, 'Indeed, she is. Now come on, Coco, I'll take your bag up and you can tell me what you've been doing since we last saw each other.'

Everyone melted away, leaving Mum and me standing in the hall.

'Are you all right?' I asked tentatively.

'Of course I am, darling, why wouldn't I be?'

'Well, it's just that the prospect of one of Douglas's ex-wives turning up for Christmas can't exactly fill you with festive joy. I'd be in agony.'

To my great surprise, she clutched at my arm with her claret-painted nails.

'*Would* you? Oh, darling, you would! I have to admit I'm not *super* comfortable with the idea myself.' She looked – and this was an absolute first for me to see – glum. 'We all have our pasts, I don't care about that, but – oh, Fallon, I do *love* him.'

Now it was my turn to surprise her, but I couldn't resist a hug.

'I know you do, Mum. And he loves you.' I lowered my voice, grinning. 'And anyway, how could she be a patch on you?'

Mum straightened up and smiled dazzlingly – *tits and teeth, sweetie.*

'Well, Fallon, that is true. Now, shouldn't you be nose-to-nose with Alexander over a glass of gin or something?'

I rolled my eyes. One thing you could say about Mum, she didn't stay down for long.

SEVEN

I ran upstairs to leave the dress on my bed and brush my teeth, then decided to go and find Alexander to see when he wanted to start work. My limbs felt heavy and my head fuzzy and I could have done with a morning curled up reading a magazine, but judging by how antsy he had been last night, my guess was that he would want to get going immediately. I couldn't blame him – Christmas was only three weeks away, and the Christmas Fayre would be sooner than that, so we did have to get a move on. I went into the Great Hall, resisting the urge to explore the minstrels' gallery, and peeked into the room where we had eaten supper last night. The Buttery, he had called it. I thought of my London flat and giggled at the idea of having such a room – I didn't even have a separate kitchen, although I had no complaints about the modern, open-plan layout. Anyway, he wasn't in there, so I went into the kitchen. He was sitting at the table with Theo, their dark heads bent over a puzzle. I had a stern word with myself about admiring the way his hair curled round at the nape of his strong neck. *Ahem*.

'Hello...' I ventured. They both looked up and gave me identical smiles.

'Hello, Fallon,' said Theo. 'Is Runcible with you?'

'She was pottering along behind, but I think she got distracted by an interesting smell in the passage. She'll be along in a minute. What's your puzzle?'

'It's birds,' the boy replied. 'I love dogs, but I really, *really* love birds. Look, it's all the different birds of prey.'

I stepped closer to the table and peered over.

'That's great, and you've done so much of it. Has it taken ages?'

'*Ages*, but we've not got much left to do. Oh! There she is!'

He jumped down from his chair and ran to Runcible, who had sniffed her inquisitive way into the kitchen. I turned to Alexander.

'I was just wondering when you wanted to get started on some work? I wasn't sure what your schedule was today, especially after Mum insisted on being taken out for lunch. Sorry about that.'

He raised an eyebrow.

'No problem. I've arranged for Theo to spend the morning with a friend – they should be picking him up in about' – he checked his watch – 'ten minutes, so shall we get started then? My office is just round to the left.'

'Perfect.'

I went back upstairs to grab my laptop, cast a final, longing look at my armchair and magazine, then headed to meet Alexander. I passed him and Theo in the entrance hall, just as Theo's friend arrived to collect him.

'Go on through,' said Alexander. 'I won't be long.'

With Runcible pattering after me, I went to the office. It was another sturdy stone room, like the Buttery, but with a window in one wall. I went round the large desk to look out; it was the same view as from my own bedroom window, the moors stretching beyond the garden. The sound of the door opening made me turn.

'Oh, hello. I was just admiring this view – again. Do you ever get sick of it?'

'Never. Even at its most bleak, it's absorbing and changes all the time, and in the summer it's glorious.'

'Well, I'd better tear myself away so we can get started. Do you want to show me where you're up to?'

'Sure. So, the gin – the one you tried last night – is distilled here on-site, by me. I'll show you the distillery later if you like.'

'How did you learn to make gin?'

'The process is easy, but I went on a course to make sure that I understood everything for commercial production. Then it was a case of deciding which botanicals to include – I wanted to use things that I could obtain locally and even grow myself eventually.'

'You want to grow juniper berries?' I asked in surprise.

'Absolutely. But that's a way off – for now I've focused on getting the blend right and marketing the finished product.'

I nodded. 'Sounds sensible. Okay, well, I've tasted the gin, which was delicious...'

'Even if it did give you a headache?'

'No, I was a bit silly to have had anything last night, especially after drinking champagne in the car with Mum on the way up. I'm not usually a big drinker, especially during the day. I'm sure your gin wasn't to blame.'

'I hope not.'

'Anyway, the product is good – can you show me your packaging?'

He had everything ready, and I was impressed. The boxes and labels were fully recycled and recyclable, as were the bottles and lids, and the design was stunning: exquisite botanical illustrations with a watercolour washed background of the moors.

'I employed a local artist to do the design,' explained Alexander. 'He's lived and worked here his entire life and I've always loved his work. That's one of his too.' He pointed to an atmospheric oil painting of the countryside that hung opposite his desk.

'Beautiful,' I said, 'and a smart business move to use a local. What are your ideas for the Christmas Fayre?'

'It's fairly straightforward. The event is held at a fantastic Victorian town hall in a market town between here and York. You rent a stall and then decorate it however you wish. There are lots of other local producers and artisans, and it's about the most Christmassy thing you can imagine outside the North Pole.'

I laughed.

'Sounds perfect. Can I see some photos?'

I looked carefully at the pictures of the hall and of past events that had been held there, then looked up at Alexander, frowning. I could immediately see a problem with the setup, but I wasn't sure if challenging his plans was going to earn me a grumpy response or not.

'What's the matter?'

I sighed inwardly and took the plunge.

'I like the look of this, but with all the other stalls, I think you're going to be competing quite hard for people's attention. There's a foolproof way to beat them off before the customers have even got inside, but it'll be quite a bit of work... and, um, money...'

I trailed off. I could already envisage my idea in glorious technicolour, but I wasn't working with an established brand that had a multimillion-pound turnover, at some fancy London event that would generate months, if not years, of income.

'What is it?' he asked in an abrupt tone.

I chose my words carefully. 'Look, I'm going to suggest something quite full on, you might think it's too much. But I believe that if you can put in the time, money – and imagination – you'll have something that will serve you well for a long time.'

'An investment?'

'Yes, although there are options.'

'Please just tell me, Fallon.'

I was hoping that offering to work with Alexander hadn't been a bad idea, but he wanted my expertise, so he was going to get it. With any luck, he would decide he didn't need my advice, after all, and I could slope off to a quiet corner for the next few weeks. I ploughed on.

'All right. I think that you should look at obtaining a vintage Citroën HY van – you know, those cute little corrugated metal things with the blunt noses? Lots of people use them for selling food and drink because they're easily adapted to let the side down for an instant bar. You could park it in *front* of the town hall decked out with lights and looking super Christmassy and catch people before they've gone inside – and as they come out again, full of festive cheer. And then you can take it around other events as well – fairs, private parties, weddings... I think it would pay for itself quite quickly – they're very fashionable at the moment.'

I looked up a photo and showed him. He studied it intently for a moment or two, frowning, then smiled.

'I think that's a great idea. We'd have to check with the Christmas Fayre organisers if it would be allowed. If I did want to go ahead, how much money am I looking at?'

This part was always difficult. I knew nothing about Alexander's finances and whether the figure I was about to announce would be instantly payable in cash or out of reach. The best thing to do, always, was to give it straight.

'They cost between twenty and thirty grand. You'd also need specialist fridges and washing-up facilities as well as fitted storage and your logo painted on it.'

He pulled a face. 'Ouch.'

'Yeah, it's a lot. I know a couple of places that sell them, so I can get you a very good deal, and look—' I opened my laptop and tapped a few buttons. 'These are the costings I did for a customer with a food business – his was much more expensive because of the cooking and ventilation requirements. He surpassed these figures in his first year and it paid for itself in two. No guarantees, of course, and it's just an idea.'

He frowned as he looked at the figures.

'Fallon, I thought you were a party planner – this is something else altogether. I'm impressed.'

I shrugged.

'I don't just do parties. And that's why I like my job and owning my own company. I've made it about more than buying balloon arches and making sure the waiting staff arrive on time. Would you like me to cost it up for you?'

'Could you? I think I'd like to go ahead, but it's a lot of money and I need to mull it over. And could we get it sorted in time?'

I waved my hand.

'Oh, don't worry about that, I always get things sorted in time.'

'Okay, but... truly, Fallon, I'm concerned about your health too. I saw a lot of stress and exhaustion when I was working at the hospital – they're serious things. This can all wait if it needs to, there'll be other fairs, events.'

He looked very concerned, his blue eyes searching mine. I had no doubt that he would drop the whole thing if I asked him to. But the truth was, despite my reservations, I was already beginning to enjoy myself, and being away from London and the office was such a relief in itself that sourcing, fitting and painting a van in record time felt like something close to fun. I also couldn't deny that spending time with Alexander – now that he was proving more reasonable than I had expected – was pleasant, and I was happy to keep that going.

'It's fine, and I would tell you if it wasn't.'

'Promise?'

'Promise. Now, what else do we need to think about?'

'The flyers are designed but not printed yet – this is what they'll look like.'

He showed me a fabulous design which incorporated the botanical feel of the labels with an art deco flavour.

'I love it. What else are you printing up other than flyers?'

'Erm... nothing else?'

'Right. Well, at the very least you need cardboard coasters. I can get that sorted – I know an amazing place that makes them out of recycled paper from local schools and offices. You'll need a roller banner as well, and what about menus?'

'Menus? What, with one item: gin and tonic?'

I rolled my eyes.

'We are *not* just going to be selling gin and tonic!'

'We're not...?'

'No. People can have that, of course, but it's Christmas and you're launching a summery drink. What we need is a cocktail – at least one. They have to be festive and fun, and they'd better stick to your 'local' line as much as possible. Something with cranberries – there must be someone growing them near here; isn't it a Yorkshire thing to have them with cheese?'

He raised his eyebrows.

'It is! How did you know?'

'I love Wensleydale. All cheese, really. We could do something with herbs and spices, maybe orange. We'll have to give it some thought. You could even sell cocktail packs so people can make them at home, and little hampers with local cheese or crackers to have with them – they'd make great Christmas presents. I can't believe we have so little time; there's so much we could do here!'

'I wish I'd thought of these things earlier.'

'Never mind, we'll do what we can. Now, what about a webpage?'

'It's taken care of. Hetty has done all that and I'm confident in it.'

'Great. I'll have a quick look this afternoon then. Local press? We need a cheesy photo of you raising a glass to lure in your customers.'

I resisted the temptation to point out that the fact he was so good-looking wouldn't do the brand any harm; I had the feeling he might not like the idea of being a male model.

'Must we? I hate having my photo taken,' he grumbled.

'We must. In fact, why don't we do it now and I'll sort out a press release? A phone photo will do and mine's got a decent camera; I use it for this sort of thing a lot.'

I was used to people reluctant to get in front of the camera, as well as people only too keen to get as many photos of themselves from as many different angles as possible, to plaster all over Instagram, and – having grown up with my mother – I knew a little something about people's best sides. Within minutes, poor Alexander was clutching a bottle of gin and trying to look professional and warm, although I privately thought that smouldering might bring in more customers.

'Okay,' I said, pleased with what I had. 'These are great, you're very photogenic. Come and have a look.'

Wow, maybe inviting him in so close was a mistake. As he leaned in and I swiped through the pictures, I could feel the heat of his body next to mine and smell a delicious nutmeggy, woody, amber scent that went straight to my head – and in a good way. I cleared my throat and tried to sound business-like.

'So, I'll look at them properly on my laptop, but I like this one – you look friendly, the kind of person all sorts of customers would like to have a drink with, or to tell their woes to as you pour them another.'

I felt, rather than saw, him nod and didn't dare turn my head to look at him as that would put our faces in perilous proximity and I wasn't sure I'd be able to resist leaning in for a lovely big lungful of that delicious smell.

'I still can't say I like posing, but you've done a great job with these, thank you. I suppose they won't be too embarrassing to have in the local paper.'

'Not remotely.'

I didn't add that they would also be appearing in the wider press, if my contacts were amenable, and possibly on some of the publicity material. I was also thinking about an Instagram or Facebook page, but maybe that could wait. For now anyway. I swiped one more time, but rather than a handsome man clutching a bottle of gin, a picture of my dear, ugly little dog sitting on the bathroom windowsill on one of the chair cushions from my bedroom appeared. Now it was my turn to be embarrassed, and I switched the screen off quickly.

'Oops, I don't think you'll be wanting that for your publicity!'

'Do you always take your dog to the bathroom with you?'

I could feel my face getting hot. 'Not *always*, but I... I mean, *she* gets lonely if I go for a long bath, and she liked looking out of the window until it got too dark.'

He raised an eyebrow, and my traitorous stomach was infested with a frantic flock of butterflies.

'I see. Well, at least she attends you in comfort.'

'I probably shouldn't have used your cushion. Sorry about that.'

I hung my head and he roared with laughter.

'Oh, Fallon, I don't mind in the least! Runcible is our guest, and she is welcome to sit on any cushion in the house.'

'Thank you. I'm sure she is very grateful. Just be glad it wasn't a bath selfie I took.'

Why, why did I say that? It was going so well.

'I can't say I would have minded that either.'

The butterflies in my stomach had morphed into a troupe of

hysterical chimpanzees, by the feel of things, and I was glad – I *think* I was glad – when his phone rang.

'Hi, Theo, what's up?'

While they were talking, I tried not to listen, even though it was clear from Alexander's end that Theo was badly upset over something. I started drawing up a rough financial plan for the Citroën, something I had done several times before, and tried to concentrate on that, rather than getting too worried about the little boy on the phone. I managed to become so engrossed in it that I didn't notice Alexander had finished his conversation.

'Fallon?'

'Oh, sorry,' I replied casually. 'I was just wondering if branded glasses would bring in enough revenue to be worth going to the effort of selling them to customers, or if we should just keep them for serving? We can't use plastic disposable ones these days and washable plastic looks horrible so quickly.'

'I'm sure you'll make the right decision. I'm sorry, but I'll have to go in a few minutes. That was Theo – something's happened and he wants to come home early.'

'Oh, okay, well, I'll carry on working and we can catch up on it later or tomorrow.' I started collecting up my things, then realised that Alexander was looking at me strangely.

'Is everything all right?' he said.

'Yes?'

'Oh right, it's just you didn't ask what had happened with Theo. It's fine, it doesn't matter.'

I swallowed and tried to keep my tone light. The last thing I wanted was Alexander pegging me as yet another hopeful mother substitute for his son. I hadn't asked because it hadn't occurred to me – *another example of why I'd be a terrible mother* – but I did hope that the little boy was okay.

'Sorry, I was totally in work mode. Is he all right?'

'Yes, I think so. He can be very sensitive, though he'll tell me about it later, hopefully. But he sounded upset.'

'I'm sorry to hear that.' There was an awkward pause, which I quickly filled with work talk. 'So, I'll get this done today and then tomorrow we need to get serious about making some decisions and spending some money.'

He nodded. 'Sure. I'd best be going then.'

'Fine. Can you let me have the distillery costs as soon as possible? I want to factor them in.'

He shrugged. 'Sure. See you later.'

He left, and the car crunched over the gravel moments later. I could tell he was irked by my apparent lack of interest in Theo's welfare, but I resisted the temptation to ask anything else, or offer to help. I liked the boy, but I didn't want to overstep. Plus, what comfort or advice could I possibly offer? Alexander clearly had all that covered without me. Thank goodness I had no aspirations to motherhood – it was becoming more and more obvious that it was the one area in which I strongly took after Jacqueline Honeywood.

I went up to my room to carry on with the work; it felt odd to be sitting in Alexander's office without him there, but I would have to be careful not to give in to the temptation to lie down for a nap. It wasn't long before the front door opened and his and Theo's voices floated through. Theo was sobbing as if his heart was going to break and the sound, unexpectedly, sliced right through me and brought tears to my own eyes. At first, I put my hands over my ears and stared determinedly at my computer screen, but the numbers swam miserably in front of me. I stood up to shut the door but made the mistake of catching Runcible's eye. She was sitting up on the bed, her head on one side, an unmistakeable look of concern on her patchy little face.

'Oh, all *right*,' I said, and scooped her up. We jogged down the stairs to find Alexander and Theo sitting on the sofa in the hallway, their coats still on, the poor child howling into his

father's shoulder as Alexander rubbed his back and spoke soothingly to him. I hesitated awkwardly at the bottom of the stairs
and Alexander looked up. I pointed to Runcible and gave a
questioning shrug. He nodded and over we went.

'Er, Theo?' I said, putting my hand stiffly on his shoulder.
'Runcible heard you were upset, and she wanted to know if she
could help.' The noise subsided, but he was still shaking. I
leaned over and stroked the bit of his cheek I could see with
Runcible's paw. 'See, she's worried about you. Will you give her
a cuddle so that she knows she's done something to help?'

He lifted his tearstained face slowly from Alexander's
shoulder and nodded. I handed him my dog and he immediately cuddled her close; she snuggled comfortingly into his
neck, a gesture of hers I had experienced the many times she
had helped me in the same way.

'Can I take her to the kitchen?' he whispered.

I nodded, knowing that he liked to curl up in the old, soft
armchair that stood in one corner of the room. Speaking quietly
to her, he carried Runcible away. I felt stunned and rather
pleased that I had apparently managed to help him. *Probably a
fluke.*

Alexander looked at me with troubled eyes.

'Thank you, Fallon, you really helped. You and Runcible, of
course.' He smiled weakly. 'Theo won't tell me what happened,
and his friend's parents weren't sure either. It probably wasn't
anything serious – in our eyes at least – but Theo does
have... difficulties sometimes with friends. There are misunder-
standings and he gets so distraught. I wish I knew how to help
him.'

I sat down next to him.

'I'm sorry. I don't know what to say other than that Theo
strikes me as a sweet, sensitive boy. Maybe telling Runcible
what happened might be the best thing for him? I know it

sounds silly, but she has a way of listening without judgement that can be immensely helpful.'

Now it was Alexander's turn to brush away a tear. He nodded.

'I expect you're right. It can be so difficult, you know, parenting. The love is so... *fierce* and yet it can leave me feeling so helpless with the desperation to get it right, whilst knowing I can't do that one hundred percent of the time.'

I didn't reply. I couldn't. Had Mum ever felt like that about me?

'Sorry, Fallon, I'm sure you don't need to be an agony aunt on top of what I'm already asking of you. How are the numbers crunching?'

I smiled in relief. This was more like it.

'Very nicely, thank you. I'd better get back to them, though, there's a lot to do.'

'Okay. Are you looking forward to the party tonight?'

'Of course! What's not to like?' I pulled a face, laughed and got up. 'How about you? Got the tux ready?'

'I see you think that all men are so uncreative as to simply shove on black tie and come as Bond. Well, maybe I'll surprise you!'

'I look forward to it.'

As I returned to the safety of work, I wondered what other surprises the evening might have in store.

EIGHT

I spent much of the rest of the afternoon in my room going through my contacts list and writing emails to set in motion our plans for the Christmas Fayre. As I had hoped, I didn't feel stressed by it; rather, it helped distract me from worrying about the party that evening. I took regular breaks, too, something I had learned was vital for preserving my energy. Although I spent my working life arranging parties and other large events, they were for other people. I was happy to be at them, working, but when it came to my own social life, I was happiest with one or two friends, or just tucked up at home with Runcible. The fact that Mum would be the main draw for many of the guests tonight was a comfort – nobody would be interested in me. I planned to indulge myself with a bit of people-watching, and maybe get to know Coco better.

When I had finished work for the day, about four hours earlier than I was used to doing in London, I decided to venture downstairs, partly for a cup of tea, partly to see how Runcible was getting on and partly to ask if there was anything I could do to help. As I came out onto the landing, Coco emerged from a room a few doors down.

'Hello!'

'Hi there.' She smiled warmly. 'I was just going to make a cuppa – do you want one?'

'You read my mind. I was wondering if they needed any help with the party as well.'

We started walking down the grand staircase.

'I shouldn't have thought so,' said Coco, looking at her watch. 'According to what Dad said, the party organisers should be here any minute now. We'll probably be better off in the kitchen.'

I followed her into the Great Hall.

'I didn't realise the party tonight was such a big deal. I was imagining washing up a few glasses or something.'

She laughed.

'Dad loves hosting, but he hates doing anything towards it, other than telling the organisers it's a Bond theme and handing them a guest list.' We went through the chilly corridors and into the welcoming kitchen. 'It's a pretty good way to do it; he gets to enjoy himself without worrying about the details. I suppose you're used to being on the other side.'

'Absolutely. Luckily, I enjoy all the behind-the-scenes stuff. Clients can never believe it, but we're all different.' I suddenly noticed a small figure curled up on the armchair in the corner of the room. 'Oh, Theo, hello. How are you doing?' His reddened eyes slid away from mine, and he seemed to shrink back into the cushions. *Oh no, I hadn't wanted to upset him.* Feeling awkward, I changed tack. 'I can see that Runcible has had a lovely afternoon with you, so thank you for looking after her. She looks very content curled up there with you.' I was rewarded with a small nod. 'Has she been out for a wee? We could take her now if you like. I've been working all afternoon, and I could do with some air.'

The boy sat silently – had I been too pushy? All the same, my little dog probably could do with going outside, if she hadn't

already. It was Coco who spoke up next, more briskly than
I had.

'Good idea. Come on, Theo, up you get. I'm putting the
kettle on, and we can all have a drink when you come back.' She
picked up his coat from where it had been draped on the back
of a chair and held it out to him. 'You'd better put this on, it's
freezing out there.' Slowly, and still clutching Runcible like a
life ring, he uncurled himself and took the coat. Coco smiled.
'Good boy. Look, Fallon, Alexander's left his coat here. Put that
on rather than going all the way back to the front for yours.'

I took the wool overcoat a little shyly and pulled it on.
There was an intimacy to wearing Alexander's clothes, and I
caught a whiff of his aftershave. Refusing to allow myself even a
hint of giddiness, I strode towards the back door and opened it,
letting in an icy blast of air that soon put paid to any flickers of
feeling beyond gratitude that I had a coat at all.

'Come on, hurry up, you two,' chivvied Coco. 'Don't let all
the heat out. I'll see you in a minute.'

We stepped outside and Theo hesitantly placed Runcible
on the ground.

'Don't worry,' I said. 'We won't be out for long. She doesn't
like the cold much, but she'll be fine for a few minutes, especially if we get moving.' I started walking. 'When I take her out
for any more than a few minutes in the winter, I put her in little
knitted jumpers. She looks so sweet.'

'Really?' asked Theo, and I felt a rush of pleasure that I had
succeeded in getting him talking.

'Really. She has a few different ones. Maybe we can take
her out tomorrow and she can model one for you.' He didn't
answer, but turned towards a small pathway which led through
some large bushes. I persisted. 'Of course, she does have a
special one for Christmas Day, but we're saving that. Runcible
absolutely loves Christmas. Her favourite thing is playing in the
wrapping paper, but she doesn't like crackers much.'

'Neither do I,' said Theo. 'They make me jump.'

'Her too. One year I pulled all the snaps out before I put them on the table and everyone was a bit disappointed, but at least she didn't get upset. I should have got her something to wear tonight – she'd look good in gold sparkles.'

Theo looked up at me and his worried face broke into a brief smile.

'Or a bowler hat,' he said. 'She could totally carry that off.'

'She could. Are you going to join the party at all?'

He shrugged.

'Dad said I could come for a bit if I wanted to, but I don't know. I don't want to spoil it.' I was about to ask him why he thought he might, when he stopped by a fence. 'There's someone for you to meet,' he said, then started calling what sounded like *'Heath, Heath, Heath!'* and banging his hand on the fence. Then, making me jump, a large and very hairy donkey appeared and nuzzled at the boy, evidently pleased to see him.

'Who's this?' I asked, taking a step back and checking to see that Runcible was all right.

'This is Heathcliff,' he replied, pulling a carrot out of his pocket and giving it to him. He crunched it up greedily and started looking for another.

'Is he yours?'

'Mine and Dad's and Aunt Constance's. She's coming to stay soon too. I like her.'

Much as I wanted to hear about the new addition to the household, I was still intrigued by the donkey.

'I like the name Heathcliff. Who named him?'

'Aunt Constance. *Wuthering Heights* is her favourite book. He was being badly treated and she rescued him. He can't live with her, so he's here and she comes to visit him. And us, I suppose, but mostly him. You can stroke him if you want to, he won't bite.' I reached out my hand and touched the donkey's nose. He immediately responded, pushing up into my hand. Encouraged, I stroked one of his long ears.

'You can give him a carrot too,' offered Theo.

I barely had time to take it from him before Heathcliff had snatched it away and devoured it. I laughed.

'They're your favourite, are they, Heathcliff? I'll have to get some more next time I go to town.'

Finally, I was rewarded with a proper smile from Theo.

'I thought you'd like him.'

'I like all animals, but he is super. He's very furry.'

'It's his winter coat, it's not so big in the summer.'

'Talking of winter coats, I'm getting cold, aren't you?' He nodded. 'Shall we go back to the house for that tea Coco's making?' He nodded again and I whistled to Runcible, who gladly came running over, giving Heathcliff a wide berth. We set off. 'I'm sorry to hear that he was badly treated,' I said. 'And I'm glad your aunt rescued him. I don't understand why people are unkind to animals.'

'Neither do I!' replied Theo fiercely. 'Animals are much better than us – they aren't cruel or confusing.'

There was a slight pause as we trudged over the hard ground.

'Do you?' I asked. 'Find people confusing, that is?'

He shrugged.

'Sometimes.' He bent down to pick up Runcible and started muttering into her hairy ear. I sensed that I wasn't going to get a lot more out of him this afternoon, but at least he seemed happier now. I pushed open the back door to see Alexander sitting at the table with Coco. He jumped up when we came in, a worried expression on his face.

'Oh, there you are. Is everything okay?'

'Yes, fine,' I replied. 'Shouldn't it be? Oh, gosh, I'm so sorry, I borrowed your coat. I hope that's all right.'

I quickly shrugged it off and handed it to him.

'Thank you, of course I don't mind. I mean, well, Theo, are you all right?'

He nodded.

'Yes, I'm okay. I took Fallon to meet Heathcliff and she gave him a carrot. Can I go and watch TV?'

'Yes, yes, of course.'

Theo disappeared and Alexander turned to me, a look of amazement on his face.

'What on earth did you do?'

'Do?' *Had I upset him by going out alone with Theo?* 'Sorry, we just took Runcible out for a quick walk and met that lovely donkey. I'm really sorry if you'd rather I hadn't.'

I took a very welcome hot cup of tea from Coco and sat down.

Alexander looked at Coco, who raised an eyebrow, but said nothing.

'No, Fallon,' he said. 'It's not that at all. I'm happy that the two – or should I say *three* – of you went out. It's just that, well, Theo had a hard time this morning with his friend, as you know, and it can sometimes take him a couple of days to get over something like that happening. Not only do you seem to have snapped him out of it, but he's taken you to meet Heathcliff. He never, ever takes anyone there: none of his friends, no one.'

I was starting to feel awkward and stood up again.

'Well, I'm glad he's all right. And I didn't do or say anything special; I wouldn't know how to. I think I'll take this upstairs – it's not long before I need to get ready for the party.'

I nipped out quickly, before I could be asked any more questions about what had just happened. I walked past Theo contentedly watching a programme about hawks, and out into the hallway, which was a different scene from when I had last gone through it twenty minutes ago. Now the front door stood open, and I could see a large van outside, from which people were ferrying crates of glasses, chairs and, unsurprisingly in the circumstances, a life-size cutout of Sean Connery. I swerved around them and jogged up the stairs, grateful that I didn't have to get involved. As I reached my room, there was a movement by my feet, and I saw Runcible there.

'Come on,' I said. 'Let's get some rest before tonight.'

The next hour was spent peacefully sipping tea and reading my book, and I was just contemplating getting ready when a brief knock came at the door before it was flung open to once again admit my mother, wearing a lavender silk dressing gown.

'Oh, darling, haven't you started getting ready yet? The party starts soon.'

'I know, but it's okay, it won't take me long and Coco's coming to help with my make-up. Anyway, you don't look very ready yourself.'

'Actually, I am.' With a typically dramatic movement, she threw off the robe to reveal what she was wearing: a skintight red catsuit with a low-slung black belt and attached gun holster. I gawked. 'Well, what do you think?' she demanded, twirling around. 'It's the original costume from the film. I can still fit in it!'

I had to speak, I knew I had to speak, but what to say?

'Um, right... wow, well, the original one, eh?'

She pulled her robe back on huffily.

'Yes, darling, and is that all you've got to say?'

'It looks amazing,' I replied truthfully. 'Has Douglas seen it?'

'Not *on* me,' she said. 'But I had it at the convention, and he admired it then. Don't look so disapproving, darling, I could have worn the bra top and see-through skirt from the harem scene, then you *would* have something to be cross about.'

I wasn't cross or disapproving in the least, but my mother loves to believe that everyone is jealous of her.

'Actually, Mum, I'm impressed by your chutzpah as much as your figure. I was just surprised, that's all. You look great.'

'Thank you. Now, you'd better show me what you're wearing, and then I need you to help me with my headdress.'

I opened the box I had collected from the Post Office that morning, shook out the long, black dress with its diamanté neckline and held it up against myself awkwardly. Despite everything, I wanted my mother's approval. She studied me for a moment.

'Hmm, it's simple but elegant. I hope it looks all right on. What shoes are you wearing?'

I turned to find them when there was another, gentler knock on the door.

'Come in!' I called, lifting the shoe box on to the bed. It was Coco who entered, looking breathtaking in a short, tight blue satin dress with a high neckline. Her hair was piled up on her head and her smoky make-up enhanced her delicate features without overpowering them. 'Oh wow, you look incredible!'

She grinned.

'Thanks. I think this is a bit '*Dr No*' – it'll do anyway.' She glanced at Mum's robe. 'Is that your costume, Jacqueline?'

My mother narrowed her eyes at Coco, and I tried not to laugh.

'No, dear, it is not. Anyway, Fallon, if you could help me with the headdress?'

I took the proffered piece of black and gold fabric and a golden cord and looked at them helplessly. Thank goodness for Coco.

'Here, let me do it. Sit there, Jacqueline, I'll have you Bond-ready in no time.'

Coco was so skilful, both at arranging the costume and at chattering away in such a friendly and flattering manner that my mother was putty in her hands in no time. By the time they were finished, she was positively glowing.

'Thank you, darling, it looks wonderful. Now, I must go and arrange some finishing touches. If you can work your magic on Fallon, then I will be even more impressed.'

As the door closed behind her, Coco turned to me and arched an eyebrow.

'I know, I know,' I groaned. 'She can be hard work, my mother, and she thinks I'm a troll.'

'Well,' said Coco briskly, 'she couldn't be any more wrong – you're beautiful – but let's go to town on the glam anyway, shall we?'

I went and put on my dress, then sat as Coco sprayed and rolled and pinned my hair, then whisked around me with brushes, pencils and sticks. It occurred to me that I had no idea if I would like her style, but it was lovely just to sit and submit to her attentions. She talked as she worked, telling me about the kitchens she had been employed in and her dreams of starting her own business.

'Have you considered doing something with Alexander?' I asked. 'He's just starting out as well, so I'm sure you could help each other.'

'Oh, Fallon, I'd *love* to, but I doubt he'd want to work with me.'

'Whyever not?'

'He's so serious, and although I am too – about my work – I'm not sure he'd trust me enough to go into business with me.'

'Well, I don't know him well enough to say, but I do know that you don't get what you don't ask for in life.'

'Maybe. Anyway, let's not talk any more about work tonight – you're ready, Miss Honeywood!'

I smiled at her nervously and stood up to look at myself in the mirror. Gazing back was what I can only describe as an enhanced version of me – I looked natural yet glamorous at the same time as if someone had applied some clever filter on a phone, smoothing out all the tiredness, lighting up my skin, plumping my lips and sparking a little fire in my eyes. My hair fell in smooth, shiny waves that curled elegantly onto my shoulders.

'Wow. Thank you so much. I look... I don't know, sort of the same but different.'

'Well, that is exactly what I was aiming for. It's like I said, you're a knockout, so you don't need disguising or changing in any way. Just a little bringing out, maybe.'

I turned and hugged her.

'Thank you. I'll just leave some food for Runcible and put my shoes on, then shall we go down?'

'Yes, people have started arriving. We can make an entrance on the stairs.'

I'd rather be making myself cosy in bed, I thought, as I kissed Runcible goodbye, but maybe the evening would be more exciting than I anticipated.

NINE

As we went downstairs, I was glad to see that, although there were plenty of people in the hallway, they were all looking at each other and not at us. We had an excellent view from the top of the stairs, and I was impressed with what the organisers had achieved in such a short time. Gold shimmered everywhere, and there were cut-outs of every actor who had played Bond, not just the Sean Connery I had seen earlier. People were posing with them for photos, enjoying themselves before they had even reached the main party area. When we got downstairs, I couldn't resist and stood slinkily next to Roger Moore, his eyebrow arched, while Coco snapped away on my phone.

'Do you want me to do one of you?' I asked. 'Which Bond do you fancy?'

She laughed.

'Not my thing, I'm afraid. If there's one of Ursula Andress, though, I'll be first in line.'

'Don't tell my mother that,' I said in a stage whisper. 'She met Ursula at a do once and was furious when she didn't know who the great Jacqueline Honeywood was.'

We giggled and I started to feel more excited about the

party, now that I had a friend to go with. We took a glass of champagne – although I was going to take it easy tonight after finally shaking off last night's headache – and went through to the Great Hall, which had been transformed into a casino, complete with various gaming tables and a mirrored bar.

'Are these real?' asked Coco. 'I can't imagine the residents of Lingfoss having many skills on the poker table.'

'They won't be,' I replied. 'I've set up a few parties like this, and it's all just for fun – you get given chips to play with, but the only thing you win is bragging rights.'

'Sounds good to me,' she replied. 'Shall we get stuck in?'

We went over to a table covered with plush red velvet and were each given a pretend thousand pounds' worth of chips.

'I'm tempted to put them all on one spin of the roulette wheel,' I said, 'but maybe it would be more fun to eke them out. What do you want to try first?'

'Let's play blackjack,' said Coco. 'At least I can count to twenty-one, which must be something of an advantage.'

We joined some other people at the table and started playing, betting small amounts and promptly losing them. I was just wondering whether to have another turn or try my luck elsewhere when Coco suddenly shouted:

'Aunt Constance!'

I looked up to see a short, squarely built woman in a brown jacket, flat cap and plus fours – dressed, I assumed, as Goldfinger – approach the table. She smiled broadly when she saw Coco and came over, bending to envelop her in a huge hug.

'Hello, niece, I wasn't expecting to see you here. I see Douglas has produced as vulgar a party as ever, but none the less enjoyable for that. Who's this?' She peered at me. 'Your latest?'

'No, Constance, sadly not. I'm single at the moment. This is Fallon – she's Jacqueline Honeywood's daughter.'

'Is she indeed? I haven't met your mother yet, but she seems to have perked Douglas up no end. He's my brother, in case you didn't know.'

I held out my hand for a bone-crushing squeeze.

'Nice to meet you. I have heard about you – from Theo. He says you rescued the donkey, Heathcliff.'

She roared with laughter.

'Yes, that's me. It's the only thing Theo's remotely interested in about me, good boy. Where is he?'

'He'll be somewhere with Alexander,' replied Coco. 'We haven't seen them yet. Are you going to have a go at some blackjack? Come and join us.'

'Maybe later – far easier to wipe the floor with everyone when they've all had a few drinks. See you shortly.'

She turned abruptly and marched away. Coco grinned at me.

'She's a character, isn't she? I'm glad she's here, she'll be staying now until Christmas. She livens the place up no end and Theo adores her.'

'I didn't know she was coming today.'

'Nobody ever knows for sure when she'll turn up. She's an archaeologist and is always disappearing off around the world to dig up something fascinating. Her husband, my Uncle Felix, died a couple of years ago and she nursed him for about six months. It was very hard on her – as you can imagine – but now she's determined to keep working and travelling as much as she can. Anyway, shall we go and try another game?'

We spent the next hour or so going from table to table, losing almost all our chips.

'I'm out,' said Coco finally, 'and I need the loo. See you in a few minutes?'

I nodded and contemplated the few chips I had left in my hand – just ten pounds. I thought I might as well blow it, so I went over to the roulette table and watched for a few minutes as the wheel spun mesmerically.

'What number are you going for?'

I turned to see Alexander standing next to me, wearing a black suit painted with bones.

'I like your outfit,' I said. 'Casino Royale?'

'You do know your Bond films – I didn't realise you were a fan.'

'Not like your father, but I enjoy them. And seeing as Mum was in one for a millisecond, I've had to sit through more than most people as she talks about all her dearest friends that she met on set.'

He laughed.

'It sounds exciting, but I can imagine that it wears after a while. Now come on, which number are you going to choose?'

'I think I'm just going to put it all on eight – for my birthday,' I said.

'Mine too!' he replied. 'I'm in March.'

'I'm in July. It had definitely better be eight then.'

I leaned over and placed my chips, then waited with rising excitement as the wheel spun and clicked round.

'Thirty-two red!' shouted the croupier and I turned to Alexander and pulled a face.

'Ah, well,' he said, grinning ruefully, 'at least it's not real money. Would you like to top up your drink as consolation?'

I nodded, and followed him to the bar, where we hitched ourselves up onto stools and accepted glasses of champagne.

'Cheers', he said, and we clinked glasses. 'Are you enjoying the party?'

'Yes, I've been with Coco – she's brilliant.'

'She is... but I wish she'd settle to something. I truly am pleased to have her here, but that's another job she's jacked in. She doesn't seem to have much staying power.'

'I think she wants to set up something of her own,' I ventured tentatively. 'She has lots of good ideas.'

He snorted.

'Ideas are all very well, but you need a lot more than that to get a business going, as I well know.'

'Maybe you could share some of your newfound wisdom with her?' I suggested, the champagne making me bold. He frowned briefly, then his face softened.

'Maybe. Have you spoken to anyone else this evening? Coco won't be back for a while, since she's offered to settle Theo into bed – it's late for him now.'

'No. I haven't seen my mother at all, but I did meet your Aunt Constance, the roving archaeologist.'

His face brightened.

'She's great. I'm glad she's here. I never thought she'd come to stay for so long, but apparently, she's writing a book on some cave sites in Belize where she's been working. She can help look after that donkey as well. Anyway, I could introduce you to a few people if you like?'

Was he so keen to be rid of me already?

I started to slide off the stool.

'Don't worry, I'm sure I can find someone to talk to...'

I was interrupted by him unexpectedly grasping my hand and giving me a startlingly huge smile.

'Please sit down again,' he hissed through his stretched lips, and I was about to shake him off when I saw Annabel – she of the floral dress and hearty casserole – closing in from the right. She was wearing a clinging red dress with a plunging neckline and looked stunning. Ignoring me, she enveloped Alexander in a Chanel-scented embrace, then put her hands on his shoulders, effectively blocking me out. I gestured to the bartender for another refill; this clearly warranted one.

'*Alexander*,' she said huskily. 'You look divine.'

'You look lovely yourself, Annabel,' he said, trying to peer round her to see me. 'Have you met Fallon?'

She turned her head to look me up and down.

'No. Now, Alex, what say we go and put a bet on? I could be your lucky charm.'

'That sounds like an *excellent* idea,' he said, snatching the half-full bottle from the bartender and standing up, 'but I'm afraid I've promised Fallon that I would show her the... er, the minstrels' gallery. Didn't I?'

'Yes, that's right,' I said, startled. Recovering, I added, 'And what better time to see it than with a party in full swing? *Lovely* to meet you, Annabel.'

Leaving her looking utterly furious, Alexander grabbed my elbow and steered me swiftly through the guests to the little space at the far end of the hall, where he drew aside the curtain that covered the stairway.

'Are we really going up there?' I asked.

'Yes, come on, let's get a breather. Annabel's a good sort – we've known each other since we were little – but she can be extremely persistent. I don't think even she would dare follow us up here.'

I picked my way carefully up the narrow, winding wooden stairs to where they opened out to the gallery, in which there were a few mismatched chairs and a small, round table.

'Do sit down,' said Alexander. 'You can see quite a lot from here, but people hardly ever think to look up, so it's quite private. One year the weather was so rainy that they couldn't do the Nativity outside, so we offered them the Hall instead. The Angel Gabriel appeared up here and made everyone jump out of their skins.'

I laughed as I relaxed gratefully into a chair covered with tapestry and sipped my champagne, letting the noisy chatter of the party from down below wash over me. Alexander took a seat across the small table.

'How are you feeling?' he asked. 'Dad told me you'd been through quite a lot.'

'I'm all right, thank you,' I replied. 'My business has grown a bit too rapidly and I wasn't able to keep up, but I'm going to make some changes and being away for a bit will make all the difference. It was good of you to say I could stay.'

He shook his head.

'Not at all. Dad is clearly besotted with your mother, and I was glad to open up the house. Theo and I are happy here, but I know we can get rather... insular. Now we've got both of you, plus Coco and Constance, so I've got more than I bargained for. Thank you again for the help you're giving me with the Christmas Fayre, it's made a huge difference.'

He smiled at me, and a wave of attraction hit a wave of champagne, which was a heady mix. I smiled back and he held my gaze. I was the one to drop my eyes first, as I searched for some words to fill the silence.

'I'm happy to help. And, well... I know you don't need saving – other than from slinky Annabel, of course – but I'm glad to be of use while I'm here.'

'Hmm, talking of slinky Annabel, I'm sorry she was so rude to you earlier. She's usually very sweet.'

I waved my glass airily.

'Oh, don't worry about that. I just pretended I was my mother for a few minutes, and it all rolled off me.'

Alexander laughed.

'Do you do that a lot, pretend you're your mother?'

'Oh, God no, we're chalk and cheese and I'm perfectly happy with that.'

He stared at me again, and I foolishly took another sip of champagne, producing the not unpleasant headiness again.

'Actually, I'm not sure you are that different,' he said slowly. 'You're both smart, beautiful women, after all.'

'Oh! Er, thank you.' I was lost for words and started looking everywhere but at those deep blue eyes. Was he flirting with me? Maybe he was just keeping up the pretence in case Annabel suddenly appeared. I stood up and started looking over the party, hoping for a few minutes to compose myself, but he came and stood next to me.

'Sorry, Fallon, I hope I haven't offended you?'

I turned to see him looking worried.

'Oh no, of course not, it's just...' It felt so pathetic to admit, but his concerned gaze and the champagne curling through me spurred me on. 'Well, normally when people compare me to Mum – which they do a *lot* – it's to marvel at how utterly different we are and how they can't believe I'm her daughter. Given that she's famous for her beauty, talent and drive, I don't come out of it well.' I went to have some more to drink, but found my glass empty. Alexander noticed and went to get the bottle from the table. He filled my glass, and his own.

'Look, I don't know either of you well. And I'm afraid I know very little about your mother or her career, and maybe that makes me unusual. I was just saying what I have seen in a very short time. I know your mother has legions of fans, but from what I've seen of you, Fallon, there's no reason why you shouldn't be equally admired. You've taken a different path – one that doesn't involve fame and adulation – but is just as impressive. Sorry, I should probably shut up now.'

I smiled, my face now very hot.

'Not at all, thank you. Now, don't you think we should join the party again? I haven't seen Annabel lately; maybe she's given up and gone home.'

'I don't want to sound unkind, but I do hope so. I've known her a long time and she's... well-meaning, I suppose, but rather...'

'Velcro?' I supplied.

He laughed.

'Exactly that. She seems to be on a mission, but I'm not going to be worn down. Theo and I are fine just as we are.'

I nodded, trying to ignore the little flash of disappointment that went through me.

'Of course you are. Let's drink to being allowed to live the way we want.'

We clinked glasses and drank, then I turned to go towards the stairs.

'Fallon!' Alexander caught my arm and I turned, confused. 'Sorry, I didn't mean to startle you. I was just going to say, let me go down first. There's a dodgy step you don't notice coming up and I don't want you to fall.'

I stepped aside to let him pass and he went down carefully, testing each stair and letting me know which one to avoid. I navigated that successfully, but when I was on the very bottom step, as Alexander pushed aside the curtain, the champagne, tiredness and high heels combined dramatically, and I tripped. I clutched at the air helplessly before falling against Alexander, who seized me firmly as he stumbled backwards past the curtain and into the little chamber. I can't say that the dizziness I felt could entirely be blamed on the shock, as I found my face buried in his warm neck. He was trying to right me, and I stood back shakily. I was just about to thank him when an all-too-familiar voice said in amused tones:

'Dear me, you two, find a room with a proper door next time.'

There stood my mother, with Douglas beside her, both smiling indulgently.

'I fell, that's all!' I said defensively, then turned to Alexander. 'Thank you for catching me, I shouldn't have worn these stupid shoes.'

'What *were* you doing behind there?' asked Mum, not willing to throw me back in the water now I was dangling helplessly on her line. 'We've been looking for you for ages.'

'I just wanted to show Fallon the gallery,' said Alexander dismissively. 'You get a good view, you should take Jacqueline up, Dad. Right, I'm going to go and check on Theo.'

He marched off before anyone could say anything else. Encouraged by his coolness, I straightened my shoulders.

'And I'm going to see where Coco is. Fantastic party, Douglas.'

For the first time in my life, I left my mother without the last word as I made as dignified an exit as I could on a slightly sore ankle and wearing a dress damp with spilled champagne.

I found Coco with Constance, sitting near the dance floor deep in conversation. I was shy about interrupting them, but seeing as they were the only familiar people at the party, I didn't feel I had much choice. I needn't have worried, as they both greeted me warmly.

'We've been talking about Aunt Constance's book,' said Coco. 'It sounds fascinating.'

'It is,' said Constance, 'but it is also not the best topic of conversation for a party, especially when I want to dance. Come on, you two!'

She stood up and strode onto the dance floor as the band struck up 'Diamonds are Forever', and Coco and I followed, giggling as we hammed up some foxy moves. That set the tone for the rest of the party, and the three of us danced cheesily, singing along to all the bits we knew, until the band announced it was time for their last song, ironically 'We Have All the Time in the World'. There were still plenty of guests chatting and drinking, but I was done for the evening.

'Time to get these shoes off. Thank you both for the dancing.'

'I won't be far behind you,' said Constance. 'I've got a lot of work to do tomorrow, and Theo is bound to want me to trek off and see that donkey.'

'Sleep tight!' said Coco. 'I'll have breakfast ready by nine, so see you then.'

I hugged them both and slipped off up the stairs, managing to avoid Mum, who would doubtless want either to interrogate me about Alexander or take a 'survivors' end of evening selfie with me for her Instagram account, neither of which I could face.

Back in my room, I took off my shoes and put on slippers with glorious relief, then woke up a very sleepy Runcible.

'Sorry, sweetheart, but you must go out one last time.'

Now seemed like a good moment to try the back stairs by the kitchen and I was soon shivering at the door, wishing I'd put something on over my dress. Thankfully, my dog was as chilly as I was and didn't hang about, and soon we were back upstairs and tucked up, falling asleep quickly despite my mind being a whirl of music, gambling chips and the feeling of strong arms around me.

TEN

I woke the next morning with sore feet but a reasonably clear head. Remembering that Coco had said breakfast would be at nine, I hopped into the shower and dressed quickly, so that I would have time to take Runcible for a walk first. I had the measure, now, of the Yorkshire weather, and put on my warmest clothes, but even then, I knew they wouldn't be good enough, and I was proved right when I pulled open the big front door.

'Brass monkeys out there, isn't it?' came a hearty voice behind me, and I turned to see Constance, in markedly more sensible clothing than mine.

'It's freezing,' I replied. 'Do you think it will snow soon?'

'Bound to, then this little mite will sink up to her armpits.' She bent down and stroked Runcible, who was wearing a smart red fleece jumper. 'Lovely little dog. Can I join you for your walk or were you hoping for some peace? I won't be offended if you are, I'll just go the other way. I like some morning air.'

The truth was, I *had* been looking forward to it just being Runcible and me, but now that Constance had appeared, I was glad of her company.

'Not at all, please do, although I wasn't planning on being

out for long. I think I need to go shopping for some warmer clothes.' We stepped out into the misty, frozen morning and crunched across the gravel, our breath puffing out in clouds. 'I was going to walk down to the village, but only because it's the only place I know at the moment. Is there somewhere else we can go?'

'Yes, yes, let's cross here, then over that stile and you can see a good bit of moorland. Stretches for miles, but we don't have to do all that today. I don't go down to the village much. Nice enough people, but they will try to rope me in to 'village activities' just because I'm widowed. Not all single women like doing flowers for the church and baking, as I'm sure you know.'

She looked at me sharply and I grinned.

'The singles scene in London is different, but I do get annoyed with people always expecting me to be looking for a husband. I guess old-fashioned outlooks die hard. Anyway, I'm happy with my business and my friends.'

'Good for you. It's different strokes. Mind you, if you find the right person and they do, too, then marriage isn't so bad. Felix and I were happy, and I liked having my son, but I can't say I was sorry when he grew past the baby stage and got a bit more interesting.'

'I'm sorry about Felix. How old is your son now?'

'He's twenty-five – I was well into my forties when I had him – and living in Japan. He's an engineer – still out there. I'll probably go and visit him next year. Having children isn't the be all and end all of life, but do be sure either way.'

'I am,' I said firmly. 'It's not for me, I'd be a hopeless mother.'

'I sincerely doubt that,' replied Constance, 'but you know best. That dog is beginning to look woeful – shall we head back?'

. . .

We got back just as everyone else was arriving for breakfast. Coco looked fresh and professional in a chef's coat and ushered us towards the Buttery.

'Do you need any help bringing things through?' I asked, but she shook her head.

'No, just sit down, I'm nearly there.'

There were pleased exclamations as the food came through: a bowl of homemade granola, fresh fruit, toast and pastries.

'Would anybody like a cooked breakfast?' said Coco. 'I'm going to have to do some shopping, but I can rustle something up?' Everybody was happy with the feast already on the table, so she took off her chef's whites and joined us. 'What are you all doing today? If anyone's going into York, I'd be grateful of a lift.'

'Alexander and I are spending the day with Theo,' said Douglas. I risked a sideways glance at my mother to see what she thought about this, but she had painted a firmly serene expression on her face which clearly wasn't going to budge. 'We're going to visit a local animal shelter,' he added, 'but definitely *not* bringing anyone home with us.' He grinned at Theo, who rolled his eyes at his grandfather.

'I know, I know,' he said. 'But it's okay, these ones are not like Heathcliff. These animals are already being looked after. I'd like to start my own shelter one day, though.'

Alexander reached over and ruffled his hair.

'Good idea. Maybe we'll pick up some tips today.'

'I shall be sequestered away in the study all day,' said Constance. 'I've got to try and get down four thousand words a day if there's any hope of my enjoying Christmas.'

'I'm going to do some work for the Christmas Fayre for a couple of hours,' I said, 'but then I was thinking of going to get some warmer clothes. If I can borrow a car, we can go to York, Coco?'

'Take mine,' said Alexander, as his sister eagerly nodded her agreement. 'Dad will drive us to the shelter – that's okay, isn't it?'

Douglas nodded.

'Of course, my pleasure.'

'In the Aston Martin?' said Theo, his eyes alight. 'Brilliant!'

'I'll get you into Bond yet!' said his grandfather. 'The Aston Martin is certainly a good place to start.'

'Just as long as you don't move him on to martinis next,' said Alexander, grinning.

'Yuck!' said Theo, wrinkling up his face, and everyone laughed.

'I will join you if I may, Fallon,' said Mum. 'I have some shopping to do myself and I wanted to visit a small apothecary that I think will look wonderful on my grid.'

'What's a grid?' asked Theo, and a few relieved faces indicated that other people had been thinking the same thing.

'It's my Instagram grid – where I put photos for my followers to see. Such a marvellous way of connecting with my fans, but also great for selling my products.'

'What do you sell?' asked Coco.

My mother looked momentarily annoyed that her empire hadn't reached that far, but she answered politely:

'Face products – serums, creams and so on. Marvellous stuff, but...' she added *sotto voce*, 'no substitute for a skilled surgeon.' Everyone laughed and she looked pleased. 'If only I could persuade Fallon to try them – they'd work wonders on you, darling.'

The laughter died down as my face reddened and I stared at my plate. What can one *say* at these moments? Short of swearing or walking out, both of which I have done in the past and have precisely no impact on Mum, I had nothing to clap back at her. Support came from Constance.

'Oh, poppycock. Fallon is beautiful, as you well know, and there's no snake oil needed to gild that particular lily.'

'I don't think she meant it like that,' said Douglas in a calm voice. 'Jacqueline just loves to help bring out the best in people.'

I glanced up to see Mum shooting a look of dislike in Constance's direction, but it was wasted, as she was oblivious and selecting another pastry. My mother rapidly composed herself and smiled at Douglas; these days even she wouldn't pick a fight with her boyfriend's sister at the breakfast table, although a few years ago I would have run for cover at this point.

'Anyway,' she said smoothly, as if nothing had happened, 'people are interested in more than skincare these days – I get asked more and more often about my wellness regime, so I shall start things off with picking up some of my favourite herbal supplements at this apothecary and putting the shop on the map at the same time.'

This was pure Jacqueline Honeywood, and I couldn't resist an innocent question.

'And what *are* your favourite herbal supplements, Mum?'

She waved her hand dismissively.

'I'm sure I'll find out once I get there. You may sneer, but it's all the rage these days.'

'And does champagne count? Maybe the grapes are one of your five a day?'

'Good champagne is splendidly pure and anyway, five a day is terribly passé, darling, it's all about thirty different plant foods for your gut bacteria now. Sounds unpleasant to me, but Acanthe is preparing some posts about it.'

Acanthe – who was named Jane at birth – is my mother's much-exploited PA who adores her and is more Jacqueline Honeywood than she is herself.

'I'm not sure that the purity of the champagne makes up for the ethanol content,' put in Alexander mildly, reminding me that until his accident he was an eminent heart surgeon, so better placed to talk about 'wellness' than any influencer, even if he was starting up a gin business. Mum sailed on regardless.

'Oh well, we can't worry too much about that. I'm thinking of becoming sober curious next year, but I don't want to do it all at the same time.'

I hid a smile. This is the woman who, back in the 1970s, had thought nothing of necking a few tapeworms washed down with Campari. Personally, I wouldn't be taking wellness advice from her, but, as ever, I admired her determination.

'Okay then,' I said. 'Let's leave around quarter to twelve, shall we, and we can get some lunch in York as well.'

A shame I'd be driving, I reflected as I finished my coffee. A swig or two of ethanol would have made a shopping expedition with my mother considerably more bearable.

We arrived in York just after twelve. Coco went off immediately as she had friends to catch up with as well as shopping to do, which left my mother and me alone for the second time in three days. I was wearing the clothes I had pulled on for dog walking that morning, and was still too cold. Mum was looking every inch the winter princess in a hat lined with real fur – 'it's perfectly fine if it's vintage, darling, stop looking so disapproving' – and a tailored red coat with a little cape.

'It's a bit early, but shall we start with lunch?' I suggested, wanting to get my strength up for the afternoon ahead. 'We could go to Bettys; the wait might not be too bad yet.'

'Wait?' said Mum. 'I don't have to wait, Fallon. Come on, where is this place?'

As we walked the five minutes or so to the tea rooms, I looked around at the impressive medieval architecture, while Mum rang Acanthe. Even I was impressed when, as we approached the iconic building, the windows of which exploded with a fabulous sparkly, snowy Christmas display, a smartly dressed man appeared, greeted both of us by name and swept us past the long, cold, jealous queue and straight over to a corner table – my mother's usual favourite spot as she could see the rest of the room and didn't have anyone behind her back.

'Please do make sure that everyone waiting has a hot drink on me,' said my mother, smiling graciously.

'Thank you, Miss Honeywood, I'll see to it immediately. How very kind of you,' said the man and disappeared, to be instantly replaced by a smiling waitress who handed us menus, then melted away again. Mum gave a contented sigh.

'What a delightful place,' she said, taking several selfies from different angles. 'I'll mention them on my socials. Now, what shall we have?'

When the waitress came back, I ordered the smoked haddock fish cakes, which came with various sides and sauces and sounded delicious, then I settled back to wait while my mother indulged in one of her favourite hobbies: ordering off-menu. She started by clocking the waitress's name badge, then began her campaign.

'Melody, hello, how lovely to meet you. Now, do you ever watch *Mayfair Mews*? You do? I'm thrilled! Don't let me leave without us taking a photo together, will you? Now, about my lunch. You understand that I do have to be very careful about what I eat, so I hope you don't mind if I ask for a few *tiny* changes? You don't? Splendid. So. The salmon salad sounds *divine*, but I must have my fish grilled, not fried, and please leave out the garlic. I will have cabbage rather than the chicory, and if you could pop on some fresh organic tomatoes, I'd be *so* grateful. The salad dressing sounds *delicious* but will play havoc with my waistline, and right before Christmas as well. *Such* a shame, but I'll just have some low-sodium soy sauce, please. Is that *too* much trouble? Oh, thank you *so* much, you're an absolute heroine! Oh, and a glass of champagne, of course. Fallon, are you going to have one?'

Resisting the urge to applaud this virtuoso performance of entitlement, I merely shook my head.

'No, thanks, just some sparkling water for me, please.'

While we waited for our food to arrive, we made small talk about the sumptuous décor and piles of festively themed goodies: iced cinnamon buns, biscuits shaped like chimney pots with Santa hats peeping out and richly decorated tins of Christmas tea. I was, remarkably, beginning to enjoy myself, when the inevitable happened.

'So, darling, what *was* going on with you and Alexander last night? I can't say I blame you, he's gorgeous.'

I sighed.

'Nothing's going on and nothing's going to go on, all right? I tripped and he caught me, end of story.'

'Well, you know what I think, darling—'

I interrupted her.

'Yes, Mum, I do know what you think, but I also know what I think. No romance with Alexander, end of story. Now can we please talk about something else?'

Inevitably that 'something else' was Jacqueline Honeywood, this time the plans for her foray into 'wellness'. I was nodding along, only half listening, when she suddenly said:

'That's it, darling! You will do it, won't you?'

'What? Do what?'

She clicked her tongue impatiently.

'Fallon, I do wish you'd pay attention. I don't know how you get a *thing* done in that business of yours. I was saying that I was worried when you first started complaining about this "exhaustion"...' *Mum had been worried about me?* This was a first, and a welcome one. I smiled encouragingly and she continued, 'I thought some journalist would get hold of it and it might reflect badly on me in some way.' *Of course.* She had been worried about *her*. Silly me. 'But now I realise that it's the most superb opportunity for both of us!'

She smiled at me triumphantly, but I didn't smile back.

'What sort of opportunity…?'

'Well, you could do some posts about how awful you've been feeling and then it could come out that I've brought you up here with me and under my guidance you've made a full recovery! I'm sure the apothecary could recommend some supplements or teas or something for tiredness. What do you think?'

What I thought was that it was the most monumentally selfish and unfeeling thing I had ever heard in my life. But what was the point in saying that? I poked my fish cakes disconsolately, my appetite suddenly gone.

'Aren't you going to finish that, darling? I can't say I'm surprised, it was *huge*.' She patted her flat stomach. 'I could never even *think* about fitting in such an enormous lunch.'

Glaring at her, I scooped up a large forkful and put it in my mouth. She continued, undaunted.

'So, we'll get some pictures of you at the apothecary, looking wan and tired, which will be easy, and then in a week or so we'll take some where you look much better, under my guidance. Don't worry, it's all a question of light – we can have you looking beautiful.'

'Mum, I do *not* want to be featured on your Instagram page for any reason, least of all looking like some sort of lost soul. I'm sorry, but it's a no.'

This firm line in the sand was nothing more to my mother than an invitation to open negotiations.

'I understand, but think of it like this: you *are* feeling terrible and I can help with that. It will be fun, I promise. I'll even see if I can get some therapists in to help out – they must have them up here? They could come to the house – that would make a marvellous backdrop for photos – or you could go to their treatment rooms, maybe even a spa. You'd start feeling better in no time and it would probably help you work more effectively with Alexander, if you were feeling better.'

I ate some more fish cake and turned the idea over in my mind. Spas and treatments and feeling better *did* sound tempting. I was so used to looking after myself, of always having a wall up when around Mum, that the prospect of being taken care of was hard to resist.

'All right,' I said, and she clapped her hands girlishly and beamed at me. 'But only on the condition that I have veto over *every single photo* of me that goes on social media.'

She pouted.

'Must you, darling? It takes the fun out of it, and we do want to see a radical transformation.'

'I get that, Mum, I know all about before and after shots, and I'll let you have your Henry Higgins moment, don't worry, but that is my condition. Oh, and no weight loss angle. This is about recovering energy, nothing else.'

She looked at me intently for a moment, then nodded briskly.

'All right then. And of course we won't talk about weight loss, it's not *à la mode* these days – or that's what everyone pretends anyway. We'll focus on self-love and acceptance, and if you lose a few pounds along the way, that can only be a good thing.'

I turned and waved at the waitress, who came over instantly. I smiled at her.

'May I have the pudding menu, please?'

ELEVEN

To my surprise, the rest of the day in York went well. Now my mother had got what she wanted, and doubtless thought she could push me into the parts she had agreed to compromise on, she was as happy as anything. We went to the apothecary, which wasn't as terrifying as it sounded: less medieval medicine and more soothing scents and sympathetic assistants, who were thoroughly starstruck by Mum and eager to help her poor daughter.

'She's the most *wonderful* businesswoman,' my mother told them. 'I'm so proud of her. But she does push herself too hard, and you can see the results.'

I silently questioned whether she was remotely proud of me, but submitted myself to being discussed and photographed while I smelled various oils and allowed creams to be rubbed onto the back of my hand. We left after forty-five minutes with three thick cardboard bags full of expensive preparations and went to embark on clothes shopping. I was flagging badly by this time, but Mum swept me along, showing such unprecedented care and interest that instead of my usual approach to buying clothes – try a few things on, get fed up, buy something identical to everything else in my wardrobe and hope for the best where fit is concerned – I came away with some gorgeous items. My favourite was a soft, knitted cream poncho with a loose roll neck, thin enough to wear under coats but warm enough to be worth it. I also had a hat, scarf and gloves and that would have been enough for me, but Mum insisted that I let her buy me a cashmere jumper in a rich emerald green.

'You don't have to, Mum,' I protested, seeing the eyewatering price tag.

'I know I don't *have* to,' she replied, whipping out her credit card, 'but have you thought that I might *want* to? You never let me do these mother-daughter things and I'm enjoying it. I hope you are too.'

I smiled my agreement and decided against reminding her why these bonding moments had never happened before: because she hadn't been there to participate. I reminded myself that even this, pleasant though it was, was only for her social media. Tiredness washed over me.

'Mum, I'm going to have to go home soon. Do you have much more to do?'

Thankfully she didn't, and we met Coco and were soon heading back to Blakeney Hall. By the time we arrived, I had perked up a little, and offered to help Coco prepare dinner. She accepted gladly and soon we were chopping onions and enjoying some cheesy Christmas music on the radio.

'What do you think about pudding?' she asked, pulling the lid off a large tin of tomatoes. 'I was going to make Christmas stollen, but I've run out of time by a few hours. There's ice cream in the freezer, but I'm not sure anyone will want that.'

'I agree,' I said. 'It's too chilly to enjoy it properly. I really love warm things at this time of year – like hot chocolate. But I suppose you can't really give that for pudding.'

A glint came into Coco's eye.

'Actually, we could, if we dress it up a bit? I know a

gorgeous recipe for orange spiced biscuits – if you can take over this pasta sauce and get the bake in the oven, then I could knock them up quickly.'

'Sure,' I said, with more confidence than I felt. 'If you tell me what to do. We should have marshmallows as well – have you got any?'

'Yes! Oh, but only big ones, no good for floating on hot chocolate.'

'But perfect for toasting – outside, if there's anywhere we could have a little fire?'

Coco grinned.

'Yes, there's actually one of those special dish things somewhere. I'm sure Dad or Alexander would get it out.'

'Brilliant! I did an amazing outside party one winter, all this sort of thing. Actually, there's one more thing we could add...'

I explained to Coco what we would need, and she told me where it all was. I assembled it on the kitchen table, and she had her biscuits out and cooling just as the pasta bake timer pinged.

'Perfect. We won't have time to ice them, but that does make them easier to dunk.'

I felt proud carrying in the dish of pasta, even though my contribution to its creation had been minimal. Everyone devoured it, and once they had finished, Coco spoke up.

'Fallon and I have come up with an idea for a different pudding tonight, and it's going to be a collaborative effort.' There were a few 'oohs', although Mum looked sceptical. Coco continued, 'Dad, Alexander, could you get the fire pit working, do you think?'

'No problem,' said Alexander, standing up. 'Theo and I were using it last week. Can he come and help? He's very good at building up the sticks.'

'Not this time, I'm afraid,' I said with a smile. 'I need him and anyone else who'd like to, to come and do another job.'

Theo glanced at his father, who gave him a nod and a big

smile, so while Douglas and Alexander headed off outside, deep
in a discussion about kindling, the rest of us repaired to the
kitchen, where I had laid out everything we would need.

'So, we're going to make some Christmas lanterns to light
our way,' I said. 'Someone can tie the string onto the jam jars as
handles—'

'Sounds like a job for me,' interjected Constance.

'Great. Then we need to mix together this big bag of coarse
salt with some of this white biodegradable glitter and put some
in the bottom of each jar to make them look snowy – Theo, I
thought you'd be good at that.'

'Okay,' he said, nodding.

'And Mum, when each jar is ready, can you light a tealight
and nestle it into the salt with tongs?'

'Certainly,' she said, no doubt relieved to be given a clean
job that wouldn't risk her manicure.

'Coco is going to make some hot chocolate and I'll take out
the biscuits and marshmallows.'

Everyone got busy and I went outside to find Douglas and
Alexander presiding over a fire that was already burning
merrily. They had arranged some garden chairs and benches so
that everyone had somewhere to sit, and found a couple of
chunks of log to serve as tables.

'Can I throw some of this on?' I asked, holding out a bag
that had been slung over my shoulder. 'It's cinnamon sticks and
some citrus peel that Coco dried out a bit in the oven while we
were eating. It should smell lovely.'

As we added the seasonal scraps to the fire, the others
emerged from the house and walked slowly towards us, their
lanterns casting a sparkling, ethereal glow. Soon we were all
gathered around the fire's warmth, mugs beside us as we darted
our marshmallows in and out of the fire on their skewers. As I
glanced round the content faces and took in the perfect wintery
scene, I also realised that not one of us had taken out our phones

to capture this eminently Instagrammable moment; we were simply enjoying it.

The next morning, I rose early again and took Runcible out for her walk, much more comfortable in my new, warm clothes than I had been yesterday. This time we walked right up to the back of the gardens, where they edged the bleak moors, and I stood for a while staring out over them while Runcible nosed around in the frosty undergrowth. I could see why great romances had been set in these atmospheric surroundings, but the wuthering of the wind didn't do much for me and I turned to go back, calling to my little dog to join me. Unusually for her, she didn't run straight back to me, but darted towards a scraggy hedge and yapped.

'What have you found?' I asked her, going over. To my surprise, a familiar face peered out at me, wearing a very serious expression.

'Theo, what are you doing here?'

'Sssh, I'm watching for birds.'

'Sorry,' I whispered, crouching down and peering into his hiding place, which gave a wide vista of the moors. 'What are you hoping to see?'

He took out a small book and showed me a couple of pages.

'I've never seen waxwings here, because they don't come every year. That's what I'm really keen on. And I love birds of prey. There's a pair of merlins I've seen once or twice, and I'd like to see them again. I've seen masses of fieldfares and redwings, of course. Look, there are some now.'

He pointed towards some small brown birds flying past and lifted a camera.

'Got them. The light's good at this time, although you wouldn't think it, would you?'

I made a noncommittal sound and half nodded, half shook

my head, having no idea about light or birds, but knowing that my feet were getting extremely cold.

'How long have you been out here?' I asked him, stamping hard to try and get some circulation going.

'About an hour,' he said. 'Look, I've got my sleeping bag, so I'm fine.' I hadn't noticed that his lower half was swathed in the thick bag. 'I think I'd like some breakfast now, though.'

'So would I and so would Runcible. Shall we go back up to the house?'

He nodded and wriggled deftly out of the bag and the hedge, until he was standing beside me, patting Runcible who hadn't fancied squeezing into the bush but greeted him now with enthusiasm. We turned for the house.

'You know a lot about birds,' I said. 'Have you always been interested in them?'

He looked up at me, his eyes shining.

'Oh yes, always. When Mum...' He hesitated. 'Before Mum...' He fell silent and stared at the ground.

'Did your mum like watching birds too?' I asked gently.

'Oh no, she thought it was very boring,' he said, finding his words again. 'She wanted me to do sports and be on teams, but I *hated* that. Dad lets me go out as much as I like, when I'm not at school or, you know, doing school stuff.'

'Do you do school stuff at home sometimes instead of going in?'

'Sometimes. Some days I just can't go. I think it'll be okay, but when we get to the gate I just can't, and Dad has to bring me home. He's at home a lot. I'm glad he's not a surgeon anymore – he was away a lot then.'

I was awash with information and didn't know what to do with it. I'm not used to talking to children and who knew if I should be urging him to go to school or commiserating about his mother? I was bound to get it wrong, but I knew I should probably say something.

'My mother wasn't around much when I was young, so I loved going to school. It felt like a safe place. I guess it feels the opposite for you.'

To my surprise, Theo reached out and took my gloved hand in his, squeezing it.

'You understand,' he said.

I wasn't sure I did, but we had reached the kitchen door, which I pushed open with not a little relief, to find Coco inside presiding over various pans and bowls.

'Come in and shut that door, it's freezing. I'm just about to serve breakfast, so go through now. Oh, and if Runcible stays, I've got something special for her.'

She put down a bowl that my little dog fell on eagerly and, needing no further encouragement, Theo and I took off our coats and headed to the Buttery.

After breakfast, I met Alexander in the study again to continue our work. I was pleased with the costings I had drawn up and wanted to show him some of the vans I had found that would be available at short notice. He was easy to work with, decisive and efficient, and after an hour or so we had made excellent progress. Offering to make coffee, he disappeared to the kitchen, while I sent a final email.

'Here you go,' he said, coming back in. 'Coffee and some amazing millionaire's shortbread that Coco made. I had to fight Constance for it, so I hope you like it.'

'One of my favourites,' I said truthfully, taking the proffered plate and mug and sitting back in my chair. 'Thank you. I must say, Coco turning up seems like some kind of Christmas miracle.'

'I agree. She gives me and Dad plenty of things to worry about, but her culinary skills are not one of them.'

We ate in silence for a moment, and I was just about to brief him on sign writers for the side of the van, when Alexander spoke, in what seemed to me a determinedly casual tone.

'I saw you with Theo this morning in the garden. He seems to have taken to you.'

'Oh, er, yes, maybe. We were talking about birds and school.'

He frowned.

'I don't know what to do about school. He's officially become a "school refuser", but nobody – including him – seems to know why, beyond some vague suggestion of "anxiety" from the school, which doesn't seem to merit much in the way of follow up. Between us and some kind friends, we've managed to keep him going here, but it's not a long-term solution, especially if my business picks up. But it's not just that. I want him to make friends and be with children his own age. He gravitates towards adults – me, Dad, Constance and now, apparently, you – and I wonder if it's the best thing for him.'

I was growing uncomfortable with the conversation. How was I supposed to know what was best for a small boy? I felt totally underqualified to make any comment, so I just shrugged.

'I don't know, I'm sorry.'

'That's all right, I'm sorry for bringing it up. I just want to help my son, and I thought he might be opening up to you. Forget I said anything. Shall we look at those decals again?'

I reached for my laptop, then hesitated. Reluctant as I was to get involved, I had had one idea which had just popped into my head and seemed unfair to withhold.

'Alexander, I don't know if this might help a little, but Theo was telling me how much he loves birds. I have a client who lives not far from here – a client I became quite friendly with when she lived in London – and she runs a bird rescue place. He could lend a hand there. It might help a little in terms of friends as they have a daughter who's a similar age, and, if he liked it, it could be a way to get him out of the house, give him something else to focus on. I don't know...' I petered out and shrugged again, embarrassed now in case Alexander thought I saw myself as some kind of Mary Poppins figure, magically solving children's problems. But his face lit up.

'Fallon, I think that's a great idea. Do you think your friend would be open to him coming over?'

'I can give her a call, but I don't see why not. She used to work at London Zoo and always talks about getting children involved in conservation. I can ask her anyway.'

'I'd be very grateful. I know I said before that I don't need any help looking after Theo, but this could make a difference. Better than a casserole.'

I looked up and his lopsided smile made my stomach flip over. This wasn't going at all how I had planned. I put on my most brisk and business-like voice.

'I don't do casseroles or kids, but coming up with ideas is my job. Don't worry, I'm not going to don a flowery apron and start making myself indispensable – I'll charge you for my help if that makes you feel better?'

I had spoken more harshly than I intended, and it was Alexander's turn to look embarrassed.

'Sorry, I wasn't trying to suggest... well, you know, that you were anything like Annabel, or that your motives were – I don't know – anything other than kind. Sorry.'

This was teeth-clenchingly awkward, but I didn't know how to backtrack. So, in true Jacqueline Honeywood style, I ploughed on.

'No problem. Shall we finish this up and I'll go and ring Sadie before lunch?'

He agreed heartily and soon we were back on solid ground in a place which made me wholly more comfortable than talk of children and domesticity: scrolling through an Excel spreadsheet, which asked nothing of your emotions.

TWELVE

'Hello, Sadie? It's Fallon Honeywood.'

'Fallon, how lovely to hear from you! It's been a while.'

'Yes, too long. How are you?'

We made small talk for a few minutes, catching up on her work with the sanctuary and mine in London, before I moved on to the real reason for my call.

'I'm not far away from you right now – I'm spending Christmas in Lingfoss. You may have seen that Mum has a new boyfriend – well, his son lives up here.' I explained that I had needed a break from work and from London, something Sadie understood only too well. 'Douglas's grandson, Theo, is a huge bird fan, and I was wondering if it might be possible to bring him up to the sanctuary? He's been having a few problems at school as well, so he's not attending much at the moment. If it's convenient for you, I think a visit could help him.'

'Of course,' said Sadie warmly. 'He's nine, did you say? Old enough to be able to help out, if you think more than just a visit would be good for him?'

I was relieved that Sadie understood.

'I'm not entirely sure, I haven't known him for very long, but that's my feeling, yes.'

'Good stuff. You can come over this afternoon if you're free?'

'That's incredibly kind, thank you. I'll check with his dad and let you know in a few minutes.'

When we all gathered for lunch, Alexander agreed that the afternoon would be perfect, and so did Theo, even though he had had a riot that morning with Douglas and Mum, who had staged some sort of crazed Christmas scavenger hunt that all three had enjoyed enormously. They had been hunting for festive items beginning with each letter of the alphabet; angel, bauble and crib were easy enough, but things got very silly around 'q' when someone suggested a small duck ornament might count as a Christmas quacker. Having described his morning in great detail, Theo was now asking about the sanctuary.

'What birds do they have? Why have they got them there – are they injured? What sort of help do you think I can be? Can Runcible come too?'

I laughed.

'I can only answer one of those questions. Yes, Runcible is allowed to come, but she has to stay on a lead. Otherwise, we'll just have to find out when we get there.'

Douglas and Mum decided to stay behind, having worn themselves out with Theo, as did Coco, who wanted to practice a recipe or two.

'I'll join, though, if I may?' said Constance. 'I'm making good progress with the book, and it won't do me any harm to get out of the house for a while.'

Theo looked around at us, his face happier than I had seen it yet.

'Yes, come, Aunt Constance. I'm hoping they might have a merlin, or even owls, but I suppose...'

His face fell and Alexander put a hand on his shoulder.

'What's up?'

'If they're in the sanctuary, it means that they've been hurt. I shouldn't be excited about that.'

There was a silence and the adults looked at one another awkwardly. It was Constance who saved the day.

'Not at all,' she said robustly. 'You're not excited about them being hurt, you're excited about the chance to see these birds close up, and to help them, and so am I. Fallon and Dad, too, I imagine.'

We both nodded vigorously. She continued.

'Sadly, in life, animals do get hurt, but wonderfully there are people like Fallon's friend Sadie who help them, and that is a cause for celebration. Now, let's get this lunch eaten so we can get there as soon as possible.'

Taking her cue, we all started eating and Douglas asked Alexander how plans for the Christmas Fayre were going, which kept us talking until it was time to get ready to leave.

The sanctuary was a twenty-minute drive away, and I saw Sadie waiting for us as we drove up the lane. Tall, with long, grey hair today caught up in a clip beneath a woolly hat, she made a striking figure against the leaden sky.

'Welcome,' she greeted us, shaking everyone's hand and stroking Runcible's head. 'Good to see this little one again, I always was a fan of your dog. Come on, let's get moving – it's cold out here and there's plenty to see and do.'

She strode off towards a large building near the house and we all trotted after her. I was glad of the prospect of being indoors again; Sadie lived on a bleak and exposed part of the moors and the wind was snatching at us viciously, turning our cheeks red and making our eyes water. She pushed open a heavy wooden door and we found ourselves inside a large, warm room lined with cages but otherwise kitted out as a vet's surgery.

'So, this is where we do any medical work on the birds, as you can see. The cages here are small and they don't stay for long. Today we've only got one bird in, came in this morning and I had to operate. Come and see.'

She led us over to a cage with a heat lamp in it and we all peered in. All I could see was a little hunched bundle of feathers, partially wrapped in bandages, but Theo let out an exclamation.

'Oh! Is it a Little Owl?'

Sadie smiled at him.

'It is. Rare for us to get one here. Not so lucky for him, but lucky for you today.'

'What happened to him?' asked the little boy, his nose pressed to the cage.

'He was found caught in some tangled barbed wire. Thankfully, he hasn't broken anything, but he has some cuts, and he needs plenty to eat and drink. We'll move him to a larger enclosure soon and he'll be able to leave us in a few days with any luck. He's one we'll need help with.'

Theo turned big, shining eyes on Alexander.

'Daddy, I might be able to help, mightn't I?'

Alexander smiled down at his son and put his arm around his shoulder, hugging him close to him.

'I should think so. But will you mind letting him go again?'

'Oh *no*, that will be the best part. He should be flying free.'

Sadie caught my eye and nodded.

'Good lad. Right, come and see our biggest inhabitant.'

I had limited interest in the birds, beautiful though they were, but as we walked around, I noticed that several of the enclosures were looking worn and that Sadie's house, where she lived with her husband and daughter, had some missing tiles on the roof and flaking paint on the window frames. The shiny Christmas garlands strung around couldn't detract from the state of disrepair. Maybe what this place needed more than anything was some sort of fundraising effort? Sadie had explained to me previously that many people in the local area disliked the sorts of birds that she was striving to save, and they were often victims of deliberate harm, but there must be some people who understood that they actually presented little threat to stocks of game birds and who would be eager to see them helped?

'You look like you're glazing over there,' said Alexander, coming up beside me as we watched Sadie showing Theo how to prepare food for a sick owl. 'Cutting up chicks not your thing?'

I smiled at him.

'It's not that, I was just thinking about how I might be able to help Sadie raise some money and awareness for this place. She does such amazing work.'

'I thought you were meant to be up here resting,' said Alexander teasingly. 'So far, you've leaped into action to help me, offered to get things moving for Coco, found what looks like the perfect activity for Theo and are now plotting some sort of raptor party as well. Forgive me for saying, but I'm not surprised you were on the road to burnout.' His eyes darkened slightly, and he looked more serious. 'You do have to be careful, though, no matter how driven you are.'

I screwed up my face.

'I know. I'm always taking on too much, but although I like the idea of doing nothing for a while, it doesn't suit me. I've even agreed to help Mum with her Instagram stuff, although that looks like it should be good for me, I promise.'

He was about to answer when a very tall man with a huge,

black beard came through the door, holding the hand of a girl around Theo's age.

'Hello, everyone,' he said in a deep voice. 'Good to see you all.' He came over and gave me a hug, which I returned warmly.

Sadie looked up from her work and smiled.

'This is my husband, Jacob, and our daughter, Linnet. Linnet, darling, do you want to come and help me and Theo?'

Without looking at anyone, the little girl let go of her father's hand and scuttled over. The three of them were soon bent over their task again, Constance now joining them, and I turned to speak to Jacob.

'Oh! I must introduce you – this is Alexander Knight, Theo's father.'

The men shook hands, and both started speaking at once. Alexander urged Jacob to talk first.

'I was just going to say that we know each other already, don't we?'

'So was I. From the hospital – I used to work as a surgeon there.'

'Of course.' Jacob turned to me. 'I'm a physiotherapist, as you know, mostly roving – I work with sports teams usually – but I do occasional work at the hospital.' He turned back to Alexander. 'I was sorry to hear about the accident. How was the rehab for the hand, are you back at work?'

Alexander stretched his hand out and shook his head.

'No, I don't think I'll get it back to surgical standard.'

'Really? From what I remember, it was an injury that would take a lot of work to recover from but would be doable. I can have a look if you like?'

Alexander shook his head.

'No, thanks. I'm going to go and see how Theo's getting on.'

He walked off abruptly, and Jacob turned to me with a frown.

'What's going on there? I hope I didn't offend him, but I'm sure that hand could mend with some good, regular physio.'

'I've got no idea. Maybe he doesn't want to be a surgeon again.'

'Whyever not? He was extremely talented, from what I remember.'

I shrugged, feeling uncomfortable discussing Alexander, but Jacob continued speaking and I couldn't pretend I wasn't interested in finding out a little more about Alexander's past. 'His wife left him after the accident – well, after she realised he wasn't going to be a surgeon anymore. I didn't know her, but no one had anything good to say about her, especially after she dumped him and her son and went off with some rich Italian. Oh well, mustn't speak ill of the dead. How are *you* getting on with him?'

I was reluctant to give Jacob, who seemed to be an inveterate gossip, anything else to work with and was making noncommittal noises when Theo called over.

'Fallon! Do come and see! We've finished preparing the meat now and we're actually going to feed a sick barn owl. Do come!'

Relieved at not having to give Jacob an answer, I hurried over and watched as Sadie took a sleepy-looking owl from a cage and wrapped it tightly in a towel, then showed us how to give it a drink using, at first, a small paintbrush to dab the water into its mouth, followed by a tiny syringe. We all had a turn, but Theo's joy at performing this task made us step back and let him take on the majority of the work. Sadie looked up.

'There's plenty more to do if you're looking for jobs? Linnet and Theo can carry on here – it'll take a good fifteen minutes to get all this into him. Jacob, you and Constance could go and sort out that hen harrier and I'll show Fallon and Alexander the kittens.'

I followed her happily, Runcible trotting along on the end of her lead. She was as sweet with cats as she was with everything, and although I still wouldn't leave her alone with young kittens, she would be perfectly fine to come along and watch. Sadie pushed open the door to another, smaller outhouse, this one with a hand-painted wooden sign on the door that said 'Nursery'. She went over to a large cage, where all I could see were blankets, opened the top and beckoned us over. We peered in and saw, to my surprise, not cats but tiny rabbits, all huddled together asleep.

'These are kittens,' she said, smiling. 'We often take in wildlife other than raptors; the RSPCA passes them on to us or people ask us for help. This large litter of six was found a couple of days ago – their mother had been killed by a dog.'

'Poor little things,' I said. 'How old are they?'

'About a week. Don't worry, they'll be fine, but they need feeding. Come on, I'll show you how to make up some formula and give it to them.'

She showed us a small kitchen area and left us with instructions, then went to leave.

'Sadie, I'm not sure about this,' I said, panicking. 'What if something goes wrong? I can't do it, I'll probably hurt them.'

She laughed.

'All new mothers feel like that, Fallon. You'll be fine, can't go wrong if you do what I said, and you've got Alexander here. He's a doctor.'

And she whisked out, shutting the door firmly behind her. I looked at Alexander and pulled a face.

'You heard her: you're the doctor, so this is on you.'

'Not anymore, and never a rabbit doctor. She seems to have appointed *you* mum, so she must trust your instincts.'

'More than I bloody do,' I muttered, picking up the tin of formula. 'Oh, come on, between us we must be able to manage this.'

We made up the milk to Sadie's instructions, then went over

to the baby rabbits. Alexander reached in and lifted one out gently.

'Do you want this one?' he asked, and I nodded, although I was still far from sure that this was a good idea. I took it from him, noticing again the livid scar on his hand, and sat on a small sofa, a towel on my lap with the rabbit snuggled into it. Alexander handed me a syringe full of milk and I held it to the rabbit's mouth. To my delight, it immediately started to suck. I looked up.

'Alexander, look, it's drinking!'

He smiled.

'Well done. Let's see if I manage as well as you have.'

He took out another kitten and sat down next to me. His rabbit also started to take its milk. We beamed at each other and then sat peacefully until the syringes were empty and the babies looked drowsy.

'Time for the next ones?' whispered Alexander, and I nodded. I hadn't suddenly transformed into some sort of Earth Mother, and I didn't want my own baby any more than I had this morning, but even I couldn't deny that sitting there in this milky quiet, feeling the warmth of Alexander's body next to me as we nurtured these minuscule creatures, was bringing a sense of pleasure quite unfamiliar to me: one that I had never found in work, no matter how satisfying it was.

We were feeding the last two kittens when the door opened and everyone else came in, dropping their voices when they saw us. Theo was over in a flash.

'Oh, look!' he whispered. 'They're adorable.'

'Would you like to finish off?' I asked.

'No, you're doing really well,' he said, with all the confidence of one who has learned how to handfeed a starving owl. 'I like watching, though.'

In a few minutes' time, the syringes were empty, and we replaced the kittens in their cage.

'We should be heading home,' said Alexander, looking at his watch. 'I can't thank you enough, Sadie, we've had a wonderful afternoon.'

'You're welcome,' she said. 'And I've been talking to Theo – if it's all right with you, he can come back and help out as much as he likes. Be glad to have him.'

Theo looked at his father with huge, shining eyes, and Alexander laughed.

'Of course he can come back, thank you.'

Theo just squeezed his father's hand and beamed.

When we got home, everyone took off their outdoor clothes and disappeared, leaving only Alexander and me in the hall. I decided to go and rest in the hour or so before dinner and started heading up the stairs, but he caught my wrist. I turned.

'Look, Fallon, I just want to thank you again. That afternoon was transformational for Theo. I think, I hope, that after a difficult period, we might have turned a corner.'

'It wasn't really me – it was Sadie who did everything.'

'Yes, but you had the idea, you had the instinct that it could help, and you were right.'

This was all feeling too intense for me, and I pulled my arm away.

'It just seemed logical. I'm not sure instinct had anything to do with it, but I'm glad it helped.'

He looked confused – he'd probably got too used to all those gushing Annabels – but then grinned.

'Have it your own way – but you made a lovely bunny mummy, you can't deny it.'

I stuck my tongue out at him.

'A one-time only special, and one that's left me needing a nap.'

And with that, I ran up the stairs to the peace and solitude of my room.

THIRTEEN

The next few days were simpler and more to my innate strengths: less nurturing of baby bunnies, more consulting spreadsheets and chasing orders. Only having one project on the go suited me and I was stimulated by the work rather than exhausted. It also didn't hurt that the time I spent working each day was severely limited by other people. Douglas and often Mum as well, to my surprise, or Constance, sometimes even Coco, were taking Theo to the sanctuary every day, which left Alexander and I a good block of time to get work done. But when Theo was home, Alexander downed tools and spent time with his son. At first, I had found this frustrating.

'What's up with you?' asked Constance one day, finding me slamming my phone down on the kitchen table with what was no doubt a very sour look on my face.

'I just want to get these labels *done*,' I said. 'We could have got the order in today, but Theo's home early because Sadie and Jacob had to take Linnet somewhere, and Alexander's gone off with him. I can't make the decision unilaterally, he *knows* that. Now it will have to wait until the morning.'

'How annoying,' said Constance calmly, switching on the kettle. 'Cup of tea? You might as well.'

'Yes, all right then,' I answered ungraciously. 'I suppose I'd better have one of those herbal things Mum's been making me drink.'

'Is this the one – linden and camomile? Sounds very soothing, I might join you in one. I've hit a rocky patch in my book.'

'Sorry to hear that.'

'Thanks. I'll get past it. I'm going to take a break and go for a walk when I've drunk this, I find the cold December air works wonders for "unsticking" me when work isn't going well.'

'My problem is that work *is* going well – I'm only stuck because Alexander isn't here.'

Constance placed a mug of tea in front of me.

'Do you think he should be working instead of spending time with Theo?' she asked in her direct way.

I flushed.

'I guess not, but time is very limited, and this is important.'

'Will anything suffer if it is done tomorrow morning rather than today?'

'No. I just wanted to get it done.'

I sighed and took a sip of tea, not looking at Constance, who I could feel staring at me intently.

'It seems that you are very driven and hard-working, just like your mother.' Now I looked up. I opened my mouth to say *I'm nothing like her*, then snapped it shut again and glared at Constance. She continued, unperturbed. 'Did she work a lot when you were a child?'

'Yes. She was always at work—'

'And not with you.' She finished my sentence for me. 'So that is why you think you, too, would be a terrible mother, as you told me on our walk not long ago.'

'That's right. Look at me, desperate to work and annoyed

that Alexander is prioritising his son. I'm *just* like her, you're right.'

Constance didn't reply, but stood and picked up her cup, placing a hand briefly on my shoulder as she left the room. I was alone with my thoughts, a place I don't find myself often, as the space is always filled with work. Turmoil raged inside me. *Was* I like her? I had spent so much of my life resenting her for her perceived abandonment of me in favour of her ambition, yet here I was, annoyed at Alexander because he was doing exactly the opposite. A picture of Theo with Runcible on his lap floated unbidden into my mind. Was what I had experienced as a child what I wanted for that sweet little boy, with all the anxiety and grief he was already coping with? All for a sign off on some labels that could easily be done in the morning? I was suddenly ashamed of myself. Is this what everyone did? Beat our fists against the unjustness of our childhoods, then replicate it? Then, for the first time since I could remember, I reached out to my phone and, rather than checking my emails, I leant on the side button and switched it off. Stress began to ebb away from me, and I gazed out of the window at the weak sunlight washing the garden. Maybe a wintery walk would be good for me too. I woke Runcible, who was unimpressed to be uprooted from her cosy spot by the stove, wrapped us both up warm, and headed out into the freezing Yorkshire afternoon.

The next day, when Alexander and I sat down in his study to start work, I was going to broach the subject of the labels, but he got there before me.

'Fallon, I realised late in the day yesterday that I never signed off on those labels. I'm sorry, I know you wanted to get it done. Anyway, I sent the email today before breakfast, so hopefully I won't have held things up too much.'

The walk yesterday had cleared my head and helped me get a few things in perspective.

'Thank you. I was worried about it then, but it actually wasn't so urgent, and I know you and Theo want to spend time together. It's important.'

'I'm so glad you understand. But I wouldn't want you to think that I'm sitting back and leaving all the work to you. I'm focused on doing well at the Christmas Fayre, but I think I can manage both.'

'Of course you can. Everything's going very smoothly, which is why I think we can look again this morning at something that isn't imperative, but I still believe would be a good idea. Do you remember I mentioned offering a special cocktail?'

'Yes! You said we should do something with cranberries.'

'That's right. Well, I've been thinking about it, and I think that something with strong local links would be a big draw. I was wondering if we might be able to forage or buy within a mile or two and use that as a selling point.'

'What did you have in mind? Surely there can't be much to forage in December?'

'Not berries and things, no, although we can buy small amounts of locally grown cranberries. But I was thinking of something different. We can forage sweet chestnuts and pine needles and quite easily make them into syrups. I bet we could do it; I've looked up a few recipes, or I'm sure Coco would help. There's that Yorkshire brand of tonic water who have already agreed to work with us—'

'Thanks to you,' interrupted Alexander. 'I would never have thought to approach them.'

'Well, it makes good sense to use local providers. I think we could make some great Christmas drinks with those ingredients. We could sugar the edges of the glasses and add a few crystallised cranberries – I bet you'd sell out.'

Alexander looked excited now.

'Fallon, that sounds amazing. I love it.'

I beamed.

'Oh, and I thought that you could also offer non-alcoholic drinks made with the same syrups. We just have to think up some fun names.'

'I like this more than ordering coasters, I must say. Well, look, seeing as we're up to speed on everything else for now, why don't we give it a trial run?'

'Today?'

'Why not? Theo and Dad won't be back for a few hours, so we could go and pick the things you mentioned and have a go. How long does it take to make the syrups?'

I laughed.

'The chestnut one is quite quick, about half an hour, and most of that is roasting time. The pine one takes longer, because you have to steep it for three hours or so.'

'So we could be drinking them tonight?'

'We could!'

'I think we should do it. Runcible, are you up for a walk?' My little dog ran over to him as he patted his knees, and he scooped her up. Seeing him be so sweet with her made it very hard for me to pretend to myself I didn't fancy him. 'There you go, you see? She's enthusiastic.'

'All right, then, let's go!'

We put on our warm clothes and Runcible's thick jumper and stepped outside, the cold momentarily taking my breath away.

'They take some getting used to, these temperatures,' said Alexander, zipping up his coat a little further. 'I like it, I've lived with it for such a long time, but some people who move here never get used to it.'

I stamped my feet and shivered dramatically.

'I'm reserving judgement for now, but I prefer it to boiling hot summers.'

'We don't get many of them up here.'

'So, where can we find the things we need? Will we have to go far?'

'There are some pine trees growing at the back – Christmas trees that Dad and I started planting a few years ago so eventually we'll have big ones for the house every year. They're Douglas firs – any good?'

I consulted the information I had saved on my phone.

'Yes, they're fine. Let's start there then.'

We walked across the frosty lawn, our feet leaving marks behind us, although Runcible's little paws barely did. The pathway through the hedges that led to Heathcliff's field veered away to the right, but we turned left and crossed a pretty stone bridge over a stream. I paused and looked down at the water.

'It hasn't frozen yet. I'm surprised, it's so cold.'

Alexander laughed.

'This isn't cold, not yet. Give it time, although the stream still may not freeze. You should see it later in the year – this is just a trickle compared to spring, then the becks all around here gush along.'

'Beck?'

'It's what we call these streams – ones with stony bottoms.'

I nodded, wishing I could see it at full flow later in the year, and we continued walking, the ground now tufty with heather, although there was also a lot of stone and brick lying around. Alexander must have noticed me looking and said:

'There was once some sort of religious building on this site, destroyed in the English Reformation, but you can see what's left. There was probably some sort of kitchen garden – that would have been perfect in the warmer weather for finding locally grown herbs.'

'What a great idea. You should work out where it was, bring it back to life and use the botanicals in your gin. It's impossibly romantic. People would love knowing their drinks were flavoured with herbs from a monastic medicine garden.'

Alexander grinned at me.

'I like the way your romanticism is tempered with good commercial sense,' he said teasingly. 'For instance, would you sell your wedding pictures to a magazine?'

'Ha. I doubt there will ever be a wedding to sell pictures of,' I said shortly.

'Marriage not for you?' he asked, and when I just shrugged, unwilling to get into the conversation, he continued, 'I agree. I went there once before and look how that ended. You do know about that, I suppose?'

I nodded.

'Yes, Mum mentioned it. I'm sorry, what an awful train of events for you and Theo to go through.'

We had stopped walking now, and he kicked at some of the old bricks.

'Yes, it was a lot to go through in a short time – my accident...' He flexed his hand, and my eyes were drawn once again to the livid scars across the palm. 'Holly leaving and then the car crash... I doubt Theo will ever get over it.' He lifted his head and looked at me. 'You can understand why I'm so protective of him. He's already suffered so many terrible experiences in his short life, I can't bear risking him being exposed to any more.'

So, no school, no playdates and now no second wife, I thought, although I didn't say anything out loud. Instead, I asked:

'And what about you?'

'What about me?' His voice had taken on an edge, warning me to tread carefully.

'Don't you want to return to practicing medicine, or to have some time for yourself?'

'My work as a surgeon took me away from home too much, and often at odd times. I'd get a call at two in the morning and have to rush to the hospital. I can't bring that kind of uncertainty back into Theo's life. And before you come up with a million solutions, I don't want to hire someone to live in or, God forbid, get married again, just so I can be a surgeon and palm my son off on someone else when he's inconvenient. I don't need or want the money or the status and by teaching students I'm still useful.'

I didn't say anything, but bent and scooped up Runcible, who was shivering by my feet. I cuddled her close to me, burying my face in her neck. Alexander spoke again, his voice more gentle this time.

'Sorry. I didn't mean to take it out on *you*. I'm just so used to people trying to fix me, I try to pre-empt it now.'

'It's okay. And for what it's worth, I don't think you need fixing at all.'

He looked into my eyes and for a moment I was transfixed, my stomach leaping around all over the place, defying my head which was screaming at me to remember the conversation we had been having *thirty seconds ago, Fallon!* I was first to look away.

'So, which way are these pine trees? I think Runcible is going to go on strike if we don't get moving again.'

We walked a little further until a scene from a picture book met my eyes: a little copse of Christmas trees, about twenty of them, all different sizes and sparkling from the chilly touch of winter.

'You planted all these?'

'Me and Dad and Theo together, yes. We still don't have one big enough for the hallway – we buy that in – but we've dug one up for the Hall now for three years. And after Christmas we put them back out here to continue growing.'

'Oh, I love that. It does seem sad that so many trees are thrown away.'

'It does. Our problem in a few years is going to be too many trees, and trees that are too big for us to handle, but we'll worry about that when it happens.'

'So you don't want me to offer any solutions now?' I asked, grinning. 'I'm sure I could come up with some ideas.'

He laughed.

'No, you're all right. If I'm stuck in ten years' time, I'll ask you then.'

'Do you think our parents will get married?' I asked him suddenly.

He raised an eyebrow. 'I think it's looking likely, don't you?'

I nodded. 'Funny how differently people's lives work out, isn't it? It will be Mum's first wedding, but Douglas's third.'

He visibly stiffened.

'She can trust him, you know. Remember that he was widowed once, and he still gets on well with Coco's mother.'

'I didn't mean it like that at all. Douglas is wonderful and I'd be delighted if they got married. I'd be more concerned that you wouldn't want him to marry her.'

'Why?'

'Nothing sinister. I mean, she's refused hundreds of proposals over the years – according to her, that is – and I can see that she feels completely differently about your dad. It's just, well, I know how she can be with her soap career and her Instagram page and now all this wellness stuff.'

'Honestly, Fallon, I don't know much about that. I just see someone who clearly loves my father. Okay, so she has her own agenda sometimes, but from what I understand, she's a self-made woman, and obviously an extremely successful one. She's never going to be some sort of surrendered wife, but that's a good thing.'

'You won't mind that she will almost definitely want a magazine taking photos of the wedding?'

He shrugged.

'I may not know much about celebrity or soap operas, but I

know how the world works.' He paused. 'Fallon, I hope you don't mind my asking, but what's it like for you having Jacqueline Honeywood as your mother? I must say, when Dad said you were coming with her, I expected somebody very different.'

'Somebody more like her?'

'More like somebody who had been so steeped in celebrity their whole life that they had been washed along by that. But you're not at all that way, and still like your mother – self-made and determined.'

I tucked Runcible inside my coat – all this standing around talking in the cold wasn't her thing – and thought for a moment.

'My relationship with Mum hasn't been the easiest. When I was little, she was working on building up her career and she prioritised that over everything else, including me. I get it, I do, I'm not a brat, but it was very clear to me that I was a nuisance, a hindrance, and very low down on her list. When she became successful, I was packed off to boarding school. I loved it and it was by far the best thing for both of us, but of course I still felt abandoned. So I did what she had done all those years before – focused on building up my career so that I could be independent and in charge of all my own decisions. Only I didn't have a child to factor in.'

'Would you have done things differently if you had?'

'Probably not. My motivation not to be dependent on Mum was too strong. She wasn't cut out for motherhood, and neither am I. Can you imagine some poor little mite being stuck with me for a mum?'

I gave a strangulated laugh at this not very funny comment, and an image of Theo cuddling Runcible flipped across my mind. *Would it be so terrible, in reality?*

Alexander looked at me for a moment, opened his mouth to say something and then clearly changed his mind. He cleared his throat and instead asked me:

'What about your father? What was he like?'

'I have no idea, never met the guy. Come on, let's get this pine picked or we won't be drinking cocktails this evening.'

I was grateful that he accepted my abrupt change of direction and immediately turned his attentions to the trees, chatting about which ones looked juiciest. As we worked, I pondered what it was about Alexander that had prompted me to have a conversation I never, ever get into with anyone. He was so kind and easy to talk to, listening without judgement and allowing me to stop when I wanted to. I sighed inwardly. If only I wasn't so worried about what damage I could do to his lovely child, he could just be perfect.

FOURTEEN

We returned home from our foraging with several sprigs of pine from different parts of the trees, as well as a small bagful of sweet chestnuts. No one else was around, so we went to the kitchen and started on our syrups.

'I hope Coco won't mind us raiding the cupboards,' I said, hunting around for what we required. 'We need an awful lot of sugar.'

'I'll text her,' said Alexander, 'and if she's near a shop, she can pick up some more; otherwise, I'll pop out later and restock anything she needs urgently. I was going to take Theo to the cinema this afternoon anyway. What are you up to?'

I wasn't sure if this was an invitation, but I wouldn't have been able to accept it anyway.

'It's the next phase of Mum's "return Fallon to wellness" scheme. Although I have to confess that I'm looking forward to this one. There's a woman in York who does special holistic massages and they do sound amazing – all scented oils and being wrapped up in cocooning towels.'

He laughed.

'Whatever floats your boat. Is she sharing it all with her social media following?'

'Oh, absolutely. The caring mother angle is one she hasn't exploited before – on social media or anywhere else – so her fans adore this new side of her and she's also getting plenty of attention from the wellness brigade. A couple of magazines have been in touch about doing articles on it, so she's very pleased with herself.'

'What about you?'

I measured some sugar into a saucepan.

'I suppose you would say "it's complicated". I can't pretend I'm not enjoying these little pockets of time with her and, if I'm honest, being the focus of her attention, even if I know that her motives go far beyond helping me. She's different when she's not working on *Mayfair Mews*, and I don't think she's ever taken so much time off before. Your dad must be having a positive influence.'

'He's a good guy.'

'Anyway, sorry for going on about myself. Shall we add the water to this?'

Alexander put down the jug he was about to fill and put both hands on my shoulders. I looked up at him awkwardly, not sure what he was doing.

'Fallon, please don't apologise for talking about yourself. I'm interested, and you're not "going on". It seems to me that you spend an awful lot of time doing things for other people; maybe you *should* talk about yourself more.'

I blushed and looked away.

'I'm not doing things for other people – it's just work, normally.'

'I know I've only known you for a few days, but I see it differently. You may not be in some traditional caring profession, but your work is all about making people happy. And since you've been here, as I said before, you've reached out to several of us, helping us. You may dress it up as "just work", but I see a very caring and selfless woman.'

I wriggled away from him and gave a slightly strangled laugh.

'Maybe I should get a flowery apron, after all,' I joked, but rather than laughing, he sighed.

'I don't mean it like that.'

I dragged my eyes up to meet his again.

'I know you don't, sorry. Thank you, it was a nice thing to say. Come on, let's make these syrups or we'll run out of time.'

We got back to work, and I ruminated as I watched the bubbling sugary water. What Alexander had said, although clearly meant to be complimentary, had made me feel very uncomfortable. Secretly I knew that there *was* a nurturing side to me, one that got immense pleasure from looking after and helping others, but if I could explain it away as 'just doing my job', it made it more palatable. If it was work, then mistakes could be absorbed as part of the process, and although I cared greatly about my clients and their happiness, I didn't make myself vulnerable by loving them. My reverie was sharply interrupted.

'Fallon! It's boiling over!'

I quickly turned off the heat and whipped the saucepan away, smiling wryly. For all my pretences, I couldn't even look after a pan of syrup!

Douglas and Mum arrived home with Theo shortly after we had both our fragrant syrups steeping. Theo was full of his morning at the sanctuary, and I was going to leave him to tell Alexander about it, when he stopped me.

'Fallon, don't you want to hear about my morning? I want to tell you about the amazing falcon I saw, right up close.'

Surprised, and not a little flattered, I sat down and listened while he described his visit. I looked around at the faces smiling at Theo as he chattered on; even Mum had a fond smile on her face, and I don't think I've seen one of those since she lent the Victoria & Albert Museum a handbag for a fashion exhibition. She was gladder to get that bag back than she ever was when I came home from boarding school at the end of term.

'And Linnet is really nice,' he continued enthusiastically. 'She doesn't talk much, but that's fine. She showed me how to pick up a hedgehog today.'

I glanced over at Alexander and found him already looking at me, his eyes moist. He shook his head as if to clear it and returned his attention to his son.

'Anyway,' continued Theo, 'I want to go back tomorrow because we're releasing a hawk – she's better now. I can go, can't I?'

'Of course you can,' said Alexander. 'Fallon and I are doing well with our work, so I'm sure I can spare a morning – if that's all right with you?' He turned to me, and I nodded.

'Yes, we've got everything in motion now, so we're just waiting for things to turn up and then we'll be busy again.'

To my astonishment, Theo, who I was sitting next to on the sofa, turned and hugged me, briefly burying his head in my shoulder. I don't think I have ever been hugged by a child – well, not since I was a child myself – and I had no idea what to do. For a moment, my hands sorted of flapped impotently, then I lowered them and patted his back awkwardly. He showed no signs of letting go and, eventually, I began to relax, until I was hugging him back.

'I'm glad you like the sanctuary so much,' I said, as he eventually broke away. He didn't reply, just nodded, then stood and went over to his father, hiding his face in his chest. For once I was grateful when Mum took over.

'Fallon, our afternoon activities await. We can get lunch, if you need it, in a little bistro near the masseuse.'

I put my head on one side and pursed my lips.

'Mum, you've known me for thirty-five years. I *always* need lunch.'

To her credit, and my eternal amazement, she smiled.

'Well, quite. I could do with a bite myself. Come along then.'

The bistro turned out to be more of a gastro pub, which suited me, particularly after the long, cold walk that morning and all the sharing of past hurts that had gone on between Alexander and me. I ordered scampi and chips and tucked in gladly when it arrived. Mum picked at a Caesar salad – no dressing – and regarded me owlishly.

'Can you really eat *all* that?' she asked, delicately removing the yolk from a hardboiled egg and putting it to one side.

'Absolutely,' I said, dipping a perfectly crunchy double cooked chip into the ketchup. 'It's delicious. Don't worry, I won't spoil your secret and credit any of my new-found rosy cheeks to this rather than your herbal tea.'

She put down her fork.

'*Are* you beginning to feel better? I know you don't think I care – you think this is all for my own publicity – but I have been worried about you, darling. You've been looking very peaky.'

The old defensiveness rose up inside me, but, for once, I checked it. Maybe what felt to me like criticism was just her way of looking out for me?

'I am feeling better,' I said. 'It was a good idea to come up here, so thanks for bringing me.'

A rare, enormous, beautiful smile – one that risked too much deepening of any nascent crow's feet around her eyes to be produced very often – came over her face.

'Oh, Fallon, I'm so glad. And you do like Douglas, don't you?'

'Yes, very much. I'm truly happy for you.'

She clutched for my hand, the one that wasn't using a fork to spear another scrumptious piece of scampi.

'That means a lot. I just wonder if maybe you and Alexander...' She tailed off as she saw the look in my eye. 'No, okay, maybe not then. The important thing is that you're feeling better. Oh! Come on, ten minutes until this massage. It's meant to be utterly restorative – I can't wait.'

'Are you having one too?'

'Well, of course, darling, I need to experience it to review it properly. Don't worry, they offered to do it side by side in the same room, but I thought it might be more relaxing to enjoy it separately.'

I grinned at her.

'I agree. And no photos of my half-naked body being pummelled going up on the grid, okay?'

She started to object, then stopped.

'Okay. Spoilsport.'

Maybe, after all these years, Mum was developing a sense of humour.

We floated home from the massage. This was worth a few dodgy photos on Mum's Instagram page, I thought, as we pulled up outside the house and I inhaled the mingled scent of lavender and rose from the essential oils the therapist had used. I smiled dreamily at her as we got out of the car.

'That was wonderful, thank you.'

'My pleasure, darling. Can I quote you?' she asked, smiling wryly.

'In this case, you absolutely can. Sinead was a miracle worker.'

'Sometimes your mother does know best.' I rolled my eyes at her exaggeratedly, and we both grinned. 'Now go and lie down or have a bath or something, extend the benefits.'

'I think I will,' I said, picturing relaxing in that sumptuous bathroom, staring out of the window as the afternoon darkened into evening. 'What are you doing now?'

'I have some work to get on with and then Douglas is taking me out for the evening, so I'll get ready for that.'

Finally, *finally*, it was my turn to needle her on the subject. I raised an eyebrow and grinned.

'Ooh, special night out, just before Christmas, that's got "proposal" written all over it.'

Mum wasn't to be outdone.

'We'll see. Just make sure you redo your make-up after that bath. Alexander is a very handsome man, and if you're going to be spending the evening together, you'll want to look attractive.'

'No, Mum, *you* want me to look attractive. I told you, nothing's on the cards there.'

She gave a satisfied smile before turning to go into the house.

'As I said, darling, sometimes your mother does know best.'

The bath was, as predicted, perfect and, as I emerged from it with twenty minutes left before the time Coco had given me for dinner, I decided that it couldn't hurt just to refresh my make-up a tiny bit. Job done, I pulled on some jeans and the cashmere sweater Mum had bought for me and headed downstairs. With Mum and Douglas out, there were five of us at the table and we had a very jolly time of it. We were all in good spirits – me after my massage, Theo and Alexander because of the success of the sanctuary, Constance because she had experienced a breakthrough with her book and Coco because she had met someone new and was going on a date later that evening. And we were all starting to look forward to Christmas.

'Fallon and I are testing our cocktails once Theo's in bed,' said Alexander. 'Would you like to join us, Constance? I'm sure you wouldn't be backward in coming forward with your opinion,' he added teasingly.

I must admit that my heart stopped just for a second when he said that: I had, it was now clear, been looking forward to a cosy evening just with him. But did I see a flicker of relief on his face when she replied:

'I am usually delighted to tell people what I think, as you know, but not tonight. I'm going upstairs with a cup of tea – don't want to interrupt the archaeological muse when she's in a good mood.'

'What are you going to call them?' asked Coco. 'The cocktails, I mean. You've got to come up with some fun names to draw people in.'

'Yes, I said the same thing!' I said. 'Come on, everyone, what can you come up with?'

There was a momentary pause as everyone thought, then Constance said:

'What about an "Open Fire"? You know, chestnuts roasting and all that.'

'Or "Home Fir Christmas"?' suggested Coco.

'"Fir-ytale of New York"?' came in Alexander, and I piped up with:

'"All I Want Fir Christmas is You"?'

We were all laughing at the terrible puns when Theo spoke up shyly:

'I've got an idea – "*Gin*-gle Bells".'

'Theo, that's brilliant!' I said, and he beamed with pride. 'We might have to take you on as a marketing advisor. We could do loads with that – Gin-gle Bell Rock, Gin-gle all the Way...'

'Gin Gin Merrily on High,' suggested Constance, to gales of laughter.

'Well, we'll try them tonight and see what feels right,' said Alexander. 'But you all get a free cocktail at the Christmas Fayre – an alcohol-free one for you, of course,' he added, hugging his son.

'If you're feeling very generous,' said Constance, 'you'll let me take Theo now. After all, you have had him all afternoon, and the muse will wait an hour or so for me. We can play that complicated board game you like and then I'll read you a story about Tutankhamun.'

'Yes, please!' said Theo, then turned to his father. 'Is that okay, Dad?'

'More than okay,' said Alexander, smiling. 'Come on, let's get this lot in the dishwasher and we can all go about our evenings.'

Once we had finished clearing up, Alexander and I gathered together some glasses, the syrups, a bucket of ice and a bottle of his gin.

'I thought that rather than sitting in the kitchen or Hall you might like to see a part of the house you haven't been in yet?' said Alexander.

'I'd love to,' I said enthusiastically, and he led me through the Hall to a small door at the back I hadn't noticed before. It led into a narrow corridor running to our left and right, with another door in front of us.

'If you go left,' he explained, 'you end up back at the kitchen and Buttery and my study. There was a servants' hall at some point, but that is long demolished. Go right and you'll find your-self on the other side of the entrance hall. There's a room there that we call the Library, but it's in a shocking state of disrepair so we don't use it.' He shrugged. 'Maybe one day I'll be able to restore it, but at least it's watertight for now. It's this room I wanted to show you.' He gestured to the closed door in front of us. 'It doesn't look like much at first, but I'll explain once we're inside.'

He opened the door, switched on the light, and stepped back to let me through. I entered a very small room with an uneven, boarded floor. The walls were plaster with some kind of crude painting on them, covered in rough timber beams. There was a small, curtainless window in the facing wall, beneath which sat a large wooden chest. Two old-fashioned, high-backed leather chairs stood on either side of a plain table. Simple though it was, the room exuded such atmosphere that I caught my breath and took a step back.

'What do you think?' said Alexander quietly, stepping forward to put the bottles and glasses on the table.

'It's... it's – *amazing*,' I said, gazing round and drinking it in. 'I don't know *why* it's amazing, but there's something about it...' I trailed off, feeling foolish for being so overwhelmed by this ugly little room. But Alexander smiled.

'You feel it. So do I. It's a very special room. It was built as a small oratory or chapel and would have been quite ornate at one time, but all that had to be stripped out during the Reformation. The chest is where the altar would have been, and the only things that remain are the wall paintings.'

I walked over and looked at them more carefully.

'What are they of?' I asked. 'They don't look very religious.'

'No, that's how they got away with leaving them there – they just look like a pattern, but they're droplets of blood and water, see? They represent the Passion of Christ – the last events of his life.'

'How incredible. I can't believe you have these in your home, paintings that were done, what, five hundred years ago?'

'About that. They are important and we've taken serious steps to conserve them, with specialist help. People are able to visit here, by appointment – mostly Catholic church groups – but I would like to make it more publicly available. Maybe one day. For now, we can enjoy them with a drink. The room was deconsecrated centuries ago, so it's not a chapel anymore.' We sat down. 'Right, which would you like to try first?'

'How about the pine? It smells delicious.'

He carefully measured out the drinks according to a recipe we had found online, adding ice and the local tonic he had found, then we both took a tentative sip.

'Oh! That's incredible!' I exclaimed, surprised that our experiment had worked. 'It tastes almost citrusy, doesn't it, but the smell is Christmas in a glass. I love it.'

'I must say,' said Alexander, taking another sip, 'I'm amazed that it tastes this good. I think we're on to something here, Fallon. It was a very good day for us, when you arrived at Blakeney Hall. You've pushed my ideas for the business beyond what Hetty and I had ever imagined, but it's what you've done for Theo...'

He trailed off, his voice full of emotion, and looked down into his glass. Relaxed by the drink, for once I didn't make a joke, or change the subject, or jump up and start looking anywhere but at him. Instead, I sat quietly and waited until he was ready to continue.

'I know you don't think you've done much, but it's not just the bird sanctuary, although that was inspired. There's something about the way you are with him, the way you talk to him and share Runcible... He's responding to you in a way I haven't seen before, and certainly not with the Annabels of this world, who try to coddle him and look at him with pity for the poor little motherless boy with his awkward father.'

'Well, maybe that's because that's not how I see him,' I said, having another sip of my delicious drink. 'Obviously he's experienced trauma, and you've been open about some of his struggles with school and friends and so on, but he strikes me as having a sweet, kind, empathetic nature – particularly with animals – and he has you and Douglas looking after him. He doesn't seem to me to be lacking anything, but I suppose my view of families and parenting might not be quite the same as Annabel's.'

'And that's what he senses,' said Alexander, his voice full of emotion. 'Your acceptance. You don't have one view of how things should be and try to force things into fitting that. You accept that there is more than one way to do things. To you that may seem normal, but believe me, it is rare and very special.'

He held my gaze and, try as I might, I couldn't drag my eyes away. My head spun and it had nothing to do with the gin; the more I looked at him, the more I happily drowned and made none of my usual efforts to strike out for the safety of the surface. He reached across the small table and took my hand, which lay on the smooth leather arm of the chair. As if they were separate from the rest of me, my fingers turned to lace themselves between his, and he rubbed his thumb gently against my hand. Every part of my body was now yearning to be closer to him, to be held, to be kissed, and surely that would have been what happened next, had the door to the oratory not opened fractionally, and a little figure slipped in, breaking the mood.

'Runcible!' I gasped, laughing. 'How did you find us?' I scooped her onto my lap and kissed her balding head. 'That must mean Theo has gone to bed then.'

'Your tiny chaperone,' said Alexander, grinning ruefully. 'Ah well, at least she won't stop us having another drink. Shall we try the sweet chestnut syrup this time?'

'Why not?' I said, holding out my glass, then settling into my chair to enjoy the rest of an evening that remained chaste, but with a spark in the atmosphere that put more of a spring in my step when I eventually went upstairs to bed than any of Mum's wellness solutions had so far managed.

FIFTEEN

The next morning, I woke early, dressed quickly and took Runcible out for a run before anyone else was up – other than Coco, of course, who seemed to keep the most bizarre hours, yet never appear tired. I greeted her, then togged up and went outside. I breathed in the misty morning air and decided to take the path down to see Heathcliff the donkey, thinking as I went how I was already getting used to being here: the cold, yes, but also the peace and stillness, the mere idea of which would have sent me into a panic when I was in the whirl of my busy life in London. *Ah well,* I thought*, it will probably wear off soon, and I'll be glad to get back to the capital and the buzz of work.* The donkey was out of his cosy shelter and came over to see us. I rubbed his head and ears and smiled when he bent low to gently greet Runcible.

'Sorry I haven't got anything for you,' I said to him, 'but I'm sure Theo or Constance or Alexander will be along soon enough with your breakfast.'

Alexander. He had entered my dreams more than once last night, and memories of the intense gaze between us, the intertwined fingers, the delicious contemplation of what might have happened next, came flooding back and with it a flush of heat to my face that was welcome on that freezing morning. As we turned to go back to the house, I hoped fervently that Mum wouldn't notice if there was any change in atmosphere between Alexander and me. She had a tendency to be remarkably observant over things you would prefer that she missed – whether you were eating or not eating, if you liked someone or had had a falling out with them, if your skin looked bad. Whereas you could be having a proper crisis over something serious, and she would sail on, oblivious. Or maybe it was just what she chose to bring attention to, rather than the thing itself; for all her declared wisdom and life experience, she has always found it challenging to talk about the important things, those that couldn't be fixed with a face cream, cocktail or magazine multiple choice quiz. I sighed. Oh well, maybe I would manage to lie low and avoid her embarrassing comments and attempts to winkle out the truth. There was also always a chance that the electricity that had crackled between Alexander and me last night would have fizzled out by now, so there would be nothing to notice anyway. *Let's hope that's the case*, I told myself unconvincingly as we approached the house; any entanglement with Alexander would be at best fun, but pointless. We both knew that.

I gave Runcible her breakfast, then helped Coco take through some trays to the Buttery. Everyone was there and I risked a glance at Alexander, who gave me a warm and spine-tingling smile that nearly made me drop what I was carrying. *Okay, so no fizzling out*, I thought, sneaking a sideways glance at Mum to see if she had noticed and was arching an eyebrow already. But no, to my relief, she was too busy gazing at Douglas like a lovesick puppy. I slid quietly into my chair and was just offering

Constance some coffee when Douglas stood up. He cleared his throat.

'Er, good morning, everyone.'

We all returned a muttered 'good morning' and he continued:

'I – that is, Jacqueline and I – are delighted to tell you that as of last night we are engaged to be married.'

That woke us all up, and we clapped and offered our congratulations as the happy couple beamed. Mum drew her left hand out from underneath the table and showed us the ring, which was huge but very pretty with an oval-shaped diamond in the middle, surrounded by smaller, pink stones.

'They're pink sapphires,' gushed Mum, making sure we all had a good look. 'Isn't it wonderfully thoughtful of Douglas? I think I'll have to speak to Alan at *Mayfair Mews* and ask him to write in an engagement for Ophelia.' She broke off and turned to Theo. 'That's the name of the character I play. I don't think I can bear ever to take it off.'

'What number engagement will that be for Ophelia?' I asked, grinning. 'Seven, eight, nine?'

Mum shot me a look across the table.

'She's a very desirable and passionate woman. And this may be *my* first engagement, darling, but only because it's the first proposal *of many* that I have accepted.' Now came the head tilt, and I braced myself. 'How many have you racked up, darling?'

I briefly toyed with the idea of inventing a proposal or two – after all, she had been so uninvolved in my life that I could easily have had hordes of suitors of whom she was ignorant – but decided that the truth was good enough for me.

'None, Mum, and that's fine by me. But I'm so happy for you and Douglas. I suppose it's too soon to talk about dates and venues and so on?'

I have had a great deal of practice in deflecting attention from myself onto Mum and it worked like a charm, as always.

'Well, we haven't got *quite* so far as picking a date or a venue yet, but we would like to celebrate our happy news as soon as possible. We thought that we could squeeze in an engagement party between the Nativity and the Christmas Fayre. I know everyone's frightfully busy, but I'm sure you could all make an exception for something so special.'

I frowned, confused by her wording.

'What do you mean?'

She glanced at Douglas, who had the grace to look guilty but didn't have a chance to speak as she fired up her steamroller again.

'Well, the thing is, darling, the people who normally do Douglas's parties – who did the marvellous Bond one – are chock-a-block. So, I – *we* – thought you wouldn't mind putting something together? It won't be huge, only about fifty people, and obviously we'll do it here, so that's the venue sorted,' she added brightly.

A jolt of dizziness overwhelmed my head, and for a moment it was the physical symptoms that preoccupied me. Was I going to faint? I was hot and my heart was racing. It took a few seconds before the cool inner voice I have finally learned to let in came drifting across the panic. *Breathe, Fallon, breathe.* Trying not to gasp for air – partly because it didn't particularly help and partly because anything that looked too dramatic would instantly be interpreted by my mother as attention-seeking in the face of her limelight – I managed to count my breaths in and out until my jangled body calmed down and the adrenaline seeped away. I glanced furtively around the table. Mum had moved on, assuming my lack of reply as agreement, and was yakking to Douglas about colour schemes. Everyone else was looking at me with some concern, even Theo. It was Constance, sitting next to me, who put her hand on my shoulder and said quietly:

'Are you all right, Fallon? Do you want to go outside for a breath of air?'

I shook my head and smiled shakily.

'I'm okay, thank you.' I turned to Mum and spoke more loudly, interrupting her ruminations over whether baby pink was too girlish for the more mature bride. 'Mum, Douglas, I'm sorry, but I don't think I can arrange your party.'

My mother's head whipped around.

'What on earth do you mean?'

A feeling of nausea crept into my stomach, but I breathed it away.

'You brought me up here to rest. I really, really need to have a break. I know I'm helping Alexander, and I am enjoying it, but that workload is tiny compared to organising a last-minute engagement party for fifty people – especially, Mum, when you are the bride.'

'Whatever do you mean?'

I hated myself for the cold feeling of fear that was creeping into my veins; I was a grown woman, but still scared of her and of that tone of voice. But I gathered my courage, injected my own voice with soothing tones and continued:

'It's not a criticism, but you are very particular – a perfectionist. I don't mind working with clients like that, but the timescale just isn't long enough to deliver what I know you would want.'

'Rubbish, I would be perfectly happy with a relaxed gathering.'

I nearly snorted with derision, but managed to turn it into a cough. My mother has never been happy with a relaxed anything. I soldiered on.

'Even if that were true, who are you going to invite? All your friends are in London. Don't you want them to celebrate with you? Why don't you have the party down there after Christmas?'

I was pleased with this idea, not least because I would be able to palm the planning off on someone else – I was aware that it was only my availability that had made Mum ask me this time. I wasn't nearly fancy enough for her in normal circumstances. Unfortunately, she waved my suggestion away.

'No, no. Douglas has lots of people up here he can ask, and it would be the perfect opportunity for me to meet them if they couldn't make the Bond party. There will be plenty who are curious to get to know the future Lady Knight.' I fought to keep a straight face. Of course, she was going to be lady of the manor. 'Anyway, this will just be the first of our celebrations. Obviously, we'll have something in London as well, in the New Year, won't we, Douglas?'

Finally, he spoke up.

'Yes, we can do that... but Fallon, I am worried about you. After all, as you said, you are our guest here and you need to rest and recover.' He turned to Mum. 'Jacqueline, I'm sure we could find someone else.'

Mum pouted and allowed tears to spring to her eyes.

'We won't, though,' she whispered, dabbing at her eye with a corner of her napkin. 'I don't know why you're not happier for us, Fallon, I would have thought it would be your *pleasure* to put a little something together for us, to celebrate our joy. All you would need to do is sort out some drinks, maybe some music, a photographer from one of the better magazines to pop in. Décor *might* be difficult, I suppose, with everyone so busy, but we can't be defeatist...'

She trailed off and looked around at us pathetically. It was Alexander who tried next.

'Jacqueline, of course we're all delighted for you and Dad, but a special party like this would be a big ask. I was already worried about squeezing in time to decorate the house for Christmas.' He turned to Theo, who had looked up from the book he was now reading in preference to listening to our conversation. 'Don't worry, we'll *definitely* make time to do the house.' Theo grinned and returned to his book, satisfied, but Mum clapped her hands in delight.

'Oh, Alexander! You are wonderful!'

'I am?' He looked at her suspiciously.

'To offer to sort out the decoration. That's the part I was *really* worried about, but you've solved it, you clever thing!'

'That's not what I—' He attempted to interrupt, but I could have told him that was a fool's errand. Mum was full steam ahead now.

'And I just *know* that you'll want to help Fallon, seeing as she's given *you* so much help – of course you will – so really, darling' – she turned to me, now – 'it will be a tiny little bit of nothing, just a few phone calls, and I would be *so* grateful.' I went to speak, but she hadn't finished. 'It's been so *lovely* seeing you and Alexander working so beautifully together, it would probably be a pleasure for you to have an extra little project.'

She gave me a catlike smile; she could continue on this theme, if she chose. So more to shut her up than anything, I capitulated.

'All right! I'll put something together, but it will be small and simple.'

'With a magazine photographer?'

'I'll see what I can do.'

I put my head in my hands. For now, she had to be satisfied with that.

SIXTEEN

I could feel myself burning with anger and embarrassment as we continued with breakfast. Now that she had me caught nicely in her net, Mum moved on to talk about what dress she might wear, and I had no need – or requirement – to join in with that particular topic. Luckily, Coco was more interested, and kept Mum diverted.

'Are you all right?' asked Constance, buttering a piece of toast lavishly and putting it on my plate. I was touched by the gesture and picked it up gratefully.

'I'm okay,' I said, glancing across at Mum to make sure she wasn't listening. 'Remember that I'm used to her.'

'Don't want to be rude about your mother,' murmured Constance, who was clearly itching to do just that, 'but she's extraordinarily manipulative. Didn't like seeing you and Alexander backed into a corner like that. I do hope Douglas will be all right.'

I gave a small smile.

'You can be as rude as you like about her – it's refreshing. I hear a lot about how terrific she is. The truth is that, like all of us, she has her good side and her bloody awful side. But from what I've seen, I don't think you need to worry about Douglas – she's besotted with him in a way I've never seen before, and I think that if he were to challenge her on something, she loves and respects him enough to compromise. Which is a word I've not associated with Mum before.'

Constance laughed.

'Well, he's a grown man, he can look after himself. And you're a grown woman and no doubt more than capable of looking after *your*self...'

'But I'm a doormat where Mum's concerned?' I supplied.

She shrugged.

'I wouldn't have gone so far as to say doormat, but you do seem flattened by her at times. Maybe anyone would be. She's a force of nature, your mother.'

'As are you, I think.'

She nodded thoughtfully.

'Yes, but I tend to direct it towards myself and my work, rather than pulling other people's strings.'

'Mum is just so convinced of her own rightness that it's hard for her to understand that other people might see the world differently. And besides, steamrollering and manipulating people has paid dividends over the years. She can be kind, too, and she's a great person to have on your side if something goes wrong.'

'I can imagine. Perhaps I just need to get to know her better.'

'Just don't get sucked into her orbit. I'm already dreading being asked to be a bridesmaid, and what monstrous outfit she'll make me wear, but you don't need any peach taffeta in your life.'

Constance roared with laughter, causing everyone at the table to look our way.

'Something funny?' asked Mum, with an arched eyebrow.

I was also giggling now and waved her away with my fork.

She frowned and returned to her dress conversation, which had already been going on for ten minutes or so – about nine minutes longer than I am able to talk about wedding dresses. I concentrated on finishing my breakfast, difficult when, at regular intervals, Constance hissed various horrors at me: Watered silk! Crepe de chine! Kitten heels! Alexander looked over at us queryingly a few times, but of course we couldn't share the joke with him.

As breakfast drew to a close, Mum turned her attention back to me.

'Are you busy this morning, Fallon?'

The truth was that Alexander and I had nothing big to do now until the Citroën turned up, but I had planned to do a proper, long Moors walk with a pub lunch at the end of it. As is her style, Mum took my lack of instant response for an answer – one which was to her liking.

'Good. I'd like to get some of your toxins flushed out: I'm taking you for a colonic cleanse!'

This was announced much as if it were a special treat, but the ripple of horror that went around the table swiftly put paid to that.

'What's wrong with you all?' demanded Mum. 'It's a fantastic way of restoring energy and the practitioners who do it are very discreet.'

I started to say that *no way* was I spending my morning doing anything of the sort when, like a beautifully trained, supportive chorus, everyone at the table spoke at once:

'I'm sorry, Jacqueline—'

'Darling, I'm not sure—'

'But I wanted Fallon to—'

'What rot! I was going to ask her—'

'It sounds amazing, Jacqueline, but—'

Yes, everyone spoke up for me, giving Mum a reason why I couldn't possibly spend the morning with a tube up my bottom, then having the entire experience plastered all over social media. I looked around the table, grinning, then raised my hands in the air helplessly.

'Sorry, Mum, as you can see, I'm rushed off my feet. In demand.' Luckily, I had managed to hear what everyone's rapid excuses for me were, and I seized on a couple. 'I'm going to the sanctuary with Alexander and Theo this morning and then I'm meeting Constance for lunch in a pub on the moors. All that walking will tire me, so I plan to spend a quiet afternoon making some preliminary plans for your engagement party. Sorry.'

'Your loss. Maybe we can do it another day.'

'Mum, to be honest, I think I'm *always* going to be too busy for a colonic cleanse.'

She would have continued arguing her corner, but Douglas swept in heroically.

'Actually, darling, I was hoping that we could spend the first day of being an engaged couple doing something special? I have booked lunch and an overnight stay at The Mottled Dog in Charlington.'

'Oh, Douglas!' She clapped her hands girlishly, my colon forgotten, thank goodness. 'That's the one with two Michelin stars – however did you get a reservation?'

'You're not the only one with contacts,' he said, smiling. 'Come on, let's go and ring *The Times* to put in our announcement, then we can think about what to pack.'

They left the room, and the rest of us grinned at each other.

'Your father is an absolute genius,' I said. 'As for my plans today, nobody has to hold me to what I said in the line of fire, but thank you all for saving me.'

'Does that mean you're not coming to the sanctuary?' asked Theo, looking disappointed.

I glanced at Alexander, then smiled.

'I'd love to come. I need to see how my baby bunnies are getting on.'

'Yay!' shouted Theo, punching the air in a way that made me feel flattered. 'I'm going to go and get ready!'

'And I'd still like to have that lunch with you,' said Constance. 'I'll be nose to the grindstone this morning, so a brisk walk over the moors and a good plate of food at the end of it will be just what I need. Do you want to join us, Coco?'

She shook her head.

'No, thanks. I've got exciting news of my own. I'm going into York to speak to someone who needs a last-minute caterer for a dinner party at the weekend. A friend of a friend put us in touch, so I hope it comes off. Oh, and talking of last minute, Fallon, if you need someone to cater Dad and Jacqueline's party, I'd be glad to help.'

I could have hugged her.

'That would be amazing, thank you so much. If you're around this afternoon, maybe we could have a look at some ideas?'

She agreed, and we all started to clear up breakfast. As I stacked plates, I thought how lucky – not to mention surprised – I was that this holiday was turning out so well. Even after such a short time I'd miss the Knights when I went back to London.

When we arrived at Sadie's, even I could see the change in Theo. He jumped out of the car almost before it had stopped and ran to ring on the doorbell of the house. Linnet appeared, pulling on her coat, and the two of them ran around to the sanctuary. By the time Sadie appeared at the door, there was no sign of the two children.

'Gone already, have they?' she asked, tugging a deep purple knitted hat down to her eyes. 'They've palled up, those two. It's been great having Theo come to visit, and I can't pretend that the extra helping hands of whoever brings him aren't welcome.'

We started walking around to the sanctuary, at a more sedate pace than the children.

'I can't imagine my mother being much help,' I said, trying to imagine her pushing raw chick meat into the gullet of a towel-swaddled owl.

'You'd be surprised,' said Sadie, pushing open the door of the room where the bunnies we fed last time were kept. 'She's not squeamish, so she makes a great vet's nurse. She assisted me with an amputation the other day – poor fox had been hit by a car. There'd be plenty of people fainting at the sight, but she was interested, and very competent.'

I raised my eyebrows. Why hadn't Mum mentioned it? I decided to ask her when I had a chance. Sadie flicked the kettle on and continued.

'But one of the best things she's done is put us on her Instagram page. Thanks to that we've had near to a one hundred per cent increase in donations, and interest from the local press. The power of these things is amazing. Right, you two are on baby bunny feeding duty again, then I've got a piece of dry-stone walling that needs fixing – you said you know how to do that, Alexander?' He nodded. 'Great. In that case, I'll leave you to it. Oh, and do use that kettle to make yourselves a coffee, everything's in the cupboard there.'

We bustled around for a few minutes, getting everything ready, then each gently lifted out a little rabbit and sat down on the sofa.

'They're bigger than last time,' said Alexander. 'They won't need feeding like this for much longer.'

We settled into a companionable silence which appeared calm although my heart was racing at the sensation of his thigh pressing against mine; we were sitting closer together than we had been last time. As we swapped our sated rabbits for hungry ones, I prepared myself to bring up what had happened at breakfast. Much as I didn't want to spend this cosy time talking about Jacqueline Honeywood, I did want to clear the air.

'I'm sorry about Mum,' I said, stroking the bunny's velvety ears as it sucked at the small syringe. 'Obviously, you don't have to do anything to help with the engagement party; it's bad enough that I was forced into it.'

'Do you find it hard to say no to her?' asked Alexander. 'Although I don't know who wouldn't – it seems almost impossible.'

I grimaced.

'She has a way of making you feel so unreasonable for refusing her that you end up agreeing. It's only later that you think of good arguments, and by then the juggernaut has moved on. I don't see her very often, normally, so it's not as bad as it could be, and it's much easier to say no over email or text message than it is over the breakfast table.'

'Dad should have been firmer,' said Alexander. 'I can have a word with him if you like?'

'No, don't worry, I'll put something together and steel myself for her inevitable disappointment. At least the time scale is dramatically limited. That brings its own problems, but it'll all be over with quite quickly.'

We swapped our rabbits again for the final two.

'I'll gladly help you,' said Alexander, 'although you'll have to just give me instructions to carry out. The Christmas Fayre has been bad enough; I don't have the first clue when it comes to organising a party. Theo never wants them for his birthday, so I haven't even been able to do that.'

I turned to him gratefully.

'If you really don't mind, then that would be brilliant – for the moral support, if nothing else.'

'Of course. And it's for Dad as well – a small step towards thanking him for everything he does for Theo and me. And Fallon...' He broke off, but I couldn't answer – my throat was suddenly tight. 'I can't deny that I'd be very happy to spend more time with you.'

Our rabbits, now replete, were dozing on our laps. Alexander caught and held my gaze again in that gorgeously unsettling way he had, that I seemed unable to break away from. His hand crept away from the rabbit and towards mine, which met it willingly. We were already so close together that I could feel his breath on my face, and it was the easiest and most natural thing for our lips to meet in a kiss that was gentle, yet set off explosions throughout my body. Those baby rabbits may well have needed to cover their eyes with their soft little paws, had the door not flung open, admitting Jacob, Theo and Linnet and causing Alexander and I to spring apart, guilt written all over our faces.

'Hello, all!' boomed Alexander in an unnaturally jovial voice, standing up and just managing to cling on to his surprised rabbit, rudely awakened from its milky snooze.

Linnet hadn't noticed a thing and bounced over to take the little creature from Alexander's hands, crooning over it. Theo followed her more slowly, looking at us thoughtfully, but was soon absorbed by the rabbit he took from me, going over to the cage with his friend to look at all the babies. Jacob, of course, wasn't so easily distracted and gave us a knowing grin and a raised eyebrow, which prompted us to get very busy clearing up the little kitchen area and jabber away about dry-stone walling.

'Do you want to come and help?' Alexander asked the children, who agreed enthusiastically, so we all set off to complete our next job.

As we worked on the wall, Alexander and I tried to determinedly avoid looking at each other, but our eyes kept meeting and each time they did, a jolt of electricity shot through me. I kept up a stream of conversation, hoping to keep things normal in front of the children, but I can't deny that I was relieved when the time came for me to go and meet Constance for lunch.

'Are you sure you can find your way all right?' asked Alexander, pausing in his work. 'I could run you over there, it would only take ten minutes.'

'It's fine, thank you,' I replied. 'I have my phone and a paper map and it's only a mile or so. But there was one favour I wondered if you could all do for me?' I touched Theo on the shoulder, and he smiled up at me. 'Could you possibly keep Runcible with you and take her back home when you go? She's tired and I don't think a hike across the moors is going to help.'

'Ooh, yes, *please*,' said the little boy, as I had known he would. 'We'd love to look after her for you.'

'Thank you.' I handed him a small crossbody bag I had been carrying. 'This is her lunch and poo bags.'

He put it on importantly.

'Don't worry, Fallon, she'll be fine with me.'

'I know she will, thank you.'

With a final glance at Alexander, I set off. The truth was that I was tired, too, but I welcomed a stride across the moors to think about that kiss and try to get my tangle of feelings straightened out.

Of course, by the time I arrived at the pub, I had answered precisely no questions about how I felt or where I wanted things to go, and when I went to join Constance at the table she had secured right next to the blazing fire in an inglenook fireplace, she noticed immediately that something was up.

'Ah, Fallon, hello. Goodness, are you okay?'

I sighed.

'Yes, I'm fine, just got a few things on my mind.'

Kind, understanding Constance didn't probe for details, but

instead pointed to the menu, written on a small blackboard near the bar.

'Maybe some lunch will sort you out. I'm trying to decide between the ham hock and the bean and mushroom pie.'

I studied the board for a moment.

'Yes, I'll have the bean and mushroom pie, it sounds delicious.'

'Good. I'll get some drinks when I order too. I'm going to have half a pint of the local bitter, same for you?'

I shook my head.

'No, thanks, I'm not a beer drinker. I'll just have a lime cordial and soda.'

Our drinks and food were soon before us, and we tucked in hungrily. Constance told me all about the book she was writing, which sounded fascinating.

'Belize is a wonderful country,' she told me. 'But the caves we're investigating are difficult to get to, so we had to set up a temporary camp and labs right next to the site so that we could stay there for weeks at a time. We made some real progress into working out what rituals the caves were used for, hence the book. It's an under-researched place and we're desperate to go back again, but that takes money, of course. Hopefully, the book will get a bit of attention and we might get some funding.'

'Let me know when it's being published,' I said, forking up some delicious, buttery mashed potato that lay in a thick coat across the top of the pie. 'I'll gladly help you throw a launch party and try to whip up some press interest.'

Constance beamed at me.

'Jolly good of you. Not sure many archaeologists get launch parties thrown by glamorous London companies like yours. Will you mind us all turning up in muddy boots and holey sweaters?'

I laughed.

'Wear what you like, it'll be your party. We can talk about it nearer the time, but you can be sure it won't be something that feels wrong for the occasion, or where anyone feels out of place. It'll be fun.'

'I don't doubt that... but Fallon, publishers of this sort of thing don't have the money for more than a pint down the pub.'

'Please, it would be my pleasure. Anyway, you can consider it a quid pro quo for the advice you're going to give me.'

'Ha. Don't know what my advice is worth, but I'll take you up on that. Alexander, is it?'

I pulled a face.

'Is it that obvious?'

'I'm usually a dolt when it comes to this sort of thing, but even I noticed that you fancy the pants off each other. So, what's the problem?'

Heat rose in my cheeks.

'I'm not sure there *is* a problem, that's what.'

'Marvellous, we can think about what we're having for pud, instead.'

I laughed.

'Okay, fair enough. He... er, I... that is, *we* kissed this morning...'

I trailed off. The pink in my cheeks was rapidly turning purple, and I wished I could turn the fire down. I am not used to these sorts of conversations, and whenever they arose with Mum, I did my best to end them as quickly as possible. But Constance couldn't have been more different, and I desperately wanted to talk over my feelings with someone. She finished chewing her mouthful and waved her fork at me.

'Excellent. Tell me more. If you want to. Always happy to talk about dogs, if you prefer.'

I shook my head.

'It's all right. It's all just a bit embarrassing.'

'Not embarrassing. Life.'

I continued, 'So, I'm feeling happy... I suppose that's what's

worrying me. I think Alexander is – lovely. And yes, I do fancy
the pants off him.'

'But?'

'But...' I stopped, feeling awful about what I wanted to say. I
looked up at Constance's plain, intelligent, calm face and felt
encouraged. What I had to say next came out in a rush. 'It's
Theo. He's a great little boy, but I've always had major reservations about becoming a mother. I just think I'd be terrible at it,
especially with a child as sensitive as Theo. And I've never been
that interested in serious relationships at all, let alone with men
who have kids. I know it's ridiculously early where Alexander is
concerned to be saying this stuff.'

I stopped abruptly and stared miserably into what was left
of my pie. I braced myself for the usual: *you'll come round to
motherhood, give it time*; *how can you not want children, you'll
love it once you do*; *aren't you jumping the gun a bit, it was one
kiss?* But Constance was different.

'I can see your dilemma, and you're right to think about it
now. There are plenty of hearts to be broken if things develop
with Alexander. As far as deal breakers go, it's a biggie. With
my most sensible of sensible hats on, I'd advise you to stop this
thing before it has properly started. Alexander comes with
Theo, it's non-negotiable.' I nodded, feeling tears pushing at the
back of my eyes. 'Deep breaths,' instructed Constance, draining
her glass. 'I'm going to get another of these – do you mind
driving my car back?'

I shook my head and grabbed the opportunity of her going
to the bar to take the breaths. I started to feel better, and more
ready for the most difficult part of my admissions, yet to
come. Constance returned, placing a glass in front of both
of us.

'I've ordered pud as well, two different ones so just take
what you like when it comes, or I'll tackle both if you don't want
anything.'

An unexpected bubble of laughter erupted from my mouth, and she looked at me quizzically.

'Sorry! I'm all about the puddings, so I'm afraid you'll only get one. I was only laughing because having lunch with you is a very different experience from having lunch with Mum.'

She raised an eyebrow.

'I'm sure. Couldn't live like that myself, but we do what we have to do. Being a glamorous celebrity comes with some upkeep, I imagine.'

'Just a bit!'

'I'm much happier scrabbling around in a muddy field and enjoying puddings, myself, but it takes all sorts. Ah, here they are.'

I chose the apple pie with custard, while Constance had the sticky toffee pudding. We ate for a moment in silence, and then she said, 'So, finish the story. I know there's more.'

'There is more. The hardest bit. The thing is, that after all these years of feeling one way and being perfectly happy... I think my feelings are changing. And I don't know how I feel about that. I haven't done some massive one-eighty: I'm not about to start baking and knitting baby bootees. It's more that it feels like a little window has opened somewhere in me, that I could contemplate...'

'You're changing.'

'Yes.' I busied myself for a moment, scraping my bowl. 'That's what it feels like, but is it true? Can one change so suddenly, and in such a big way?'

'We do change, and there's no shame in that. We should embrace it, not fight it, but of course it can feel slippery and terrifying, so of course we run scared. And these changes that feel so huge, well, often they're pretty much in line with who we already are, even if they don't feel that way.' I looked at her curiously, not sure what she meant. 'There are plenty of ways to skin a cat, my dear. Motherhood doesn't automatically equal a love of baking and flowery aprons. If it does come to you, you'll do it your own way, and that won't be any better or any worse, but it will be the best thing for any child involved – that you just be yourself. Look at me: hardly the catalogue version of a mummy, but I loved it, deeply, still do. Had to bat off a few opinions along the way, but that's true of everything in life.'

'But that's it!' I burst out. 'Being any sort of mother is fine, but the loving it deeply bit. How do you guarantee that? How do you know you'll be able to be selfless, to give the child what they need?'

'Being selfless and giving a child what they need are not necessarily the same thing. An exhausted, resentful, frustrated parent is no good to anyone. But you muddle through and do your best and make mistakes and try to sort them out. I suppose you're thinking about Jacqueline?'

'Yes. I understand what she was doing with her career, and why, and I appreciate that, I do, but I felt so unwanted and even now she still always makes me feel like I'm not good enough. She's always trying to upgrade me in some way. What if I do the same? Become a mother and then get bored with the whole thing?'

For a moment or two, Constance regarded me in silence. Finally, she said, 'I can see why you're worried. But we don't have to repeat patterns, especially when we recognise them. You already have your life, your identity, your success. From what I know about the situation, Jacqueline was very young when she had you and was still chasing those things. It's very different. And she loves you, you know, very much. She's just hopelessly clumsy at showing it. But I see her looking at you, see the pride when you talk about your work, or when you helped Theo out with the sanctuary. I can see the inner glow she has for you.'

'*Really?*' I spluttered.

She nodded seriously.

'Really. It doesn't take away the fact that your childhood wasn't ideal, but it's true. I know it might be an impossible ask, Fallon, and this is by no means a directive, but you did ask for my advice...'

She looked at me questioningly.

'I did. Please say whatever it is.'

'You might consider – just think about – letting some of that resentment go and allowing her to be a mother to you *now*. You push her away, you know, and it's not helping either of you.'

I swallowed, feeling those annoying tears pricking again.

'I'll think about it. All of it. Thank you.'

I reached across the table and took her hand. She squeezed mine hard.

'Let yourself be happy, see where it takes you. And, for some more traditional advice, let me tell you that Alexander is one of the best men I have ever met, and Theo one of the best kids. You'd be a bloody fool to let them go.'

I let my mind bring up an image of the two of them and my heart swelled with hope.

SEVENTEEN

Breakfast the next morning was a quiet affair, with Mum and Douglas away. I hadn't seen Alexander since our interrupted kiss, as when I had arrived home with Constance after lunch, I spent a couple of hours with Coco, who then suggested going out to a restaurant in York where a friend of hers was working. It had been good to be out and, as I had driven and Coco was staying out to go clubbing with her friend, I had got to bed early, drunk nothing but elderflower cordial and consequently woken up with a clear head and more energy than I'd had in months.

'What time did you get home last night?' I asked her, as we carried through the breakfast things.

'This morning, more like,' she said, grinning. 'It was just past two. I hope I didn't wake anyone up.'

We all shook our heads.

'I wish I still had that stamina,' said Constance. 'Funny now how I can dig and work all day in stupid temperatures and be fine, but if I'm in bed later than ten thirty, I feel it for a week – and show it. You, darling Coco, look as beautiful and fresh-faced as ever.'

Coco put her hands in a 'v' shape under her chin and pouted, and Constance laughed.

'Theo being born did it for me,' said Alexander, hugging his son. 'I've never quite been the same since. Having worked plenty of nights in surgery, you'd think I'd be perfect for getting up at night with a baby, but it was more punishing, I'm sure of it.'

'Did Mum get up in the night too?' asked Theo.

There was a tiny pause. I had rarely heard her mentioned.

'She did,' replied Alexander, his voice light. 'But these things are often a two-person job.'

'What are you all up to today?' asked Coco.

My phone pinged.

'Ah ha!' I said, reading the message. 'Well, we are going to be extremely busy, as it happens – if you can bear to forgo a morning at the sanctuary, Theo?'

'Has the van arrived?' he asked, his face lighting up with excitement.

'It's about five minutes away,' I said, 'so we'd better finish up our breakfast.'

We did so, quickly, and the five of us were pulling on coats and opening the front door when the vintage Citroën HY van came slowly up to the front of the house, followed by a small red car.

'Fallon?' asked the woman who had been driving the van.

'That's me,' I said, going forward and shaking her hand. 'And this is Alexander, the proud new owner.'

I introduced the rest of the family to the woman, whose name was Tara, and the man who had followed in the car behind, Greg.

'Come and see your new van,' said Tara, and led us around. Alexander and I had, of course, seen plenty of photos, but seeing it for real was exciting. It had been painted in shades of pale green and purple, to represent the heather on the moors, and the painted signs and decals with Alexander's logo were immaculate. Greg went inside to open up the side flaps and we all oohed and aahed at our first glimpse of the inside of the van. The back wall was tiled with cream metro tiles above a wooden countertop which would soon be filled with bottles. Glasses were stored hanging in racks and there was a fridge under the counter. A small sink was fitted to the left.

'It's adorable!' said Coco. 'And I love the lighting. I never realised it would be so cool. Can we come inside?'

'Maybe just two at a time,' said Greg, smiling, and he came out. I stood back to let Alexander and Theo be the first inside, but Alexander put a warm hand in the small of my back and said:

'You come, too, Fallon, I'm sure the three of us will fit just fine. You made this happen, you should be one of the first in.'

Unbelievably touched, I didn't reply for fear of my voice cracking and giving away the strength of my emotions. I let him steer me gently inside, where we marvelled at the clever way everything fitted in so neatly and looked so very smart. I got a couple of glasses down for Theo, who pretended to serve Constance and Coco drinks.

'I'm afraid we only have gin, madam, not whisky,' he said to Constance, his face wreathed with smiles. 'But I can make yours extra enormous if you like.'

She roared with laughter.

'That's my boy! Always liked a bartender with a heavy hand.'

I sneaked a look at Alexander, who was gazing at his giggling son with bemused wonder. Constance and Coco toasted each other, then took their turn looking inside the van with Theo, while Alexander and I completed the paperwork. We waved Tara and Greg off until their little red car was out of sight, then all beamed around at one another.

'It's an absolute bloody triumph!' said Constance, thumping

Alexander on the back so hard he coughed. 'You'll be the talk of the Christmas Fayre.'

'Thanks to Fallon,' he said. 'This was all her idea.'

'Not my wallet, though,' I said, 'and not my risk. All credit to you for going with it. I'm glad it looks so good.'

'Where are you going to keep it?' asked Coco. 'In one of the outbuildings?'

'Yes,' replied Alexander. 'I've made a space in the old garage, and we'll keep it there. In fact, I'll take it round now and then we can get on with stocking and decorating it. Theo, will you go with your lovely aunts and get dressed for the day, and Fallon and I will see you round the back in ten minutes?'

The little boy nodded happily, gave his father a quick hug, and the three of them went back inside, leaving Alexander and me together. I instantly went into efficiency mode, awkward at being alone with him.

'Right, you've got the key, haven't you? Let's start her up! I'll go and shut the flap.'

I scuttled away before he could reply and secured the back of the van, feeling it judder as he turned on the ignition. I trotted back around to the passenger side and started to hop in. Of course, I had forgotten that the van was left-hand drive, and I almost ended up in Alexander's lap.

'Whoa, steady there!' he said as I half fell back out again. 'Are you okay?'

'Yes, yep, fine!' I called as I dashed around to climb in the other side. 'Wrong driver's side,' I explained sheepishly, as I buckled myself in.

He laughed.

'We're both going to do that a lot over the next week or so,' he said, and started to move the van slowly forward. We chugged around the side of the house to the stone outbuildings where the distillery was housed, then he stopped, jumped out and opened a pair of large double doors on one, before getting back in and expertly reversing the van inside. He quieted the ignition and turned to me.

'Fallon, before Theo comes back and we get busy, I just wanted to say that yesterday – well, that is… I'm feeling very happy.' He reached across and took my hand. 'No pressure or anything, that's it.'

I squeezed his hand and didn't even try to curb the huge smile that was spreading across my face.

'Me too.'

'Good.'

Then he leant across and kissed me again, and all the same fireworks as yesterday fizzed and exploded like crazy inside my body, maybe more. We broke away and he cupped my face in his hand. I could feel the uneven scar against my cheek. He gazed at me as if I were the most precious thing he had ever seen, and all I could do was lose myself in his eyes. Who knows how long we would have stayed like that, the cramped cab of the van and the oily smell of the dark garage the most romantic scene I had ever experienced, if Theo had not come running across the yard outside, yelling that he had finished getting dressed. We stepped out and greeted him and I surprised myself by discovering that I was looking forward to spending the day with him.

'Right, we've got lots to do,' said Alexander, switching on the overhead lights to reveal a space that was bigger than expected. 'The Christmas Fayre is approaching quickly, but we've got plenty of other commitments – including visiting the sanctuary – so we need to get lots done today.'

I knew that he liked to keep afternoons free to be with Theo, of course, and with the visits to the sanctuary and the Nativity rehearsals that would soon be starting up, we were pushed for time. But rather than feeling stressed and resentful, as I doubtless would have done a few weeks ago, I was energised by the challenge.

'Absolutely. Now the first thing to do is make sure we have some music.' I pulled my phone out of my pocket. 'And as luck would have it, there is a cheesy Christmas playlist here ready to go.' I tapped the screen a few times and pressed 'play' and the strains of 'I Wish It Could Be Christmas Every Day' floated reedily out of the phone's speaker.

'I can improve on that,' said Alexander and, reaching up to a shelf, brought down a small speaker. 'Bluetooth,' he said by way of explanation. I took it from him, tapped a few more times and soon the song filled the small space.

'*Now* we're ready to get started,' I declared. 'Alexander, you and I should maybe get going on stocking the bottles, and Theo, do you think you could be in charge of the blackboard?'

He nodded eagerly.

'What do I have to do?'

'Come back up to the house with me and we can get everything you'll need,' I said, smiling at his and Alexander's confused faces. This was a surprise I had prepared for both of them. As we started walking, Theo, to my great surprise, grabbed my hand and started chattering away about Christmas, telling me why robins were traditionally the birds of the season and wondering if all the creatures at the sanctuary would be given stockings. Luckily for me, he was more delivering a stream of consciousness than wishing to hold a conversation, because my poor brain was too busy trying to adjust itself to holding a child's hand to be able to formulate coherent sentences. I felt a curious mixture of alarmed, awkward and incredibly touched. Even I, with my little experience of small people, could appreciate that Theo's taking of my hand was, particularly for a child who seemed to struggle with social stuff, a gesture of warmth and trust. That was nice. At the same time, I was terrified of responding incorrectly and offending him – was I holding his hand too tightly, or too loosely? How did we let go? Would Alexander mind this small intimacy, or might he think I was 'doing an Annabel' and trying to close in on his little family?

'Where's the stuff?'

'Huh? Oh, right, the stuff.' We had arrived back at the house and Theo dropped my hand to open the big front door. 'It's upstairs. You stay here and I'll run and get it.'

I jogged up the stairs – well, up the first few stairs, until I got out of breath, then walked the rest of them, berating myself for not doing enough exercise – and to my room, where I collected the items I needed.

'Here they are,' I said, back in the hall again, and handed Theo a slim folder of papers, and a box of chalks and chalk pens. 'You take these, I'll carry the blackboard.'

We set off again back to the outbuildings, our hands now too full to entertain any more hand holding. There was Alexander, lugging a heavy box of bottles, which he put down when he saw us.

'What have you got there?'

'It's a blackboard, which you can put on a stand outside with all the prices and choices written on it,' I said, putting it down and starting to unpeel the cardboard that wrapped it. 'I thought Theo could do the writing – I've printed out all the details – but look!'

I stripped off the packaging to reveal the board I had had printed with the same design that Alexander had on his labels as a border.

'Fallon, it's beautiful!' he said. 'This is going to look amazing, what a great idea!'

'Thank you,' I said modestly. 'I'm glad you like it.' I noticed that Theo was biting his lip, a worried habit I had noticed in him before. 'Are you all right?' I asked. 'You don't have to do the writing if you don't want to, it's fine.'

He shook his head but didn't speak. I crouched down next to him and, after a split second's hesitation, took his hand. 'I can see something's worrying you. Please tell me what it is, and I can help. Look, Runcible wants to know too.'

My little dog had trotted over, and I picked her up. Theo's lips raised a fraction at the corners, and I waited patiently. After a moment, he spoke.

'It's just that your board is very pretty, and I don't think my handwriting is good. I don't want to spoil it.'

'Oh, gosh, what a relief!' I said, and he looked at me suspiciously. 'I thought you didn't want to do it, when this is the job I had in mind for you all along. Because, you see, I've seen your handwriting, and it is just perfect for this sign – it's very neat and clear.'

'My teacher said I should join it up, but it's too difficult. Everyone else can,' he added miserably.

'Well then, thank goodness everyone else hasn't been asked to write this board,' I said firmly. 'Joined up handwriting would *ruin* it. I want your best not joined up. Would you do that?'

The shadows fell from his face, and he nodded eagerly.

'Yes, please. Can Runcible help?'

'Of course she can, but her paw-writing is very messy, so she had better stick to advising you, if that's okay.'

With that little hurdle jumped, I set the board up, got out the papers and showed him how to do his writing with chalk first, to make sure the spacing worked before going over it with chalk pen.

'You're a genius,' muttered Alexander when I went over to help him with the box. 'I thought we'd lost him for a moment there.'

'I think it was probably more down to Runcible than me,' I replied. 'But I'm glad he's happy.'

We busied ourselves for the next few hours filling the cabinets with gin and the fridge with tonic and a few other mixers in case people required them. After that I left Theo and Alexander attaching the now-finished blackboard to its stand

and tackling a tangle of fairy lights while I went and collected some more pine and sweet chestnuts, Runcible pottering along with me. I then returned to the house to get big pots of syrup bubbling away and set the dishwasher going to sterilise glass bottles to pour it into. I toyed with the idea of making enough to sell alongside the gin and was looking up the logistics of doing this in the time we had available when they came in through the kitchen door. I looked up.

'All finished?' I asked.

'All finished,' said Alexander. 'Those fairy lights were a pain, but you were right, they look great now they're up.'

'It smells delicious in here,' said Theo, putting his nose in the air and sniffing.

'I'm glad you like it,' I replied. 'I thought we could have some of the old batch just with tonic to see what it's like. I'm thinking you could sell it as a cordial, then, as well as the gin, if it works well on its own. But I don't think there's time before the Christmas Fayre to get it organised.'

'You could do it in time for the Burns Night thing in January that Dad's doing,' said Theo, peering into one of the large saucepans.

'Ooh, don't scald yourself,' I said, turning the pot handle. 'Burns Night? I'll be back in London then, but I suppose I could work something up.'

Two pairs of dark blue eyes turned towards me.

'Are you going away?' asked Theo. 'I suppose you're only here on holiday, I forgot.'

He crouched down to pat Runcible, and I stirred the pans needlessly to give myself something to do.

'Well, we don't need to think about any of that now,' said Alexander in an overly jolly voice, dropping his hand gently on Theo's shoulder. 'I think Fallon's idea of tasting the syrups is a good one, and we should have some lunch too. Come on, Theo, you can help me put something together.'

The atmosphere eased as we all went about our different jobs, and before long, we were in the Hall, a tray of toast, cheese and some leftover roasted vegetables in front of us.

'I like eating in here,' said Theo. 'It's more comfortable than the Buttery.' He turned to me. 'We're only eating in there all the time because of guests – we usually have lunch on our knees in here.'

Alexander laughed.

'We do. You don't mind, do you, Fallon?'

'Of course not. And it's so cosy with the fire. Here you are, I've brought a few glasses each because I want us to try each flavour with tonic but also with warmed apple juice.'

'This is going to be the best cocktail bar in Yorkshire,' said Theo, and we all beamed around at each other, the firelight flickering over our happy faces.

EIGHTEEN

As we finished off our simple but delicious lunch and were congratulating ourselves on the syrups, my phone rang. Fishing it out of my pocket, I saw that it was my business partner, Sam.

'I'm sorry, I have to take this,' I said, worried. He had promised he would only call if there was an emergency. I ran out to the little room at the end of the Hall, which I had since learned was called the screens passage, and tapped the green button.

'Hello, Sam?'

'Hi, Fallon, how's it going?'

'I'm having a good time up here, thanks. Is everything all right?'

We chatted for a few minutes, then I returned to the Hall to find Alexander and Theo looking concerned.

'Nothing to worry about,' I said, helping them put everything on the tray. 'Sam just needed my advice on how to hurry up a particular supplier without offending them so badly they refused to work with us again. Luckily, I know them of old, so I think it'll work out okay.'

'The thought of work going on in London without you hasn't stressed you out too much?' asked Alexander.

'Not at all. In fact, I feel quite energised by sorting that out. Being away even for this short time has made me feel much better, and working with you has helped me keep a balance. I was more worried about getting bored and stale.'

'Did you think it would be boring up here?' asked Theo.

'Well, I did wonder,' I said honestly. 'But I was wrong, wasn't I? Even when I'm not working, there's plenty to do – more than I expected – and if there's a moment to fill, then there's always Mum.'

But Theo wasn't to be distracted.

'But you *are* going back to London after Christmas? I thought you liked being here with us?'

I glanced at Alexander. I could feel myself on uncertain ground here.

'I do, of course I do. I love it here. But...'

I trailed off, alarmed by the little boy's stricken face. This wasn't part of the plan. Alexander stepped in.

'Theo, love, Fallon has her home and business down in London. Of course she'll need to go back to them.'

'Like Grandpa does?' asked Theo, his face brightening. 'Go down to them sometimes, but then come back here?'

'I'd love to come back,' I said firmly, which I thought was true but also non-committal. 'Now, what are you planning to do this afternoon? I think I'm going to go into York. I'm dying to have a look around the Christmas market, I haven't had time yet.'

'Can we go, too, Dad?' asked Theo. 'They might have the wooden birds for the Christmas tree that they had last year, and I'd love another one to go with the blue tit.'

Alexander looked at me questioningly and I smiled.

'I'd love some company. I'm going to leave Runcible here,

though; shopping isn't her thing. See you out the front in ten minutes?'

We took the lunch things into the kitchen, then I let my little dog outside briefly, before settling her into her basket and kissing her goodbye on her tufty head.

'We call it the St Nicholas Fair here,' said Alexander, as we passed the shops festooned with twinkling lights and approached long rows of sweet wooden chalets, stuffed to the brim with enticing Christmas trinkets and food, a huge Christmas tree watching over proceedings.

'Dad, I can hear the carousel!' cried Theo, and we all stopped to listen to the cheery, tinkling music. 'Oh, can I go on that first?'

'Why not?' said his father, and we edged through the crowds to find the golden merry-go-round, resplendent in a pretty shop-lined square, its colourful horses bobbing gracefully.

'Pity you didn't sign up for this one,' I said, as we joined a short queue. 'It would have been the perfect place to sell your gin.'

Alexander pulled a face.

'Maybe next year. The Christmas Fayre feels quite big enough for me – for now anyway. Are you going on?'

'Huh?'

'The carousel!'

I looked at the glittering ride, its colours, music and nostalgia an enticing invitation.

'You know, I've never been on one?' I said to Alexander. He frowned. 'Nope, never.'

'Well, one of the beauties of having children,' he replied, 'is you get to do all sorts of stuff you missed out on the first time, and nobody bats an eyelid. It's terrific.'

'Are you going on?'

'Damn right I am!'

'Oh, you have to come, too, Fallon!' said Theo eagerly. 'It's not too fast, you won't feel sick, I promise.'

I smiled at his kindness.

'Well, in that case I will give it a whirl.'

As the ride stopped and the passengers alighted, we stepped up onto the shiny metal platform and chose three brightly painted horses in a row together, so that Theo could go in the middle.

'Look, Dad, look, Fallon, their names are painted on their necks! Mine is called Lily, but I wish she was called Runcible. What are yours called?'

I looked.

'Oh! Mine is called Dancer, that's pretty.'

'More traditional for reindeer,' said Alexander, grinning. 'Mine is called Boniface, which makes me regret not choosing that for you instead of Theo.'

Theo shrieked in horror, and we all laughed. I was feeling quite giddy and we hadn't even started moving. When we did, it was glorious. The lights on the shops became streaks, punctuated with the happy faces of people waiting for their turn on the merry-go-round. The music jangled cheerfully around me as the golds, reds and greens of the horses reflected off the central mirrors of the ride until I was enveloped in a fairground embrace. All I could see clearly were Theo's and Alexander's faces, both wearing huge smiles as they occasionally shouted to each other or to me. I wrapped my arms around the barley twist pole emerging from my horse's back and hugged it with joy, reluctant to let go as the spinning slowed and the carousel finally came to a stop.

'Wasn't that *brilliant*?' said Theo as we climbed off our horses.

'It certainly was,' said Alexander. 'Did you enjoy it?' he asked, touching my shoulder briefly.

'I loved it!' I said. 'I'm going to make sure I go on one of those whenever I can from now on, to make up for lost time.'

'They always have one here at Christmas,' said Theo. 'So, you'll have to come back every year.'

I nearly said that we had carousels in London, too, but stopped myself. Instead, I said, 'Wasn't there a tree decoration you were looking for? Shall we see if we can find them? And to continue my theme, I'm going to have some candy floss next, if anyone cares to join me?'

We plunged into the crowd and spent the next hour going from stall to stall choosing tree decorations, buying and eating all manner of sweets and biscuits and deliberating over potential presents for our friends and family. I was spilling over with happiness, and might have let myself fall into it completely, had it not been for the mistake that stallholders kept making.

'Are you getting that for Mum? Ooh, you'd better look away!'

'Why don't you check with your mum?'

'Would Mum like to try something as well?'

It felt rude to correct them, although I did, and it added a certain strain to the afternoon – for me at any rate. Alexander and Theo barely acknowledged it, so I was alone in my awkwardness, not sure if I should make a joke of it or even apologise. Therefore, it was with some relief that Coco's clear voice cut through the crowds.

'Theo! Fallon! Alexander!'

She came through to where we were trying to choose between different intricately painted tin stars with lights inside and patterns of holes punched in them. We all hugged.

'When are we decorating the house, Alexander?' she asked. 'And where is this star going to go?'

'We'll do it this weekend. The big tree is coming then.'

Coco turned to me.

'It's always fun. We all join in and it's the perfect house for Christmas.'

Alexander decided on a star, then said, 'I think it's probably time to head home.'

He nodded at Theo, who I could now see was looking tired.

'Can I squeeze in too?' asked Coco.

'Of course,' replied Alexander, and we started making our slow way back to the car. We were temporarily distracted by a shop window display when Coco's phone rang. She walked off a little way to take the brief call, then returned, rolling her eyes.

'Is everything all right?' asked Alexander, as they continued walking.

'It's Mum,' said Coco. 'She and Maurice are going to "drop in" for a few days, which probably means they'll stay for a month.'

'It'll be good to see her,' said Alexander, then turned to me. 'She was married to Dad when I was in my late teens, early twenties, so she saw the worst of me and was always brilliant about it.'

'You were a faultless big brother,' said Coco, smiling. 'I was so in awe of you.'

He grinned.

'You were a pretty nice little sister yourself, even if you did make all my friends admire your Barbies with their new outfits every time they came round.'

Coco giggled.

'Those poor dolls – thank goodness I didn't go into fashion!'

'Why didn't it work out between Douglas and your mum?' I asked Coco.

'The lifestyle didn't suit Mum at all,' said Coco. 'She hated going back and forth to London all the time and didn't enjoy the social scene there at all. And she was never comfortable living in Blakeney Hall. When they separated, we moved to a little chocolate box cottage, all uneven walls and beams you bump your head on, and she was much happier. She's still there, with Maurice now.'

'That's it in a nutshell,' said Alexander, as we entered the car park. 'Ironic though, given...' He broke off. 'What floor was the car on?'

As we went to look for it, I was dying to know what he had been going to say. I looked at Coco with her long, lilac hair, piercings and exquisitely pretty face and tried to imagine what her mother would be like. Very different from Jacqueline, of that I was sure.

'I hope Mum's nose isn't put out of joint too badly,' I said, as we pulled out of the garage. 'She's not very good when it comes to confronting anyone's past, including her own.'

'Well, Mum's a huge fan of *Mayfair Mews*, if you think that might help? She's dying to meet Jacqueline, which is another reason I think her "few days" are more likely to be a month.'

We all laughed.

'It will help,' I said, although privately I thought it might take more than that to mollify Mum. I comforted myself with the image I had produced in my head of Coco's mother: a plump, homely lady of a certain age, glued to her soap operas, living with her cats and Maurice in rural bliss. It didn't seem likely that I would have to referee a Dynasty-style diva war and I relaxed and joined in the chatter as we drove home.

We got back to Blakeney Hall just after five and found Mum, Douglas and Constance having tea in the Hall.

'Do join us,' said Douglas, standing up and ushering everyone into seats. 'We brought back some Fat Rascals from our little trip.'

I was taken aback, particularly when the others all made

various expressions of delight. Alexander must have seen my face.

'Fallon, have you ever had a Fat Rascal?'

'Er...' I replied.

'They do sound horrible, don't they?' said Mum. 'But I can confirm that they are delicious.' She twinkled at Douglas like a schoolgirl, and he smiled soppily back. She turned to me again. 'I could only manage half of one, of course.'

She patted her flat stomach complacently. Alexander continued, 'Fat Rascals are traditional up here. They're cakes made with pastry offcuts, sugar and dried fruit and flavoured with winter spices – cinnamon and so on. Would you like to try one?'

'Yes, please, they sound amazing,' I said, and was handed a plate with an enormous bun on it. I could see why Mum had only eaten half; a normal meal for her was smaller than this bun. But I tucked in with relish, hungry from my busy day.

'Dad, has Mum been in touch?' asked Coco, between mouthfuls.

Douglas glanced at my mother before replying.

'Yes, she has. She and Maurice will be here any moment, I think. I hope she doesn't disapprove too much of these shop-bought cakes.'

'With any luck, she'll knock out some of her own,' said Coco. She turned to me. 'Mum's Fat Rascals are the best I've ever tasted, but that's true of all her baking.'

I glanced over at Mum, who was sipping her tea and looking remarkably calm. I suppose she had come to the same conclusion as me: Coco's homely-sounding mother wasn't much of a threat. It was then that there was a loud knock on the door.

'She's here!' exclaimed Coco, and ran out, followed at a more stately pace by Douglas. In a minute or two they returned, with a friendly-looking man and a woman with neatly coiffed blonde hair, merry eyes and a wide smile. I recognised her instantly.

'Estelle Knight!'

I turned to Mum, who had blurted out the name. It was very unlike her to do something so gauche, and I could see that she was shaken. For this was no dowdy homemaker who had walked through the door, but Estelle Knight, doyenne of the most popular baking show in the country: *Bake for Britain.*

'Jacqueline Honeywood!' Estelle returned, and went over to Mum, who hastily put down her cup and stood up. As she held out her hand, Estelle bypassed it and went in for a hug. Mum was used to being embraced by overkeen fans, although she didn't enjoy it, so took this sudden physical contact in her stride, patting Estelle's back before delicately extricating herself.

'Can I pour you a cup of tea?' Douglas asked.

'Yes, please, Maurice and I are parched,' she replied in her strong Yorkshire accent, so familiar from hearing her console contestants over sunken soufflés, or berate them gently for careless crème Anglaise.

She beckoned him over and introduced him to Mum and then to me, before we all sat down again, and Douglas refreshed our cups from the enormous Brown Betty teapot.

'I'm sure Coco has told you how excited I am to meet you, Jacqueline,' said Estelle, reaching for a Fat Rascal and biting into it with no evidence of distaste at its commercial pedigree. 'I'm a big fan of *Mayfair Mews*, always have been. I hope you're going to share some of the show's secrets with me.'

'Of course,' said Mum politely. This is something she is often asked to do, and she has a stock list of 'secrets' that she reveals. 'I'm afraid I'm no baker, but I have also enjoyed *Bake for Britain.*'

'You must come on one of the charity celebrity ones!' said Estelle. 'Do say you will, it would be grand.'

I could no more imagine Mum baking on TV than I could

see her living in the jungle for three weeks on a diet of caterpillars, which she has turned down more than once. But she wasn't about to make herself look like the bad guy. There were other people who could take the blame.

'That sounds super, but all those sorts of requests must go through my agent, I'm afraid.'

Estelle nodded, but I wondered just how long it would take Mum to get her phone out and text Mags to put her on the alert.

'I'll get the show to get in touch,' she said. 'And maybe in the meantime I could get you ahead a little? I'm happy to give you some lessons while I'm here. And we have so much to talk about! Coco told me that you and Douglas are engaged, congratulations! I'm sure you'll make a much better hash of it than I did. Poor Douglas, he had to drag me to London, I was much happier up here in the kitchen. But I love a wedding. I can't wait to chat to you all about it. Ooh, maybe I could make the cake, do say you'll let me! And did you know Maurice is a hairdresser? He'd do all the coiffing, wouldn't you, dear?'

Maurice nodded enthusiastically, but then Douglas spoke up, thank goodness. I might have helped out, but I was too busy trying to stifle my giggles behind my teacup at the worsening look of horror on my mother's face. No one had touched her hair other than her own hairdresser, Linda, for nearly thirty years.

'Estelle, give us a chance,' he said. 'We've barely been engaged forty-eight hours. What's happened at the house anyway? It's always good to see you – both – but what has precipitated this sudden visit?'

As she started explaining, Alexander, Coco and I all stood up and reached for the teapot. Coco got there first.

'It's empty,' she said. 'I thought I'd get a top up.'

'Me too,' Alexander and I replied together, and we all grinned.

'Come on,' said Coco, 'let's go and sort it out.'

We scuttled off to the kitchen like naughty children and shut the door behind us before dissolving into laughter.

'Oh, my goodness, my mother's *face!*' I said. 'Sorry, Coco, Estelle is lovely, but Mum looked like a trapped rabbit! Why didn't either of you tell us who your mother was?'

Alexander and Coco looked at each other, grinning.

'Sorry, Fallon,' said Coco, 'we couldn't resist the surprise. And anyway, you know what it's like having a famous parent, there's no good time to casually mention it.'

'It was a good surprise,' I agreed, 'but I thought you said she liked a quiet domestic life?'

'That is true,' said Coco, filling the kettle. '*Bake for Britain* is filmed up here and she goes home every night. She does do the odd appearance or event in London, but they're few and far between. She prefers opening country shows and judging local cake competitions. She's been a genius at working out balance for herself that way.'

'Let's get this tea in before it stews,' said Alexander. 'I guess your mum and Maurice's arrival means we'd better get on with the Christmas decorations?'

'You bet,' said Coco, then turned to me. 'They love Christmas a bit *too* much, those two. Just you wait, she'll have you teetering on a stepladder hanging tinsel swags before you know what's happened.'

I smiled as I followed them back to the Hall. Despite Mum's nose being put out of joint, I couldn't help feeling that Estelle and Maurice had brought a great deal of fun with them.

NINETEEN

The large breakfast table was quite full now, with nine of us there the next morning. Douglas had gone to help Coco in the kitchen, and they had waved the rest of us away, so we sat and drank coffee – or in Theo's case, orange juice – and talked about what we were going to do that day.

'It's the dress rehearsal for the Nativity this afternoon,' said Alexander, 'so Dad and Theo are going to be tied up doing that. Fallon, I wondered if you'd like to come and see the place the Christmas Fayre's being held? I promised the man organising it that I'd pop by so that we could decide exactly where the van would go.'

'Good idea,' I said.

Secretly I was excited that Alexander and I would finally have some time together, just the two of us, and by the way he was smiling at me, I could guess that he was of the same opinion.

'I'm cracking on with the book,' said Constance, 'but I don't mind taking you and my laptop up to the sanctuary this morning if you like, Theo? As long as Sadie doesn't expect me to mop the brows of sickly little mice, I'm happy to do that.'

Giggling at the image, Theo agreed enthusiastically. Douglas and Coco came in then, with heaving trays of food, and there was the usual bustle as we jumped up to help them put it all out. I was just trying not to dive into the heavily buttered toast with indecent haste when my phone rang. Sam again. I tapped the green button and ran out of the room.

'Sam, hello, everything okay?'

Of course, it turned out that everything was not okay, and I went back to join the others with a heavy heart.

'Are you all right?' asked Coco as I sat down.

'Sort of,' I answered. 'That was Sam. Another problem, but this time with a client. I'm afraid I'm going to have to go back to London and sort it out.'

A silence descended over the table, eventually broken by Alexander.

'It's funny,' he said. 'I'd almost forgotten about London. You can't deal with it from here?'

'Unfortunately not. It's a regular but tricky client who is all but threatening to pull her business from us if I don't go and coordinate the event in person. She had plenty of notice that I wasn't going to be there, and was fine with it a few weeks ago, but she isn't now.' I shrugged. 'Keeping people happy is part of my job description.'

'Poor you,' said Estelle. 'I suppose you can't just dump them?'

'Not really,' I replied. 'Although I've been tempted more than once.' I sighed. This was the last thing I wanted or needed, but there was no question over whether I should go or not. 'I'm sorry about this afternoon, Alexander, I was looking forward to it.'

'When will you be back?' asked Theo, the faintest tremor in his voice. 'It's the Nativity tomorrow evening.'

I bit my lip.

'I don't know, sweetie, I'm sorry.' He looked so disappointed that I wanted to cry, but I didn't want to make a promise to him that I wasn't sure I'd be able to keep.

'Oh, for heaven's sake, I don't know what everyone is looking so morose for.' My mother's voice cut across the table. 'Fallon has to look after her business and is doing what she needs to do. Clients can be difficult, but that's their prerogative when they're paying the bills. Chin up, darling, it's just a little trip to London, not to the gallows. If you're going to be successful, you need to learn to juggle.'

I was irritated by her patronising tone of voice.

'Like you did, you mean?'

'That's right. I suppose you're insinuating that I didn't do it well, that you *suffered*? You were always fine, and I *had* to work – to put food on the table and then to send you to an extortionately expensive school, not to mention for my own sense of pride and well-being.'

'I wasn't fine, you know,' I said calmly, aware that everyone was listening, but prepared to have this conversation with an audience rather than continuing to bottle up the truth. 'I was lonely, and I hated being palmed off on your random acquaintances.'

'That was only for a few years, until you went away to school. And anyway, my "acquaintances", as you call them, were wonderful. Look at Jason! So relaxed and never minded the late nights.'

'Do you even know Jason's surname? Did you know it then? Jason was relaxed because he smoked so much pot – and he offered it to me *when I was ten*.'

'Jason was the most marvellous character – he would never have harmed you.'

'Jason was a criminal.'

'What twaddle. He was awfully charming. Anyway, I don't know what suddenly makes you the authority on motherhood. You've clearly chosen your career and that is fine, darling. I applaud you. Sometimes, you have to disappoint people to work, that's just how it is. Theo, you'll be all right, won't you? The rest of us will be here cheering you and Douglas on.'

Theo nodded miserably but didn't speak. It was at that moment I made up my mind.

'Don't worry, Theo. I will get back, I promise.'

He looked up, his face brightened as if the sun had come out.

'Really?'

'Really. It's only a few hours on the train and the event's tonight. Of course I'll be back, I wouldn't miss it.'

Constance put a hand on my arm.

'Not too knackering for you, all that travelling?'

I could have cried at her concern. Why couldn't that have been Mum's line?

'Not at all, it's only once. And maybe there's a possibility of a few Fat Rascals to take with me? They'll give me plenty of energy.'

'I'll pack them up for you now,' said Coco. 'And Mum's going to teach me how to make them, so there will be a fresh batch waiting for you when you get back.'

'There you go,' I said, smiling at Theo. 'If I needed any more motivation, that's certainly it. Right, I'd better go and get my stuff together and check the train times.'

Mum looked up, a sour expression on her face.

'Maybe you could put some thought into our engagement party on those long train journeys, darling.'

I gave her my sweetest smile but left the room without replying. It was only when I was alone that I buried my face in my hands. How on earth was I going to keep all these people happy?

.   .   .

As I was gathering some things into a bag, there was a tap on the door.

'Come in.'

It was Alexander.

'How are you doing?' he asked.

'All right, thanks. There's a train at quarter past ten to King's Cross, which only takes a couple of hours. I was just about to look up the number of a cab firm, or can you recommend one?'

'Don't be daft, I'll run you into York.'

'Are you sure?'

'Of course. Constance will take Theo to the sanctuary in her car.'

'Thank you, that would be great. It already feels weird to leave you all behind to go to the sanctuary and deal with the Christmas Fayre while I head to London. It feels a long way away.'

I was overwhelmed with a confusion of feelings and stared into my bag, unable to corral my thoughts and decide what else I needed to take with me. Alexander pushed the door shut, came over to me and slid his hand around my shoulders.

'We're going to miss you.'

I looked up at him.

'I will do my absolute best to get back for the Nativity. I'm sorry that Theo is so worried about it – I had no idea how much he wanted me there.'

Alexander gave my shoulders a squeeze, then dropped his arm and stepped away.

'He has become attached to you very quickly,' he said evenly. 'I've been surprised – it's unusual for him.'

Not sure how to respond, I slipped through the curtain and down to the bathroom to give myself some breathing space. I grabbed the toothpaste to give myself an alibi when I returned – unnecessary as I had plenty at home in London – and sat down on the edge of the bath for a moment, gazing through the window at the beautiful but bleak moors. Having Alexander's son become attached to me was not something I would have even dreamed of, let alone encouraged, and now that it had happened, I wasn't sure how I felt. Scared I may be, but even so I had a responsibility to Theo, not to let him down. I liked him so much, and I couldn't deny that I had an odd feeling of what I can only describe as protectiveness towards him. *Well, that's normal,* I told myself, standing up and taking some deep breaths. *You'd feel like that towards anyone you liked – adult or child – particularly if you knew they were a bit vulnerable. It's not pretending to be anything you're not, just – kind.* Feeling slightly better for this pep talk, I went back up to the bedroom, brandishing my toothpaste.

'I think that's everything,' I said, aware of a slightly false brightness in my voice. 'I will make sure I'm back for the Nativity tomorrow.'

Alexander nodded and we headed downstairs. Coco presented me with a food parcel that would last a week rather than a train journey and I said my goodbyes, getting an extra hard squeeze from Theo and a brave smile coupled with troubled eyes.

'You will be back tomorrow?'

'I'll be back tomorrow. See you then.'

Once Alexander and I were on the road, I spilled out what had been worrying me.

'I'm not sure I should have made that promise to Theo, that I'll be back in time. I mean, I should be, but now I'm feeling terribly anxious that something will go wrong.'

Alexander glanced at me.

'It's difficult with kids. You want to make everything right for them, but it's only too easy to make promises you can't keep. I've done it myself plenty of times, but it gets easier. When Holly – Theo's mum – left, it was almost impossible to get it right, and she broke promises almost faster than she could make them. I felt complicit in that. She would say she was coming to visit, I would tell Theo, and then she wouldn't turn up, leaving him with a strong sense of betrayal from both of us. And then she died, which at least stopped the uncertainty, but also robbed him of any hope.'

I dabbed at a tear that was threatening to fall.

'That's so awful, I'm sorry. I honestly don't know how you do it. I mean, I don't know the first thing about parenting, but in those circumstances...'

He shrugged.

'It was hard. Parenting is hard, but amazing as well. And I wouldn't say you don't know the first thing about it.' I stayed silent, unsure what he meant. 'You're good with people, Fallon, sensitive and warm. Children are people too. I mean, I know it's a bit more complicated than that, but that's what's at the heart of it.'

'It's the 'more complicated' part I struggle with,' I said. 'What about *wanting* to do it, being prepared to take on the complications? I do deal with other people well, but I go home at the end of the day and have my space and time, without worrying that they're suffering because of that.'

We pulled into the car park, and I went to open the door, but Alexander's hand on my arm stopped me.

'I hope it goes well in London. I'll text you about the Christmas Fayre, send some photos.'

I nodded, wondering if we were going to kiss. But neither of us made the move.

'Do,' I said, pushing down a sudden surge of disappointment. 'I'll see you tomorrow.'

I stepped out of the car and headed towards my platform – back to London and doing what I did best.

TWENTY

I arrived at King's Cross at lunchtime. Full from Coco's care package and my body zinging with adrenaline from being plunged back into London's energy, I didn't bother to stop for lunch but instead headed directly to the office. Even as I did so, a voice in my head urged caution; I knew from past experience that if I carried on at too fast a pace, then a crash would surely follow, which was precisely the cycle I had been attempting to extricate myself from. With this in mind, I slowed down my walk and deliberately started to take in everything that was around me. London at Christmastime is a jewel box of delights, and I took in the pretty shop displays and lights. The seasonal theme of the area of London I was walking through was 'Gingerbread House', and there were huge, cheerful figures suspended around the streets. Many were, as you might expect, 'cookie cutter' examples, but you could also spot the ones that represented public figures; I particularly liked the cluster of 'royal' gingerbread people, complete with the children and a dog. One bakery had fashioned an entire Nativity scene for their window, which reminded me of my determination to get back to Yorkshire in time tomorrow, and another shop had recreated its entire façade as a gingerbread house, complete with icing snow and an enormous Liquorice Allsort in place of the door handle.

The building our office was based in had more modest decorations, but the tree in the foyer looked cheerful enough with its candy canes and twinkling lights. I greeted the security officer on duty and jogged up the stairs to the first floor, pushing open the familiar door.

'Fallon!'

'Sam! Talitha! Good to see you!'

We all hugged and then I threw my bag in a corner and grabbed a chair.

'Okay, so has anything changed since your last email?' I asked.

'Nothing,' said Sam, pulling a face. 'Lindy is still refusing to go over the final details with me and told Talitha on the phone that she was considering cancelling the whole thing unless you saw to it personally.'

Lindy Dixon was a glamorous but extremely highly strung supermodel who had been a client for about a year. We had done three events for her in that time and this Christmas bash was fairly small in comparison to those. I had done most of the preliminary work and everything had gone smoothly. I had had no concerns about Sam taking over the final execution of the party, with Talitha's support, and Lindy herself had been happy about that. Until yesterday. I sighed.

'All right, well, she's got me here now. I left a message to let her know I was on my way down, but I've not heard back. Is everything in place?'

'Yes, nothing has changed. The venue stylists are all going to start turning up in' – he checked his watch – 'just under an hour. The band is on their way and the caterers are all fine. I chased up a few final guests a week ago to check they understood the dress code and pointed them in the direction of

Marcella in case they needed any help. Yours is here by the way
– do you want to try it on?'

I glanced at my watch.

'Not now. I'm going to get hold of Lindy and then we
should head over. Marcella knows my measurements well
enough. Does it look good?'

'It's ravishing,' replied Talitha. 'Beautiful fabric, kind of
sparkly and shimmery but tasteful. You'll love it.'

'Well, that's something,' I replied. 'Thank you for sorting it
out at such ridiculously short notice. There wasn't anything in
my wardrobe that would have worked for a 'Frozen' theme.'

'No worries, Marcella's amazing.'

That was true. Marcella was a designer we used to provide
us with rented outfits we could wear to look the part at our
clients' parties, and we recommended her to guests who were
struggling with a particular party theme, or who wanted something unique. She had a lock-up somewhere full of clothes that
she altered to make sure that they both fitted perfectly and
would be one-time-only outfits, only to be swiftly reimagined
for the next customer. She had won awards for both design and
sustainability and was a thoroughly nice and very calm person.
In a business like mine, contacts – or I would even say friends –
like Marcella were gold dust.

Sam gathered together everything we would need while
Talitha organised a taxi and I left a message for Lindy, and in
five minutes we were on our way. The venue, a nineteenth-
century banqueting hall in Marylebone, would take about half
an hour in the traffic, so we sat back and had a good catch up.

'So, how are you getting on in deepest, darkest Yorkshire?'
asked Sam. 'I hope you're feeling better. I'm so sorry for dragging you down here like this, but I didn't want to risk the whole
thing going belly up.'

'It's fine,' I said. 'You did the right thing. Lindy's a pain, but
she's a good client, so it's worth it not to lose her. And Yorkshire

is beautiful, much nicer than I thought it would be. There are quite a lot of people in the house and I'm busier than I envisaged, but I am feeling refreshed and much less stressed – mostly because I could rely on you and Talitha to look after everything brilliantly.'

I explained how I was helping Alexander out with the Christmas Fayre and that I now also had Mum and Douglas's engagement party to arrange.

'And how's Jacqueline?' asked Sam. 'I know you were worried about spending this much time together.'

'It's going all right,' I said carefully. 'She's quite heavily diluted by Douglas and everyone else, but she still finds plenty of ways to be *Mommie Dearest*. But then again...' I paused, remembering what Constance had said, that she thought Mum *did* love me, '...she is trying, in her own way, to help me get back on my feet. She's into wellness now, and she's insisting on herbal teas and experimental treatments, although I drew the line at having a colonic.'

Sam laughed.

'That is so Jacqueline. Did she want to put a photo of it on the 'Gram?'

I pulled a face.

'Probably. But the rest of the family saved me from that particular humiliation.'

'They're nice, then? What's it like living with a kid?'

'He's brilliant. I'm really surprised how much I like spending time with him.'

I tried to keep my voice neutral, but Sam and I have known each other for years and I wasn't going to get anything past him.

'And?'

'What do you mean, "and"?'

'And, Miss Honeywood, I can tell there's something else. Ooh, it's a man, isn't it? The handsome lord of the manor?'

'Well, technically Douglas is Lord of the manor, and I wouldn't dare muscle in on Mum's fiancé, even if I wanted to.'

'Too true. But doesn't he have a son...?'

I capitulated.

'Yes, he does, and yes, you're right. There is – oh I don't know, *something* there.'

'Something?'

'We've kissed, a couple of times.'

Sam grabbed me and hugged me.

'Fallon! Too exciting! So, what else?'

'Well, the little boy – Theo – is Alexander's son, and you know how I felt – *feel* – about being a mother. I know it's early days to be thinking about that stuff, but I don't want things to get messy. I think it's better that I just stop whatever this is with Alexander before it's started. Not that it even really *has* started – he didn't kiss me goodbye when he dropped me at the station.'

Sam made a sympathetic face. 'You really like him, don't you? I can tell.'

I nodded.

'He's wonderful. He's kind and quite serious, but with a real sense of humour. He takes stuff in his stride. He's been through a lot, but he's not bitter or defensive, he's just moved forwards. He loves Theo so much and he's an amazing dad. I never thought I'd even notice something like that, let alone find it attractive, but I do. It showcases his character – loyal, empathetic, patient and capable.'

Sam giggled.

'Sorry, Fallon, but only you would include 'capable' on a list of adorable character traits in your ideal man.'

I grinned.

'Fair point, but it *is* appealing. He doesn't want, or need, to be looked after, but then, of course, on the flip side of that—'

'Is his son,' filled in Sam.

'Exactly. Who obviously comes as part of the package. But

the thing is, Sam, I adore that little boy, and I seem to somehow have clicked with him. He likes me too.'

'Of course he does.'

'But you know how I feel.'

Sam nodded. 'People have children all the time and don't bring them up like their parents did. Look at my dad. Do you think I'd ever do what he did?'

We had had this conversation before, and I was well aware of Sam's aggressive, violent father. I shook my head.

'Of course I don't. But the thing with Mum is… it's not like she was straightforwardly bad, or anything. Although I struggle with it, and wish things had been different, I not only appreciate but applaud her drive and passion for work. She didn't mean to get pregnant with me, but she had me anyway, then made the best of it. I have a choice and it seems reckless to *choose* to take on a child when I do want to work and make a success of it.'

'But with Jacqueline it wasn't just the work, was it? It was the careless way she treated you, left you with all sorts of people and had a hard time showing you much love or affection – unless it was through criticism.'

I was reminded again of what Constance had said.

'That's true. I think I'm beginning to take on board that she did – *does* – love me, but eight-year-old me never saw that.'

'And that's the crucial part. That's what you do understand and wouldn't repeat. You can be a mum, Fallon, and work hard and care about that work. People do it all the time. You may be like Jacqueline in your drive, but you're very different in most other ways. You're soft where she's tough, and I know what a caring person you are. Maybe your childhood has even brought that out more in you, maybe it's your father's side, who knows? But please don't miss out, darling, from fear. If your gut is leading you towards Alexander and Theo, then let it do the talking.'

I nodded, still feeling unsure.

'Maybe. Oh, Sam, it's good to see you.'

'You too. Now tell me all about Jacqueline and Douglas! Is the engagement public knowledge yet?'

'Not yet, so you're sworn to secrecy.' I had no qualms about trusting Sam. 'I think Mum's going to do some soft-focus Instagram announcement, all very J Lo, this week sometime.'

'Sounds fab. And do you think the marriage will last?'

'I hope so. I've got a lot of time for Douglas. He "gets" Mum and can see what she needs and who she is besides *Mayfair Mews*' biggest star, but he's also quite firmly his own person. He doesn't try to dominate her, or compete with her, or show her off, which must be pretty refreshing. God knows she's been with some shockers in the past.'

'She has. Remember Gavin?'

We both pretended to puke, causing the taxi driver to raise his eyebrows in the rearview mirror.

'Gavin was the worst,' I said. 'I think he thought Mum was some sort of prize he'd won, which made him special in some way. He didn't last long.'

'Not beyond the second time he got stroppy because a restaurant didn't have room when he tried to reserve a table in his own name, but came up with one when she took the phone from him. I know she can be a pain, but I do love your mum at times.'

'Also, Douglas is the longest relationship she's ever had, other than with her hairdresser...'

'And you.'

'And me, but she's known Linda longer! She's never lived with a man, let alone been married to one, but I have a feeling the two of them will be okay.'

'Good. Are you going to organise the wedding?'

'I hope not. The "small and intimate" engagement party is bad enough. But you can come as my plus one.'

'Yes, please! Although maybe handsome, capable Alexander will fill that role.'

'He'll be there anyway, for his father, so you're on the list! You would be anyway, Mum adores you. Anyway, you know I wouldn't ditch you for any man, ever.'

'I know. Do you want some help organising the engagement party?'

I groaned.

'Yes! All the help! Seriously, though, if I need to, can I call you?'

'Darling, I'll do better than that. Why don't I come up? It sounds as if you've got plenty on your hands with the Christmas Fayre and you know me and anything to do with weddings – I love them.'

'And Mum loves you! I bet she'd be thrilled if you were there. Are you sure you can spare the time?'

'Of course. After tonight there's only that bank Christmas party tomorrow and the birthday on Wednesday and they're both going very well. I'd love to come and help, Fallon; I hated seeing you knocked sideways by work. There must be a local pub I can stay in.'

I was prevented from answering by the taxi drawing to a sudden stop.

'Here we are,' said the driver and we jumped out, made sure we had everything and headed inside.

The hall was empty but looked spectacular, nonetheless. It was made from white marble, with carved columns sweeping up to the moulded ceiling; huge arched windows dressed with enormous curtains, tied back now to let in the winter light; and an unusual mezzanine level or gallery running around three sides, behind the columns. We were greeted warmly by Judy, who managed the space and several others like it in London.

'Let me show you backstage,' she said, leading us to a door at the back of the hall. 'There's a kitchen, loo and small sitting room where you can leave your things and set up your laptop. It's yours for the whole evening.'

As we settled in, my phone rang: Lindy. I answered it with some trepidation in my heart, but sounding as breezy as I could.

'Lindy, hi!'

'Oh! Fallon! You are in London, aren't you? Do say you are.'

'Of course I am, don't worry. Now, are you all ready for tonight?'

'Are you *there*? Are you overseeing it all? It's not that I don't trust Sam, you know that, he's so wonderful, but I am so much happier to know it's you. It was giving me a great deal of anxiety, knowing you were so far away at such an important time.'

'I'm here at the venue right now,' I said soothingly, 'and everything is going to plan. In fact' – I looked up at Sam who was mouthing at me and pointing – 'the venue stylists have just arrived, so I must go and make sure they get everything exactly right. Do you want me to check in with you again later?'

'*Would* you? I'd be so grateful. And you will check that they bring the blue carpet for my guests? I couldn't *bear* it if it was any other colour.'

'Of course I will. Now go and relax, then get ready and don't worry about a thing. It will all be perfect.'

'I know, I know. Goodbye then.'

I hung up with some relief and ran out to greet the stylists, with no time for lingering thoughts about what a difference there is to people where what is crucially important in life is concerned.

In the end, the party was indeed perfect. There were the usual behind the scenes hiccups, but nothing that Sam and I couldn't handle and nothing that Lindy ever knew about. I moved around the venue almost constantly, checking that things were going smoothly. Most people present would not have known that I wasn't a guest, dressed in the glorious shimmering blue and silver gown that Marcella had produced at the last minute and smiling at everyone with confidence. But if they had looked closer, they would have seen that I had a discreet earpiece to keep in touch with Sam, and that the glass of champagne I carried was never sipped, let alone in need of a refill. It was past three a.m. when I was finally able to hug Sam goodbye, change my silver stilettos for some comfortable flats and sink gratefully into a taxi home. For the first time since I had stepped off the train, I had the chance to check my personal messages, and saw one from Alexander:

> I hope things are going well for you in London.
> The Nativity rehearsal went well, even Heathcliff
> behaved. We all miss you here.

I bit my lip. The evening had been busy, but that hadn't stopped creeping thoughts of Yorkshire and Alexander and Theo. I had pushed them away easily at the time, but now that the adrenaline was ebbing away, I wished I was with them at Blakeney Hall, sitting by the fire. The phone pinged again, a long and effusive message from Lindy, thrilled with her party and full of promises to recommend me to all her friends, as long as she always came first, of course. Difficult though she could be, I was happy to hear from her and to feel the satisfaction of a job done well. The tug between two such different worlds was making my head spin, and I was glad when we pulled up outside my block of mansion flats, removing the option for me to reply to either message right away. I walked up the front steps, into the carpeted hallway and across to my own front door, letting myself in to the familiar, if slightly musty-smelling space. I headed straight for the bathroom then bed – maybe I would feel less confused in the morning.

TWENTY-ONE

I woke earlier than I would have liked the next day, but despite feeling groggy and weary I couldn't get back to sleep. I dragged myself out of bed and stumbled to the kitchenette to make a cup of coffee – black, of course, as I had nothing fresh in the house. I peered into the package of goodies that Coco had made for me the previous day and decided that, although squashed, the single Fat Rascal that was left would make a perfect breakfast. Missing Runcible, missing Alexander, missing Theo – in fact, missing everything about Yorkshire and feeling sorry for myself – I sat on the sofa and put on the TV for some company. A morning magazine show wittered on about how to wrap awkwardly shaped presents while I picked up my phone and returned to last night's messages. Lindy was easy to deal with. I replied saying how delighted I was that she had enjoyed the party, that I hoped to work with her again soon and wishing her a merry Christmas. Then Alexander's. I decided to keep my tone friendly but cool, as he had, and said:

> I miss you all too. I hope Runcible is okay. The party all went well in the end, thank goodness. Looking forward to the Nativity this evening.

It wouldn't win any literary prizes, but it did the job. Feeling revived by breakfast, I turned the TV off and went around my small flat, opening the curtains. Letting in some light gave me a small lift, but looking out at the view just brought more confusion. It was one of the reasons I had rented the flat, and I had always loved seeing the elegant architecture of the buildings opposite and, if I peered down the road, being able to see the tops of the trees in the nearby park. Now the view seemed small as I remembered looking out from my room at Blakeney Hall and letting my gaze wander for miles over the empty, wild moors. I sighed and turned my attention indoors again. The flat was in a sorry state. So had I been, when I left it, having no energy or inclination for cleaning and tidying. *If Alexander could see this*, I thought, *he'd know the truth about what I'm like: a complete mess who can't keep up with her own life even when it's just one person she has to think about.* Maybe, I thought, with a wry smile, I should send him a photo of it to put him off? Not that he needed much putting off, I thought, casting my mind back to that stilted goodbye. But I rallied. I forced a smile to my face, which became a genuine grin as I realised a large benefit to my current situation: the entire flat was the size of one room in Blakeney Hall, and even I could manage to get it straight in an hour or so. I rolled up my sleeves.

A clean and tidy flat was a tonic, and even more so once I had had a shower, washed my hair and dressed. My phone rang as I was stuffing my things back into my bag and I grabbed it.

'Hi, Sam! How are you doing this morning?'

'I was going to ask you the same thing. Are you exhausted?'

'I am, but I'm all right. I enjoyed it and it went well. Thank you so much for all your work on it.'

'Well, thank *you* for saving the day. I was ringing to ask if you fancied lunch – my treat. We can debrief on last night and work out what you need for Jacqueline's party.'

I looked at the time.

'I'd love to meet you for lunch, but I must be away by two. I promised I'd get back to Yorkshire for a thing this evening.'

'We can manage that. See you at the Kingfisher in ten?'

'See you then.'

I gathered my last few bits together, locked up and set off on the short walk to mine and Sam's favourite café. As I walked into the familiar smell of coffee and cooking, was greeted by name and led to my preferred table, my worries about Yorkshire slipped away. Sam arrived shortly after, and we ordered a large brunch and bottomless coffee before getting down to business. I filled him on everything I had done for the Christmas Fayre and then we moved on to Mum and Douglas's engagement party.

'She claims it will just be small and she's not fussy, blah blah, but we all know the truth.'

Sam laughed.

'Yeah, I've never known Jacqueline to go low-key in her life. We can't believe that for a second. Did you say you had someone to do the catering?'

I nodded.

'Yes. Douglas's daughter from his second marriage. She's an amazing cook. And, in fact, I can't believe I didn't tell you this yesterday – we were so busy! Her mother is Estelle Knight and she's staying too!'

'*The* Estelle Knight?'

'The very same. I bet she'd help with the food, but we'd better keep it on the downlow from Mum.'

'Jacqueline had her nose put out of joint by her arrival?'

'A bit. Poor Mum, I don't think she was expecting the home-body of a second wife she'd heard about to, in fact, be rivalling her for stardom.'

'Did Douglas never tell her?'

'Maybe he did, and she wasn't paying attention, or maybe he just didn't dare. Or maybe he thought Mum already knew. I don't know him well, but it's possible it just didn't occur to him. She wasn't *the* Estelle Knight when they were together and he's not at all interested in celebrity. Other than James Bond, of course.'

'Well, we can see if she'd help. Maybe a fun theme for the food might be some sort of chic Yorkshire thing, referencing local food but making it all look super sophisticated.'

'What, you mean like tiny little bite-size Yorkshire puddings? I love it!'

We talked for a while longer about possible party ideas, then I glanced at my watch.

'Oh no, it's much later than I realised. I said I'd be back for the Nativity, and I was cutting it fine already.'

'Don't worry – go, go! I'll be in touch and see you soon.'

I dashed out of the café and, to my relief, stepped onto a bus almost immediately. This was only the first step of my journey to King's Cross, but at the underground station I was also lucky and soon speeding along the Piccadilly line. I checked the time again: *I should, all being well, make the last train I can catch to get back in time for the Nativity*. At my stop I was ready by the doors and leaped out, running all the way to the main part of the station where, thanking the gods of technology, I scanned my e-ticket and jumped onto the train with a couple of minutes to spare. I sank into a seat, exhilarated by the success of my journey, and took out my book to enjoy a couple of hours' peace.

Everything went smoothly until we were nearly at Peterborough, when the train juddered to one of those heart-dropping stops when you know all your plans have been laughed at. Indeed, a minute or so later a voice came booming over the tannoy:

'Ladies and gentlemen, sorry about this, just a small issue with the signals. Shouldn't be long until we're off again. In the meantime, do make yourselves comfortable and ask our staff if there's anything you need help with.'

A grumble made its way around the carriage as everyone shifted in their seats and prepared themselves for a long wait. They, like me, didn't believe a word of the jaunty announcement; we all knew that we'd be sitting there for hours and that there wouldn't be a member of staff in sight. But what could you do? I looked at the time again. It was almost inevitable now that I would miss some, if not all, of the Nativity. I tapped out a quick message to Alexander to let him know my predicament, pushed my phone back into my bag and stared gloomily out of the window into the rapidly darkening afternoon. I thought about Theo, getting ready for his performance and being told by his dad that I wasn't going to make it. I hoped he wouldn't be too disappointed. I thought of the night before, the glamorous party and all the energy it had taken to get there. I thought of the pleasurable debrief I had had with Sam over lunch, always one of our favourite parts of a big job. *I shouldn't have gone for that lunch*, I told myself. But I had wanted to, and I had gone, despite knowing that it would jeopardise my chances of getting back to Yorkshire in time. So, for all my thoughts about Alexander and Theo, despite my growing feelings for both of them, I had put myself and my work first. *Now who does that remind you of?* I asked myself viciously. The tannoy crackled back into life, and I steeled myself for another cheery broadcast that we would be sitting there for at least half an hour more. But even as he started speaking, the train jerked into motion again, and to everyone's surprise we heard:

'Hello again, ladies and gentlemen. Many apologies for that short delay, but we're on our way again.'

Hardly able to believe my luck, I looked again at my watch. If there were no more problems, I should make it just in time. I considered firing off another text to Alexander, but didn't want to risk further delay and then having to send another text, which might start to look a bit crazy. And besides, he hadn't replied to the first one yet. Instead, I found the number of the local taxi firm and rang them, arranging a car for what I desperately hoped would be my accurate ETA.

There were no more holdups, and when I stepped out of the overly warm train into the bitingly cold late afternoon air, I immediately saw my car and scuttled over to it.

'Lingfoss, is it?' asked the driver, and I agreed, almost throwing myself and my bag into the back seat. 'I'm afraid I won't be able to get you all the way in,' he added, pulling slowly away. 'The Nativity's on there today, you know?'

'Yes, I know, that's what I'm going for.'

'Cutting it a bit fine, aren't you?'

I took a breath.

'Yes, unfortunately. How close can you get me?'

'Well, the main street's all shut off to traffic, all the way to the church, but I can drop you by the bus stop. Can't get much closer than that.'

I agreed with some relief, remembering the bus stop where I had first seen Coco, right by Meg's café, but still spent the journey leaning forward in my seat, urging him on silently to a speed he was never going to achieve.

After an infuriatingly leisurely ten minutes, the driver pulled his car over to the side of the road and came to a stop. My eyes darted from side to side, seeing only dark, cold fields on either side, rather than the welcoming lights of Meg's café or, indeed, any sign at all of the village. A cold chill suddenly ran through me as I wondered if the deceptively cheery driver had, in fact, brought me into the middle of nowhere for his own nefarious reasons. I sneaked a surreptitious glance at the lock on the inside of the door and saw that, mercifully, it was open. A silence stretched out as I started planning my escape, only to be broken by a polite cough which, quiet though it was, made me jump out of my skin, so wound up was I by my lateness, tiredness and creeping anxiety.

'We're here, love,' said the driver, eyeing me uncertainly in the rearview mirror.

'*Here*!?' I said, my brain struggling to catch up with reality from its adrenaline-fuelled visualisation of me dashing across the moors with the elderly driver in hot pursuit.

'At the bus stop?' he said, the eyes in the mirror now looking rather worried.

'Bus stop?' I repeated, starting to panic now that he was the one irrationally scared of me.

'Yes, love, the bus stop where we agreed I'd drop you. I can't get you in a lot further, it's impossible to turn and the road will be shut off soon. It'll only take you a few minutes to walk it, though.'

I looked out of the window again and now saw a scruffy wooden pole by the side of the road, a battered sign on the top announcing that this was the stop for the H62. Just not the stop I had been expecting. I pulled myself together.

'Right, sorry, thank you very much.'

I grabbed my bag and got out into the freezing air. I was spotlit, briefly, as he backed his taxi away, then he turned the car and was gone, leaving me in the lowering darkness, the lights of Lingfoss glowing in the distance.

'Okay...' I said out loud, to rally myself. 'It can't be further than half a mile and you still have' – I pulled out my phone and lit up the screen – 'ten minutes before it starts. You can do this.'

I hefted my bag over my shoulder and started walking briskly down the road. He hadn't been wrong when he said there was nowhere to turn – it was very narrow and I was thankful that there wouldn't be cars coming in the opposite direction, as the road had been closed off. My confidence was short-lived, however, when I saw the unmistakeable glow of headlights coming my way, and at some speed. Whoever it was must have pulled out of a house or road before the block. This time the adrenaline really meant business: if I didn't get out of the way, and quickly, I'd be hit. There was no way the driver would see me in my dark clothing until he was right on top of me. To my left was a steep bank, topped with trees and dense bushes, but to my right I saw a space with a wooden fence. I darted to it, threw my bag over, and clambered over myself, falling hard on my hip but just in time, as a large car shot past. With no time to waste, I leaped up, then sat down again abruptly on the hard ground, overwhelmed by a rush of blood to the head.

Breathe, I reminded myself, and spent a moment or two steadying myself, trying to take in smooth breaths rather than gulping down the freezing air, until my heart had steadied and my legs felt less wobbly. I stood up slowly and looked around. A field, and one which I hoped wasn't inhabited by anything fierce. I decided to take my chances and continue walking through it, with the road safely on the other side of the fence. I broke into the nearest thing approximating a jog that I could manage and glanced at my phone again. Although it felt as if hours had passed, I still had time to make it. My steady pace was soon broken by another fence but, now a veteran of such things, I scaled it efficiently, feeling pleased with myself. Until my landing, that is. Or to be more accurate, the landing of my right foot in something soft, squishy and not particularly fragrant. Lifting up my foot, I shook it free of much of the debris and tried to wipe the rest off on the grass, although I couldn't see what I was doing.

You'd think it would have the decency to freeze solid, I thought, then was clutched by the idea that, as it most definitely was *not* frozen, it must be fresh, which would mean that there was some sort of livestock nearby, possibly something that wouldn't take kindly to me stumbling around in its field in the darkness. Invigorated by this fresh terror, I set off again, improving on my previous pace and trying not to think about my soiled shoe. It was with relief that I saw ahead of me the lights of Lingfoss, and knew I was only moments from my desti-nation. Ahead of me stood one more fence, which I hauled myself over, trying to see what lay in wait on the ground for me to land in. I checked my phone clock one more time: three minutes. I was going to make it.

My chest was sore now from heaving in the chilly air, and I decided to exchange my jogging for a brisk walking pace in the hope that I might look rather less flustered and sweaty when I arrived. I was on the high street, now, and could see a big crowd of people waiting. As I approached the back, I could hear music starting up. At least I had made it in time. Just. I edged my way through to the side of the crowd where I could now see Mary pottering about, doubtless about to be interrupted by an angel with some seriously life-changing news. I cast my eyes around the crowd, spotting Mum immediately, who had clearly decided to go incognito in a flamingo-pink trench coat. Her eyes met mine, then instantly rolled heavenwards as she tapped her watch. I pushed down my feelings of injustice and impatience and continued looking, hoping to spot Alexander. And suddenly, with a lurch in my stomach, I did. He had found a spot near the front and was looking nervous. I was about to try to catch his attention, when I saw Annabel standing next to him. I hadn't clocked her until this point, and now she rested a leather-gloved hand on his arm, gave it a little squeeze and muttered a few words. He smiled at her and looked a little more relaxed. Annabel, of course, was looking immaculate in her country chic outfit of a fitted, quilted jacket, tight jeans and conker-shiny knee-length boots. I glanced down dismally at my down jacket, scuffed from the journeys I had made, leggings and trainers. The outfit that had been perfect for train travel and dashing around London and, as it turned out, clambering over fences, but that I had hoped to change out of before seeing everyone again. I sighed and returned my attention to the action on 'stage', which was, in fact, the middle of the road. Gabriel had delivered his news and Mary was now persuading a bemused Joseph that her pregnancy was the result of divine intervention. Luckily for her, after a quick nap and another angel visitation, this time in a dream and played with great verve by the butcher, Ted, Joseph was convinced, and they started making plans to head to Nazareth. It was at this point that Theo and Douglas made their grand entrance, leading Heathcliff around the corner and offering him up as transport. They hefted Mary on board and started walking down the high street, with the crowd shuffling after them. I was behind Theo so had no chance of letting him know I was there, but I saw Annabel give him a little wave and the sweetest of smiles. She was a better bet than me, I mused, as we stopped outside the pub, The Keeper's Arms, which had its own starring role as an inn with no room. I couldn't even arrive on time, let alone looking the part, whereas she had probably had the date circled in red on her calendar for months, and doubtless made mince pies from scratch for after. The play continued, with the audience moving to see the stable scene and then a little further, where subtle lighting had been rigged up on the edge of the moor to show the shepherds – complete with real sheep – watching their flocks by night. The final tableau, back at the stable, was beautifully staged: someone had even come up with a real tiny baby for Mary to hold. Life-hardened old cynic I may be, but even I found myself surreptitiously wiping my eye as the strains of 'Away in a Manger' started up, and we were all encouraged to join in.

When the performers had taken their bows, the vicar popped up to thank everyone and invite us to go for refreshments –

Annabel's mince pies, I thought, meanly – and mulled wine in the warm pub. It looked as if it would take a while for the crowd to move back there, not to mention the returning of babies, sheep and donkeys that needed to happen; maybe I had time to nip up to the house, leave my things and freshen up? I was just going to start wriggling through the crowd again, when a hand caught my elbow.

'Where are you going, darling?'

'Oh, hi, Mum. I was just going to run back to Blakeney Hall to sort myself out; I'm a mess after all that travelling.'

She looked me up and down with the slight crease to her forehead that is the closest she can get to frowning, thanks to the Botox.

'I shouldn't worry, Fallon, no one will notice any difference. Come along. Everyone was terribly upset when they didn't think you were going to make it.'

It was too much to hope that she might be pleased to hear how I had beaten the odds to be there at all, so I refrained from comment and followed her into the pub, combing my fingers through my hair as I went in a feeble attempt to look more put together. Mum was immediately swallowed into the throng, while I stood there a little hesitantly, hoping to see a familiar face. Thankfully, I spotted Alexander, minus Annabel, and made my way over.

'Hello! Hi, Theo.'

I gave them a little wave and received very tight smiles in return.

'Hello, all right?' said Alexander, his voice tight and his hand moving to Theo's shoulder.

I thought I might cry. All that panic, all that worry, all that scrambling across fields to get there on time and then be met with a face that was colder than the weather outside. My hip complained where I had landed on it, and I gave it a rub.

'Yes, although I had an awful journey. I was on time and

then there was a delay when we just sat there. Then the taxi dropped me miles away, so I had to come cross country.' I saw his face relax a tiny bit and pushed on, trying not to sound defensive. 'But I was just in time and saw the entire Nativity.'

'Did you?' asked Theo. 'Did you see Heathcliff?'

'I did indeed, he was brilliant, but not as brilliant as you. I didn't realise that you were on stage, as it were, for so long.'

Theo's smile became a beam now.

'I'm glad you made it,' Alexander said seriously, his eyes on my face. 'How were things in London?'

'Oh, it went very well. It was all pretty full on, but the client was happy, and I think we'll get more business from her and maybe from some of her friends. It was a late night, though, I'm tired.'

'Will you be all right with the Christmas Fayre stuff?'

'I'll be fine. Are *you* all right?'

Theo had drifted over to Coco, who had looked after Runcible during the performance, and Alexander glanced over at him before replying.

'I'm fine, yes, but Theo was very upset when he thought you wouldn't make it. I know it wasn't your fault, but he does take promises incredibly seriously, you know.'

I cringed with guilt, but also felt slightly put out.

'I *know*, I do understand that, and it was silly of me to tell him I'd definitely be here, but I could hardly help my train being delayed.'

He shrugged.

'I know. Would you like a drink?'

Grateful that the subject seemed to be closed, I asked for a white wine spritzer, which wasn't very seasonal but was just what I needed after the events of the past few hours. While I waited for him, I watched Theo as he knelt by the fireplace, Runcible on his lap, both looking blissfully content. I sensed someone approach and turned, ready to take my drink from Alexander, but it wasn't him.

'Hello,' said a cool voice. 'We haven't met properly. I'm Annabel.'

She held out a slim hand, which I shook with my sweaty, grimy one. I was amazed she didn't wipe her hand afterwards, but she was far too well-bred to do something like that. But even she couldn't stop her perfect nose wrinkling at the odour that was wafting up from my shoe now that it was warming up. She glanced down, but I kept staring resolutely ahead, hoping to brazen that one out.

'Hello,' I replied. 'Yes, I remember you from the James Bond party. I'm Fallon. My mother is marrying Douglas.'

'Yes, I know. Are you enjoying your stay at Blakeney Hall?'

'Yes, everyone is so welcoming. I had to pop down to London yesterday and I did miss them.'

'I'm sure. It seems they missed you too. Theo was most distressed when he thought you wouldn't make it back for the Nativity.'

I nearly asked her what business it was of hers but bit it back. She was already looking down her elegant nose at me, and I didn't want to give her any more ammunition.

'Yes,' I agreed instead. 'He's a sensitive boy and we get on well.'

'Not *too* well, I hope. He is clearly looking for a mother figure and it wouldn't do well for him to find one, only for her to disappear back off to the other end of the country once Christmas is over.'

I suppose someone who lives nearby – someone like you, perhaps? – would be a better idea?

Again, I took a breath.

'I couldn't comment on that. All I can say is that Alexander seems to be doing a wonderful job on his own, and there doesn't seem to be a mother-shaped hole in their lives at all.'

Annabel laughed.

'Oh, of *course* there is! What they need—'

'Actually, Fallon's right. Theo and I are just fine as we are.'

Alexander had appeared behind us, without either of us noticing. He handed me my drink and I took a sip, looking at Annabel over the rim of the glass. *Wriggle out of this one, Annabel*, I thought.

She smiled beatifically.

'But of course. You're both marvellous. Do give some thought to that dinner I mentioned, won't you, Alexander?'

He nodded curtly and she glided away.

'I'd better go and find Dad,' said Alexander. 'See you later.'

And he was also gone, leaving me standing alone with a glass of wine I no longer wanted. I went over to the fireplace and put my glass on the mantelpiece, then crouched down.

'Theo, I think I'd better take Runcible back now, she's looking very tired. You do too. Do you want to come with us?'

He shook his head.

'It's okay, I'll find Dad. Thanks for coming back in time for the play.'

I hugged him.

'I wouldn't have missed it for the world.'

I kept an eye on him until I was sure that he had found Alexander, then pulled my coat around me and headed out into the night, suddenly overwhelmed with exhaustion and with the events of the past twenty-four hours pinging around my head. Despite my excuses, I knew that I could have been back safely in time. Instead, I had proven myself once more to be self-seeking, work-obsessed and narcissistic. Alexander and Theo clearly hadn't been fooled. They were seeing the truth now: they were far better off without me.

TWENTY-TWO

I had an appalling night's sleep that night; I went through phases of sleeping very heavily, then waking suddenly, only to thrash uncomfortably for a while before dropping off again. When I woke in the morning, I felt sick, groggy and tearful, and my appearance in the mirror only made me feel worse. There were dark shadows smudged under my eyes, and my skin looked dull and heavy.

'Thank goodness for no doggy judgement,' I said to Runcible, who looked at me as lovingly as ever as I pulled on some comfortable clothes, popped her in a warm fleecy jumper and dug out my sunglasses. The day was grey and overcast, but I would need them to prevent my face from frightening any innocent folk I might meet. 'Come on, we're going to Meg's café for some breakfast.'

Opening my bedroom door, I could feel how quiet the house was, and guessed that no one, except for Coco maybe, was up. I tiptoed downstairs and slipped out of the front door, then marched off down the drive with a mixture of triumph and relief. It was cowardly to hide away like this, but after my hectic trip to London followed by the confusing and lukewarm reception I had, deservedly, received back here in Yorkshire, a solitary breakfast seemed to be in order. A brisk walk to the village in the freezing morning air would perk me up and hopefully bring some colour to my ashen cheeks. I passed The Keeper's Arms, quiet now after its busy night, and thought I might as well pop in and book Sam's room. Maybe I should book one for myself at the same time? I didn't know if I was still welcome at Blakeney Hall, or if I even wanted to stay there any longer. I decided against it, for now, and advanced to Meg's café, my stomach rumbling.

'Good morning, Fallon,' she said, smiling her wide smile. 'Take a seat. What can I get you? Same as before?'

Remembering the delicious, cooked breakfast, I nodded.

'Yes, please. It was perfect.'

I took the same seat as I had previously, although the rest of the café was empty, and gazed out of the window, losing myself in my drifting thoughts, then jumping slightly when Meg came over with a tray bearing a brimming plate, teapot, mug and a bowl of water and some biscuits for Runcible.

'Thank you,' I said, putting them on the floor under the table. 'That's so kind.'

'Dear little mite, couldn't let her go hungry. Now you shout if you need anything else.'

I set to my breakfast with a vigour I didn't know I had in me that desolate morning, and I was soon feeling stronger and more cheerful. I still had that horrible dragging sense of exhaustion, but at least my spirits were lifting. As I sipped the fabulously strong tea, I took out my phone, which I had put on silent, and looked at my messages. There was one from Alexander, which I opened immediately, so as not to draw out the suspense.

> Hi, thought I'd see you at breakfast this morning. T went looking for Runcible and I guess you'd both gone out. I'm ready to get those ads finalised if you are?

I drummed my fingers on the table. *Men are so annoying.* What was I supposed to glean from *that* message, other than, well, that he was ready to do the ads? I sighed. I'd better just treat it like any other job.

> Popped out for some air and breakfast. Back in twenty minutes. See you then.

And that would have to do.

As I walked through the gate at the bottom of the drive, I saw Douglas driving off with Theo: going to the sanctuary, I assumed. I gave them a wave and a cheerful smile, glad that I still had my sunglasses on. Surely, they would conceal my true feelings: sad, resigned and disappointed in myself. I slipped in the front door, hoping my mother wasn't anywhere nearby to tell me how awful I looked, and started walking through to Alexander's office. I knew I had to pretend I was fine with our fledgling relationship being over and prepared myself to say that, making it clear we could continue to work together with no hard feelings. Tears welled up in my eyes just at the thought of uttering those words to the man I had so quickly come to like, admire and – let's face it – fancy like crazy, but I was sure I was doing the right thing. What good was I to him? A hopeless prospect as a wife and mother – even though he had made it clear he was looking for neither – and a workaholic. Not to mention scruffy, especially next to the luminous Annabel. No, any further entanglement with Alexander was bound to bring pain and disappointment all round.

I pushed open the office door and caught my breath for a moment when he looked up at me and gave his gentle smile. Even in the dull wintry light, his good looks were undeniable, and a little voice in my head suggested I hold those thoughts of quitting, at least for a while. His smile broadened as I stood there.

'Bit too bright for you, is it?' he asked.

'What?'

'The sunglasses?'

'Oh!' I had forgotten I was wearing them and quickly pulled them off. 'Sorry, I'm a bit tired today.'

'Would you like a coffee? I brought the jug in.'

'Yes, please. Don't tell Mum, though, she made me promise to stick to those herbal teas, but they make me feel less radiant than ever.'

He laughed.

'You don't need them. Here you go.'

He handed me the coffee, which I took gratefully, then we got to working on the finals for the ads that were going in the local press. The work absorbed me, and mitigated the agony I was feeling as Alexander and I worked. I could smell his nutmeggy cologne, and every time our eyes met, I longed to keep gazing at him, be kissed by him again. But instead, I looked away resolutely, back to the project, and fiercely pushed aside my feelings with firm reminders of reality.

As we finished up and sent off the ads, I could see that Alexander was fiddling unnecessarily with the bits and pieces on his desk, so I waited – what was he working up to? My patience was rewarded.

'Look, Fallon, I just wanted to say that I know Annabel was being a bit... tricky last night. She's very confident in her beliefs about what is best for Theo and me...'

I was surprised by this apology, given how chilly he had been with me last night.

'That's one way of putting it.'

'Quite. Her heart is in the right place, I think, but she is rather...'

'Pushy?'

He grinned.

'I was going to say "persistent", but you've got a point. Anyway, it looked like she was getting to you a bit and I overheard the last bit of it. I just didn't want you to – well – pay any attention to her.'

I nodded. 'I've come across a few Annabels in my time, but she is unusually direct. She's very determined, isn't she?'

'I can't understand why, though. I mean, Holly left me when I had my accident and made it very clear that I was damaged goods. Our marriage was already struggling because I didn't want to do the whole social round. Annabel's already made it clear that she doesn't think much of the new business; she actually asked me if artisanal gin was legal as if I was sitting on the side of the bath with a wooden paddle. When I assured her it was totally legit, she raised an eyebrow and said, "Wouldn't whisky have more cachet?"'

I laughed. 'Maybe she doesn't think you're quite such a good 'cachet', after all.'

'Ha. If only. But I can't understand her, what she thinks I have to offer. Unless it's just being lady of the manor and hoping to mould me into something better, given time.'

He looked bewildered and I longed to reach out to him and explain in detail just exactly what I thought was so appealing about him. I swallowed.

'That stuff – the new business and your hand and the parties – doesn't matter, does it? I think she sees what a kind and hard-working man you are. And what a good father. Some women go crazy for that.'

'Some women?'

I paused. I had given myself the opening I had wanted, without meaning to.

'Yes. Some women. I'm not fussy when it comes to gin or whisky.'

He reached out his hand to touch mine.

'Look, I'm sorry that I was a bit snippy about you being back in time yesterday. I know you did your best. I get worried for Theo, and I overreacted.'

I moved my hand away.

'No, you were right. I cut it too fine, and I didn't have to. I could have been back with proper time to spare, even accounting for the vagaries of the train companies. I was too caught up in work and I left late. Although the good news is that Sam is coming up to help with the engagement party.'

He nodded, barely seeming to have heard me.

'Can we forget about the Nativity, Fallon? It all ended well, so we can take it from here, surely?'

My heart leaped and my first thought was to agree… then I thought of how unsure everything had been and how worried I had felt, so much so that I had barely slept. Pushing back tears, I shook my head slowly.

'I don't think so. I can't tell you how much I'm enjoying my time here, how I love Theo and, well, how happy I was when things changed with you.' I shut my eyes for a moment, trying to hold back the emotion. 'But I saw the pain and the worry I caused just with that one incident. Alexander, I'm not cut out for this. Hey, I'm Jacqueline's daughter, after all!' I gave a sort of strangulated and mirthless laugh. 'I think I'm better on the periphery. You two are doing just fine without me.'

Alexander looked at me, confusion in his eyes.

'We are. But – it was beginning to feel better *with* you.'

I looked miserably at my hands then back up at him.

'And you,' I whispered. 'But people don't change that much – enough. I can't risk it, Alexander, hurting you both.'

I stood up quickly and left the room, not wanting him to see the tears in my eyes and to see that I wasn't certain I was making the right decision, not at all.

TWENTY-THREE

When I left Alexander, the only thing I could do in that moment was to get out on the moors again. I had found them so healing over the time I had been at Blakeney Hall, even if that was partly down to the cold shock therapy you experienced every time you stepped outside. I grabbed my coat and almost ran back to the kitchen, hoping to avoid seeing anyone, but the house seemed deserted. Runcible had curled up in her favourite warm spot near the Aga, nestled in one of Theo's jumpers that he had left downstairs and now didn't have the heart to claim back from her. She blinked up at me sleepily.

'Don't worry, darling,' I said, my voice shaky. 'You stay put – you look so happy there.'

I pushed open the back door and started to tread the familiar path across the garden. At the bottom, I decided to turn right and go and visit Heathcliff. There he was, chewing comfortingly on some hay. I clicked to him, and he came wandering over for me to scratch his head and stroke his silky ears.

'Hello, boy,' I said. 'Getting over your star turn last night? I'm surprised Jacqueline hasn't had words about you stealing her limelight. Or maybe she's getting used to a few celebs being in the house and she'll be inviting you to a joint colonic soon.'

I babbled away at him in this manner for a few more minutes before he removed himself back to his hay and I took my cue to leave. I was on the moor in a matter of minutes and took a route straight across, with the house behind me, so that I was confident I wouldn't get lost. As I had hoped, the brisk weather and brisk walking improved my spirits, and although I can't say I was feeling exactly cheerful by the time I turned to go back to the house, at least I was feeling less inclined to go down the whole wailing and calling 'Heathcliff!' route. It would only get me a donkey around here anyway. A little lump of sadness had lodged itself deep in my throat, but I was sure now that I had made a good decision for everyone's sake. Mum had always emphasised the importance of believing in your own choices and sticking to them, and although that sometimes made her come across as brutal, or inflexible, it was good to lean on it now. She had always pushed forward, leaving behind the things and people that hindered her or made her uncomfortable, and look how successful she had been, without regrets.

Lunch that day was a little subdued and Alexander and I avoided each other's eye, both engrossing ourselves in conversations with the people next to us, in his case Coco, in mine Constance. Both were polite enough not to appear surprised at our sudden passionate curiosity about their lives. I was just running out of questions to ask about archaeology in Belize – probably a considerable relief to both of us – when she grabbed her opportunity.

'What have you got planned this afternoon? More work or are you resting after your trip to London?'

'Neither. I was going to ask if I might borrow your car. My business partner – and friend – Sam is arriving to help with planning the engagement party and I want to pick him up and take him down to The Keeper's Arms where he's staying.'

I hadn't realised that Coco and Alexander had stopped talking and were listening to me, until Alexander's voice came across the table.

'Why is he staying there? Unless he prefers to. He's very welcome here, we've got plenty of room.'

'Oh, thank you. I didn't want to ask, being a guest myself, but that's kind... I hope the pub won't mind?'

'They'll be fine. And I'll still help with the party, Fallon, we did say we'd tackle it together.'

'Oh, absolutely. I just thought three heads might be better than two, and Sam knows Mum well.'

He nodded and stood up.

'Great. I'll look forward to meeting him later.'

Then he left. Coco and Constance both looked at me questioningly, but I ploughed on.

'That's kind of him. You'll like Sam, I think he's great.'

'Good, it will be fun to have someone else staying,' said Coco. 'We'll be almost full. Come on, I'll help you sort out the room, get sheets and so on.'

I smiled at her gratefully.

'And of course you can take my car,' said Constance. 'I'm still chained to my book, so I won't be going anywhere.'

'Thank you.'

We cleared the table, then I followed Coco upstairs, Runcible at our heels.

'How many bedrooms does this house have?' I asked, as we walked down the corridor in the opposite direction from my room, up three stairs and through a large sitting room full of old-fashioned, chintzy furniture, that I hadn't seen before.

'Ten,' said Coco, 'although they're not all furnished. Oh, and another few up in the attic if you're desperate – old servants' quarters. There's been talk over the years of making that space useable in some way, but no one's ever done anything about it. It's nicer up there than it sounds; loads of light, but it's very cold in the winter. Maybe one day Dad or Alexander will sort it out. Here's the room I thought Sam could use. Constance and I are over this side as well, so he won't be isolated.'

She pushed open the door to reveal a medium-sized bedroom with dark floorboards and wooden panelled walls, painted cream. A large bed, stripped of its linens, stood against one wall and there was a heavy oak wardrobe. A large stone fireplace was opposite the bed and a door near that stood half open, showing a bathroom.

'He'll have a nice view here of the front garden,' said Coco, going over to the window and looking out. 'Oh! There's Theo and Douglas back from the sanctuary.'

I walked over as she wrenched the iron catch and pushed open the window, then we both leaned out, waving and shouting. I held Runcible up to give Theo a wave with her paw, which made him laugh. We pulled our heads inside again and Coco shut the window firmly, then opened the huge wardrobe and pulled out some sheets. We set to making the bed, chatting about this and that, including the engagement party.

'Mum and I would love to do the food, if you think Jacqueline would be all right with that?' said Coco, throwing me a pillow to put in its case. 'I wondered if she'd be uncomfortable with Dad's ex-wife helping, but they seem to have been getting on well while you were in London – they've even gone off shopping together today.'

'If you would, then that would be amazing,' I replied. 'It would be a weight off my mind, both in terms of finding someone but also finding someone good. Choice is almost non-existent by this stage at this time of year. And even if Mum did feel odd about it, I promise you that will be overcome by the kudos of having Estelle Knight catering her engagement party.'

'Oh good, Mum will be so pleased!'

'Have they really been getting on?'

I found it hard to imagine my mother bonding with the homely Estelle.

'They have. After that first awkward meeting, they got talking about people they know in common, and Mum told Jacqueline that she follows her Instagram account slavishly.'

'That would have gone down well.'

'It did. So Jacqueline picked up her phone and followed Mum on the spot, and started asking about baking.'

'I don't believe it!'

'I saw it with my own eyes. She said she'd never mastered even the basics—'

'True.'

'—but surely it couldn't be that hard.'

I laughed.

'That sounds more like Mum. I hope Estelle didn't mind?'

'Oh no, she's more than equal to that sort of thing. She calmly said that the basics weren't at all hard, it was working at *her* level that was reserved for the very talented.'

'Brilliant. Mum'll be whisking up complicated pavlovas in no time under that sort of challenge.'

As we were smoothing the bed down, the door opened, and Theo came in. We both greeted him, but he bypassed us and went straight to Runcible, who he fussed over for a minute or two before turning back to us.

'I had a good morning at the sanctuary,' he said. 'The police were there because someone shot a buzzard.'

'How exciting,' I said. 'I hope they catch whoever did it.'

'They will,' he said, with all the innocent confidence of the very young. 'And they let me sit in their car. Grandpa will show you the photo. And then,' he continued in a complete non-sequitur, 'I told Dad that he is being very silly.'

'What do you mean?' asked Coco.

'Well, I asked him a few days ago if Fallon was his girlfriend and he said no, but he was thinking maybe she might be soon and did I mind? I said of course I didn't. Then today I asked him again and he said no, and you weren't going to be. Is that true?'

He fixed me with a gimlet glare. I glanced awkwardly at Coco.

'Er, well... yes, it is.'

'Why?'

As has been established, I don't know many – any – children and have no idea what to say or not say to them. So once again I opted for the truth.

'Well, you saw the upset I caused yesterday. I was busy working and couldn't be here properly for either of you. That's what me – my life – is like.'

'You care more about work than us?'

I could feel a sweat breaking out on my lower back.

'Well, no, I wouldn't put it like that, exactly...'

I trailed off feebly. Theo was unmerciful.

'You probably think I'm too young to understand, but I do, and I think you're both silly. Dad worries about me a lot, but I worry about him too. I think he's lonely. I think that because I am often lonely as well, so I know what it's like. So I would like him to have a girlfriend. But not Annabel, because she treats me like a baby. You don't. We both like you and I know you like us too.'

'That's true—' I put in, before he continued with this uncharacteristically long speech.

'We don't need someone to look after us, we can already do that. But it is nice to have you here. If you like working, that's okay. But it's good to do more than just work.' He regarded me seriously, then added, 'I love Runcible too.'

I swallowed down tears.

'I know you do. Oh Theo, it's all a bit more complicated than that.'

'I don't see why. I think you and Dad are just *being* more complicated.'

I opened my mouth to attempt a reply to what seemed like a sensible argument, when Douglas popped his head around the door.

'Ah, there you are, Theo. I've got our very late lunch ready, come and have it before it's teatime.'

Without further comment, the boy stroked Runcible's head and followed his grandfather out of the room. I gave Coco a half-smile, and she raised her eyebrows at me.

'Good to hear Theo finding his voice,' she said. 'And for what it's worth, from the little I know about it, I also think that you and Alexander are being very silly.'

I must have looked startled, because she quickly apologised.

'Sorry, I didn't mean to be rude, and I know I shouldn't intrude, but it did seem as if you and Alexander were getting on so well.'

I sighed.

'We were. And when Theo puts it like that, it's so, so tempting. I do like Alexander a lot and I never thought I'd feel such – well, such a connection with a child as I do with Theo. But it's just too much responsibility, and it's not going to work. I had a tiny little dry run the other day, a chance to show that I could put them first, and I didn't take it. If I failed that, it's just a portent of what I'd be like if I were to let things go any further with Alexander.'

Coco pursed her lips.

'You know best, of course, and I don't know the details of what happened, but I *do* know that you did make it back in time for the Nativity. So, I'm not sure why you're saying you failed: you didn't.' I stayed stubbornly silent. 'If you think you failed because you weren't there for an hour beforehand making mince pies and soothing stage fright, well, I don't think anyone expected you to be, did they?'

I had to concede that she had a point.

'No, but isn't that who I would need to be, if I took on Theo?'

'Not at all. You'd need to be there for him, sure, but you don't have to morph into the Waltons. I'm sure you already know how to be present in life for people who matter to you.' Now *she* was looking stubborn, and fierce, and I could imagine her dealing with the head chef who had groped her. 'Sorry to be so forthright, Fallon, but I had high hopes of my brother and you. I'm not trying to force you into anything, or stop you being who you are, but I think you've convinced yourself of something that just isn't true.'

'It's okay.' I gave a small smile. 'I appreciate you saying it. Look, I'd better go to the station to get Sam. Thank you for helping me with his room, and for the pep talk.'

Her face softened.

'You're welcome. Just think about it all, won't you?'

I nodded, and went out, back through the chintzy sitting room and downstairs. I was just getting Constance's car keys from the hooks in the hallway, when Mum appeared. She was wearing, to my intense astonishment, a blue apron with white polka dots. My eyebrows hit the ceiling.

'Is something wrong, darling?'

'Only that you appear to be wearing an apron, Mum. Are you auditioning?'

'Oh, don't be so ridiculous. I'm wearing it because Estelle and I are about to do some cooking. She's teaching me how to make mince pies.'

'You?'

'Yes, me. Are you sure there's nothing wrong, Fallon? You seem to be very confused. Are you sure you should be driving?'

'I'm confused, Mum, because you are wearing an apron and having a mince pie-making lesson with Douglas's ex-wife. It's not very... *you.*'

She waved her hand at me dismissively.

'Oh, darling, one can't be constrained. Change is healthy, you know. If you don't step out of your comfort zone once in a while, then life is very boring. You should try it.'

'I do it all the time! Look at me rushing to London the other day – that was hardly comfortable.'

'Ah, but it *was* your comfort zone: dashing off to solve a problem for a demanding client. You love it. You found it far more uncomfortable to let yourself be needed by Alexander and Theo, and to enjoy that. That's why you were so late back.' I stared at her, unable to find any words in reply. 'Pretty basic psychology, darling, but I do also know you well, even if you think I don't notice. I *am* your mother.'

I was going to make some retort, but then, disarmingly, she smiled.

'And I love you, you know. Right, better go – these mince pies won't make themselves. They will be ready for Sam to have one for tea. I know *he'll* appreciate my efforts, such a dear man.'

She swept away, leaving me alone in the hallway clutching the keys and with my head spinning in utter confusion. Who had taken my mother and replaced her with this incisive, apparently loving, baker? I glanced at my watch. There wasn't time to think about it now; I was going to be late and, for once, I was grateful for that. At least it gave me an excuse not to think about the several bewildering conversations I had had that day. Maybe later I'd find myself chatting to Father Christmas about his beard care; today, nothing else could surprise me. I hoped.

TWENTY-FOUR

I drove slowly to the station, everything that had happened that day swirling around in my head. I pulled into the short stay car park at York Station and took a moment to admire my surroundings; being inside the station itself, the car park was beautiful with its curved roof, rows of brick arches and circular windows. Mind you, the fact I could park at all was pretty beautiful, I thought, locking Constance's car and heading for the concourse. The last time I had driven in London, it had been a choice between parking a twenty-minute walk from my destination or paying over ten pounds an hour to park any closer. I sat down in a small café and texted Sam to let him know where I was, then settled down to wait, scalding my lips with hot coffee as I watched the people go by and listened to someone bashing out Christmas carols on the nearby public piano. Only ten minutes had passed when he arrived. I stood up to hug him.

'I know it's only been a day or so, but I'm so glad to see you!'

'Me too, but it's bloody cold up here.'

'I know, I had to buy a whole new wardrobe. I did warn you. Do you want a coffee to warm up?'

'Why not?'

He sat down and I ordered another couple of hot drinks as he filled me in on the final pieces of work he had done before shutting up the office for Christmas.

'So, how's the handsome one-day-to-be-lord-of-the-manor?' Sam asked.

I pulled a face.

'Not sure.'

'What's happened? I thought things were going well. You didn't believe your own publicity about being like Jacqueline, did you? Oh, Fallon!'

I spilled out the story of how I'd been late back and upset Theo, but even to my own ears it was sounding a bit thin, especially in the light of the various talkings to I'd had that day.

'...so I decided it was the best thing to do...' I trailed off miserably.

'And can I divine from the look on your face that you no longer think that?' asked Sam tartly.

'Oh, I don't know. I was very sure, and now I just feel confused. But can you *really* see me making a decent job of motherhood?'

'Well, for a start...' He began ticking things off on his fingers, which was always a bad sign with Sam. I was in real trouble. 'For a start, you've only known this man for a few weeks, so aren't you jumping the gun a bit?'

'I know that's how it seems, but what's the point of starting something if I can't see a future in it?'

He snorted, unimpressed.

'Secondly, we have already had the conversation about you being – or *not* being – like Jacqueline. Thirdly, the situation is completely different. And fourthly – oh, it doesn't matter what I think. What do *you* think, truthfully?'

'Well, part of me thinks Theo might have been right – we've been silly.'

Sam folded his arms in triumph and sat back. 'Right. So now the question remains: what are you going to do about it?'

I raised an eyebrow.

He drained his coffee and continued, 'Okay. You know I'm here for you, whatever you decide. Actually *here*, in this freezing outpost!'

I laughed.

'I think you'll find that York is not only a pretty important city, but incredibly beautiful and vibrant,' I said, sounding like a tour guide.

'Ah, gotcha! You're defending it! London might lose you yet.'

'We'll see. Come on, let's get back to the house.'

'I can't wait.'

Twenty minutes later, we were pulling up on the drive and as I put on the handbrake, I turned and grinned at Sam, who was gazing up at the house in amazement.

'What do you think?'

'The photos you sent didn't do it justice – it's huge.'

'Yup. Incredible, isn't it? And, even better, you're staying here.'

He turned to me.

'What? I thought I was at the pub in the village.'

'Not unless you'd prefer to be. When Alexander heard I'd booked you a room there, he practically insisted I cancel it and invited you here. Is that okay?'

'Okay? You bet it's okay! My mum won't know what to do with herself when I send her the pictures. She never misses an episode of *Escape to the Country* now Dad's not there to tell her what she is and isn't allowed to watch.'

Sam's mother had finally kicked his abusive father out about six months previously and, according to him, she was now blissfully happy.

'Another thing she's enjoying, I'm glad.'

'You won't be when she rocks up on the doorstep.'

I laughed and opened the car door.

'I wouldn't mind – I like your mum.'

Once inside the house, we left Sam's bags at the foot of the stairs and went into the Great Hall, which was empty.

'I don't know where everyone is,' I said. 'Maybe Coco will be in the kitchen. She's lovely.'

'Coco?'

As we continued through, I quickly explained the various relationships amongst those staying at Blakeney Hall, and when I pushed open the kitchen door, I was glad I had, for everyone had congregated there, watching Estelle give Mum her cooking lesson.

'Sam! Darling! How gorgeous to see you! Look, I'm all floury, did you ever think you'd see the day?'

Sam went and gave my mother a kiss.

'I didn't, but I'm sure you'll brush it off for cocktails later,' he said with a wink.

I introduced him to everyone else and he was greeted with their customary warmth, especially by Alexander who said how pleased he was to have Sam at the house rather than the pub and thanked him for the help he would give with the engagement party. We were found chairs and presented with cups of tea to watch Act Two of the lesson which, with Estelle and Mum in starring roles and Coco tasked with taking photos and video clips to show everyone's best side on their social media accounts, was more like an episode of *Mayfair Mews* than a simple class in how to make mince pies.

'Now, Jacqueline,' said Estelle briskly. 'You have successfully made your pastry. Do you remember the name of the technique we used?'

'Rubbing in!' said Mum, with a dazzling smile, playing her role of star student to the max.

'Good. And now we're going to briefly work our pastry, then cut it. Ready?'

There seemed to me to be an unnecessary amount of flour now flying around, making, no doubt, for excellent photos. I noticed Mum surreptitiously dab a little on the end of her nose before turning, laughing, towards the camera. Cheesy it may have been, but I also admired her savvy. And what's more, it did look as if they were having fun. Was she right, was coming out of your comfort zone a good thing? Or was I just beguiled by the Jacqueline Honeywood Show and would find her ordering macrobiotic smoothies for delivery again tomorrow, with nothing changed?

'There we go, next we're going to put the filling in and after fifteen minutes in the oven and a little cooling time they'll be ready to eat,' announced Estelle. 'Now, who's going to do the washing up?'

'I will!' said Theo, who had been laughing throughout the whole thing.

'I'll help you,' said Constance, standing up. 'Then hopefully we'll be here for first tastings,' she added, grinning at the little boy.

'Shall we go and put together our ideas for the party?' I said to Sam and Alexander.

'Yes, let's,' said Alexander, 'but don't finish off those mince pies without us!'

We went through to his office and sat down. I brought up the list of ideas so far that I had on my phone, while Alexander asked Sam about his journey. I peeped over the top of my phone as they chatted, thinking how kind and warm Alexander was, welcoming this stranger into his house with open arms. *Oh well,*

I will soon be back in London and life would go on, I thought firmly, before saying, 'Right, here's what we've got so far.'

They jumped at my sudden business-like tone, but turned to listen.

'Okay, so, Estelle and Coco are going to do the catering, thank goodness. And even better, they're going to liaise with Mum and Douglas about what food they want, the budget and so on. Alexander, you said you knew the local wine merchants – are you good to talk to them about drinks?'

'Yes, I can do that. I'll just need some guidance on how much for the number of people coming. I'll provide the gin, of course.'

'Great. Numbers are still up in the air, I'm afraid. Mum and Douglas gave me a list almost immediately, which looked suspiciously modest. I sent out "save the dates" but since then she's added at least thirty people, most of whom live in London. I have no idea how likely it is that they'll make it, given that it's a two-hundred mile journey a week and a half before Christmas.'

'I'd put my money on most of them being here,' said Sam shrewdly. 'Who's going to want to turn down an invitation to Jacqueline Honeywood's engagement party, even if it is in the middle of nowhere? No offence,' he added, glancing at Alexander.

'None taken. I can't be bothered to travel five miles for most parties, but I guess Jacqueline has a certain pull.'

'Can I see who she's added?' asked Sam. I handed him my phone and he cast his professional eye down the list. 'Clever Jacqueline,' he said, grinning. 'She's not bothered with some of her nearest and dearest – saving those for the London party, I suppose – but she's added a fair few gossip writers and ladies who lunch, all of whom will be very useful for spreading the word about Her Future Ladyship's exclusive stately home bash. I'd guess most of these will sack off whatever else they've got planned and make the journey. Is there a magazine coming?'

'Well, I think that's why she's added these people. Everything was too crammed already to offer anything more than a photographer for the diary pages, so these people will boost the publicity nicely.'

Alexander shook his head.

'This is a new world to me. Forgive me, but it all seems so... cynical.'

'It is and it isn't,' I replied. 'She knows that she has to keep bolstering her public profile, for the good of her career, so any opportunity is ripe for using. Look at how she pounced on her poor, broken daughter in order to produce some kind of Fairy Godmother transformation she could bung on her grid? But I don't think it's always for show.' I paused, not quite sure how to express out loud the new feelings I had had recently about Mum. I decided to steer away from the subject of our relationship. 'She really, really loves Douglas, I can tell. We may not be that close, but I know her well – or, at least, I've known her for a long time – and I've never seen her like this. I honestly believe that you could strip away the title and the stately home and the magazine deals and she'd still marry him in a heartbeat. It may not be her usual *modus operandi*, but it's the real thing.'

Alexander nodded slowly.

'I'm glad. I thought so too. Thank you, Fallon.'

I dropped my eyes and returned quickly to my list.

'Right, so our big focus now is getting the invitations printed and sent out, which is panicking me. We've so little time, but they're both insisting on "proper" invitations, not digital ones.'

'I think it'll be all right,' said Sam. 'Because of the save the dates, we already have an idea of who's coming, so we've got a rough idea of numbers, and we can ask for replies by email, rather than post. If they don't mind printed envelopes, instead of handwritten, I've got a friend who does lovely stationery and owes me a favour. He'll get something classic out tomorrow if I give him a ring. Or do they want to design them?'

'Classic will be fine with Dad,' said Alexander.

'And I'll take this one if Mum complains,' I said. 'Please make the call.'

We went on to plan for waiting staff, chairs and tables, flowers and entertainment, until we all had something to follow up.

'At least they didn't insist on it being themed,' I said. 'That would have been a step too far.'

'Don't say that too loudly,' said Alexander, with his lovely smile. 'Dad might hear you and you know his weakness.'

'I'll be careful. I wouldn't put it past Mum to dig out that Octopussy outfit again.'

Sam laughed.

'Your mother is priceless. I hope she likes the job we do on the party – maybe she'll finally hire us once we're home? Talking of which, I must confirm my train ticket for Sunday.'

'You're welcome to stay for Christmas, Sam,' said Alexander. 'We'd be glad to have you.'

Before I could stop myself, and before Sam had a chance to reply, I waded in.

'Actually, Sam, I was thinking of coming back with you. I'm feeling much better now, and London is such fun at Christmas – we could go out for lunch together, seeing as your mum's away?'

Both men were staring at me in surprise.

'What about the Christmas Fayre?' asked Alexander. 'If you go on Sunday, you'll miss it.'

In my confusion, I had forgotten all about it. Alexander looked so hurt and worried that I was desperate to run to him, throw my arms around him, tell him what a fool I was being. But, unable to stop myself, I just carried on.

'You'll be fine without me,' I said, trying to sound casual, but knowing my voice sounded strangulated. 'All the prep will be finished and all you'll have to do is drive up, park and sell. You'll be a hit. You don't need me.'

You don't need me. The words that summed up everything I had been agonising over, that sounded so confident but felt so painful. I could feel the familiar throb start up behind my left eye and I put my hand to my forehead.

'Fallon...' said Sam, knowing the signs. 'Do you need to get something for your head?'

I nodded and left the room quickly, offering an ironic word of gratitude to the gods of headaches for their timing, whilst knowing it was me who was responsible for triggering it with my own stress and stubbornness. Most people, I thought as I took some tablets and put a cold flannel on my forehead, would have followed their hearts, seen if things might work with Alexander. Why did I find it so impossible to do the same?

As typically happens, I was overcome with a tremendous fatigue and fell asleep, waking a couple of hours later to find the room dim, lit only by the screen of a laptop where Sam was working. I sat up cautiously, dislodging Runcible, who had snuggled herself in comfortingly beside me. Sam looked up.

'Hey,' he said quietly. 'How are you feeling?'

'All right, I think,' I replied. 'I took my stuff quickly, so it didn't get too much of a grip.' Anxiety suddenly flooded me. 'Oh no, I was going to start looking round for bands, so I'd better get on with it now.'

I went to stand up, only to be subjected to a wave of dizziness and forced to sit down again quickly. Sam put his computer to the side and came over to join me, putting an arm around my shoulder.

'It's fine, Fallon. I got the invitations sorted, so I've been looking into entertainment. Although,' he said with a wry smile, 'everyone who's got back to me so far has been booked up for months, so I've no idea what we'll end up with. It's just the flowers left to do, and I have a couple of names – you could call them tomorrow.'

I rested my head on his shoulder.

'Thank you. I'm so glad you're here. Sorry to have bailed like that; I didn't even show you where your room was.'

'It's okay, Alexander took me up. He's a nice guy.'

I know! screamed a voice inside me. *I know!* But I didn't reply. Sam continued:

'I'm still worried about you. You seem better than you were, but you're still not okay. What was all that about coming back to London with me for Christmas? That's not what you want to do, is it?'

Tears started leaking out of my eyes and trickling down my cheeks.

'I don't know. He's still being so nice, and he hasn't tried to change my mind. I think he's decided I was right to break it off, and now it's too late even if I did want to change my mind, but I don't know if I do or not.'

I was properly sobbing now, and Sam squeezed my shoulder and let me cry. He was unembarrassed by tears and had given me a wet shoulder or two in the past, so I didn't mind bawling all over him. For a moment, my head responded by flaring with pain again, but it soon ebbed and began to feel clearer.

As I quietened, he said, 'Judging by the way he was looking at you, I don't think it's that at all. If he's not arguing, I reckon it's because he's a decent man who is respecting your decision, whether he likes it or agrees with it or not. A unicorn.'

This set off a fresh round of sobbing.

What had I thrown away?

TWENTY-FIVE

The next few days passed painfully, awkwardly, politely. Alexander carried on being incredibly nice and courteous, but distant, and Theo veered between affection and avoidance. Each time I noticed him deliberately pulling away from me, my heart cracked a little more; maybe at some point it would be shattered. The headache had taken twenty-four hours to pass, making me feel drained and dizzy and giving me the perfect excuse not to stay up late. I was deeply relieved to have Sam there, who was such a familiar and comforting face and who was taking on the brunt of organising the party and, more importantly, liaising with Mum over it. Her sudden fancies and exacting requirements didn't faze him in the least, and he simply reported back to me every day with what had finally been decided, and how many people had accepted the invitation that day. Alexander had been fairly quiet on the subject of sourcing the wine, so I assumed that was going well. I had managed to scare up a band that I was deeply unsure of, but that Meg at the café in the village promised me would be a hit.

. . .

By the morning of the party, I was feeling better, although the nagging feelings of missing Alexander and doubting my decision refused to go away. But I needed to push them down and get on with things, even if this would be the last time I would see Alexander before our parents' wedding. I was still planning to go back to London the next day. Today was a day for focus, for leaning into the work that had been both my saviour and my destroyer over the years. Everyone was at breakfast, and there was a fizz of festivity in the air.

'Are you sure there isn't anything I can do?' asked Constance. 'I've finally tamed the hydra that is my book, so I'd be glad to help.'

'Have you cut off all nine heads?' asked Theo, who had recently developed an enthusiastic interest in Greek mythology, even though his fascination with birds of prey showed no signs of wavering.

'Eight, I reckon,' said Constance. 'But the ninth can wait.'

'In that case,' said Alexander, 'could you take Theo up to the sanctuary today? I think we'll all be needed here for the final preparations, is that right, Fallon?'

I jumped slightly and blushed when he said my name, but managed to stammer out:

'Yes, yes, please. And Theo, I have a job for you too. Would you mind taking full charge of Runcible today? I know she'll be safe with you, and far better off than being here with strangers coming in and out all day.'

He beamed with pride.

'I'd *love* to, thank you. I promise I'll look after her.'

'What are you two doing?' asked Constance, addressing Mum and Douglas. 'I assume you won't be heaving chairs around here?'

Mum smiled graciously.

'No. Fallon has kindly suggested that we take a relaxing day off so that we can enjoy the evening.' I grinned surreptitiously at

Sam, whose idea this had been. None of us needed Mum there as we prepared the party. 'We'll be back in time to get ready. In fact, darling, I was hoping we could do that together, in your room?'

I didn't look up as she said this, assuming she was talking to someone else, but Constance gave me a dig in the ribs and nodded across the table at Mum.

'Oh, me? You want to get ready with me? Er, yes, all right, that would be, er... nice.'

She raised one eyebrow a fraction, then smiled.

'Good.'

Was that it? No dig, no insult, no suggestion that she wanted to get ready with me only to make sure I didn't let the side down? Maybe she *was* a changed character.

'The party will go beautifully,' said Estelle, 'but I think that Coco and I had better clear breakfast, if you've all finished, as we need to get started. Our first delivery has already arrived.'

We all jumped up to help – well, most of us jumped up to help – and the bustle of the day started.

By half past five, with the guests due to start arriving at seven, Alexander, Sam and I stood back and looked at the Great Hall.

'It looks stunning,' I said, with satisfaction. 'I have to admit that when this whole idea was mooted, I thought we'd be lucky to manage a few packets of peanuts, some tinsel and a Christmas CD.'

Alexander laughed.

'Well, that's all I would ever have come up with. You two are a complete powerhouse – I can see why you're so successful.'

He smiled warmly at me, and I smiled back. Much of the awkwardness of the past few days had fallen away that day as we worked, and I could feel my resolve crumbling, only for that insistent inner voice to pipe up that it was *work* that had cheered me up, and nothing had changed.

'They'll love it,' said Sam, putting his arm around my shoulder and giving me a squeeze.

I believed that they would. We had decided to feature the Christmas tree, and have a golden theme, giving a nod to Douglas's precious Bond movies, with heart decorations liberally sprinkled throughout to emphasise that it was an engagement party. Huge swags of fir, cypress, holly and ivy hung from the walls and above the fireplace, and we had placed a mixture of around two hundred real and battery-operated candles around the room. A specialist company had come and strung up thousands of soft gold fairy lights, the staff clambering nimbly up huge ladders to attach them to the ancient walls. The fire had been lit and blazed away merrily. Massive bunches of mistletoe were suspended from every doorway, as well as at various points around the room, waiting to catch unsuspecting couples, or maybe couples-to-be. The family's furniture had been heaved away to the sides of the room and small, high tables stood everywhere, draped in subtly sparkly gold fabric. Each table also bore candles and small vases of evergreen sprays hung with tiny gilded wooden hearts. A large table covered in a crisp white cloth stood to one side half full of sparkling glassware, with the other half soon to be laden with bottles of chilled champagne and other drinks. Up in the minstrels' gallery, the band I had hired had set up their things and were due back half an hour before the party started.

'They look awfully young,' I had whispered to Sam, when we had greeted them and were watching them lug their speakers and instruments up the small wooden staircase.

'They're practically toddlers,' he had replied, stifling a giggle, 'but their videos online were great, and all the reviews were so glowing. It'll be fine.'

Delicious smells had been wafting out of the kitchen all day, but Estelle and Coco had fiercely guarded their domain, only emerging to furnish us with overflowing doorstep sandwiches and warm Fat Rascals to fuel us for more work.

'Right,' I said, pulling my eyes away from the twinkling, inviting room. 'Mum and Douglas will be back soon, and we don't want them to see any of this. I'll go and wait for them.'

I had only just put my head around the big front door to check when their car came crunching up the drive. I ushered them indoors and straight up the stairs, leaving Sam and Alexander to rush around with some more decorations for the entrance hall and the front of the house.

'It looked a bit plain downstairs, darling,' said Mum, shrugging off the coat I hadn't given her time to remove downstairs. 'Are you sure everything will be ready?'

'It will be perfect,' said Douglas, taking the coat. 'I have every faith in these two. Now, you two go and get ready and I will see you, my beloved, later.'

I averted my eyes while they kissed passionately goodbye for the hour or so they would be apart, then led Mum to my room where she had earlier left everything that she would need.

'Would you like to use the bathroom first?' I asked, perching on the side of the bed.

'Thank you, darling, I will have a shower,' she said, collecting up some bottles and a sponge bag. 'I won't be long.'

With a sigh of relief, and suspecting that 'not long' could be up to half an hour, I lay back on my bed and grabbed my phone to watch some mindless TV while I waited. But it hadn't been five minutes before there was a little knock on the door, and I raised my unwilling eyes from the screen. Hopefully, this wasn't going to be problems with the party.

'Come in.'

The door opened a tiny bit and in trotted Runcible. I jumped off the bed and scooped her up for a cuddle, pulling the door wider at the same time.

'Theo! Thank you so much for looking after her. Have you had a good day?'

'Really good!' he said, his eyes shining. 'We're planning our own Christmas party at the sanctuary with edible stockings for all the birds and animals, and then Constance took me to Bettys tea rooms to celebrate nearly finishing her book and I had three cakes.'

'Sounds amazing! What did you do with Runcible when you were there? I didn't think they allowed dogs in.'

'They don't, unless they're assistance dogs, but Constance put Runcible in her bag and told them she was her therapy dog. She looked so sweet with her nose poking out that nobody minded. She had a lovely time.'

'I bet she did. I'm so grateful to you for being such a good doggy-sitter.'

Theo flung his arms tightly around my waist in the sudden way that he had, and mumbled, 'I'm going to miss her when you're gone.'

A lump formed in my throat, and I hugged him back, whispering, 'She's going to miss you, too, Theo. Very much.'

'Does she have to go?'

'I – I don't know.'

He pulled away slightly and looked up at me with a tearstained face.

'Really? Might you really not go, Fallon? I know Daddy doesn't want you to, and neither do I.'

I have never been so glad in my life to hear my mother's acid tones breaking in.

'Darling, have you made *no* attempt to get ready while I've been in the shower?'

We both turned to her, then glanced at each other with suppressed grins. She looked magnificent but ridiculous in a cream silk robe, her hair swathed in some sort of plastic cap to protect her blow dry, and her face smeared generously with purple cream.

'Sorry, Mum,' I managed to get out. 'I'll hop in the shower now. Thanks again for looking after Runcible,' I added to Theo. 'I'll see you at the party later.'

He nodded and left, and I scuttled down to the bathroom before Mum could offer me any of her beautifying concoctions to try.

When I emerged, she was looking much better with the goop and the plastic cap gone, sitting in front of the mirror applying foundation with an expert hand.

'What are you wearing tonight?' she asked. 'I know it wasn't much notice and I wasn't sure you'd brought anything suitable. Maybe the dress you had for the Bond party?'

'Actually, I picked something up when I was in London,' I said, taking the long bag out of the wardrobe and unzipping it. 'The amazing woman who we rent dresses from sorted it out for me with about ten minutes' notice. I had to carry it all round the Nativity, but I think it was worth it.' A little flutter of excitement rippled through me as I pulled the dress out of the bag: Marcella had outdone herself, and surely even Mum couldn't find fault with this. It was a floor-length dress with a fishtail hem that pooled around my feet and a deep V-neck, and it was covered with gold sequins. It wasn't very 'me' and it wasn't remotely subtle, but it was showstopping, and I hoped Mum would be pleased, hoped that I had finally got it right. I wasn't disappointed.

'*Darling*,' she breathed, standing up and coming over to feel the fabric and the weight of the dress. 'It's *stunning* and you will look wonderful in it. Oh, thank you, thank you for making such an effort for my party. You *are* happy for me, aren't you?'

An unprecedented look of vulnerability crossed her face, and I gave her a hug as sudden as one of Theo's.

'Very,' I said. 'Douglas is perfect for you and you're so happy. I'm thrilled for you both.'

She hugged me back, before returning to business.

'Now, what shoes are you going to wear with it, show me. And I have the most marvellous eyeshadow you must use. Oh, come here, let me do it for you, it'll be quicker.'

All Mum's years in the entertainment industry had taught her a thing or two about make-up, and as she stroked the products skilfully onto my face, I couldn't understand why she didn't do this on social media, instead of all the 'wellness' that she favoured. I was sure people would welcome her expert tips, but maybe she didn't want to reveal the secrets behind the magic? I began to relax as she worked – maybe it was time to try and build our relationship up a little? I was finally beginning to feel that I could leave the past in the past. Something similar was clearly on her mind too.

'Fallon, being with Douglas, and having you here has given me cause for some reflection. I do know that I wasn't always the best mother when you were young, and I regret that. But you do understand, don't you, that I cannot regret the pursuit of my career?'

I nodded, feeling an odd surge of adrenaline at this unexpected turn of events.

'But what I do realise is that I failed to find a balance, when I could have done, I think. And, well, the thing is...'

My eyes met hers in the mirror and didn't break away. We were drinking each other in as if meeting for the first time.

'The thing *is* that I was hoping it wasn't too late to regain it, maybe, with you? A balance. Of some sort. I'd like that.'

I turned around and met her eyes with no mirror in between.

'I'd like that too,' I said quietly. 'Very much.'

'Not too much water under the bridge?'

'No. And if you can make mince pies, then we can do a little thing like this, right?'

She smiled a smile of pure relief and how could I do anything but smile back?

'I'm so glad, Fallon. Thank you. And won't you think about staying for Christmas? I'd like to spend it with you.'

I turned back to the mirror and this time gazed into my own troubled eyes.

'I don't know, Mum. I want to, but... I just don't know. Do you mind if we don't talk about it tonight?'

It must have taken her a superhuman effort, but she didn't argue.

'I'm sure you'll do the right thing. Now, what about lipstick? Or maybe a gloss?'

I submitted once again to her attentions and tried hard not to think about what the right thing might be. I had no idea.

TWENTY-SIX

Seven o'clock was fast approaching and Mum was still adjusting her already perfect make-up. I was ready and had stolen enough astonished glances at my own reflection that I was worried I'd lose my nerve and wash away this version of myself – glamorous, glowing, subtly sexy – in favour of a familiar black dress and some flat ballet pumps. I was used to dressing up for events, but as well as the gold sequins, which rippled down my body in an outrageous wave of glitz, Mum's hair and make-up job far surpassed anything I could achieve on my own. It was hard to pinpoint exactly what was different, because I didn't look overdone or even remotely like my *Dynasty* namesake, not that that would have been such a bad thing. There was something in her choice of colours and the way she had applied everything, that defined my features in an unbelievably flattering way and seemed to light up when I smiled. But I was used to being on time for events I hosted, and I was starting to feel nervous.

'Mum, shall I go and get Douglas? It's so nearly time.'

She turned to me and reached out her hand which, after a second's hesitation, I took. We rarely touch, Mum and me.

'Darling, if this wasn't my engagement party, I would be proud to enter it with only you at my side.'

'Well, you mean with me in this dress.' I hadn't wanted to snipe at her, but it came out, the usual old defensiveness. I braced myself for a cutting reply, but instead received a gentle squeeze of my hand.

'Fallon, you have every right to be angry at me. Until recently, the most important thing to me would have been your dress – or at least that's what I would have told myself. But I've always been so proud of you and would have loved to have you with me no matter what you were wearing.'

'So, why didn't you?'

She paused.

'I should have done. I have been too caught up over the years in creating, then being, Jacqueline Honeywood. She came before everything else, at first because she had to, and then because I was so terrified of losing her after all she had done for me – for us. But inside, Jackie Woodcock has always adored her only daughter and it's time Jacqueline caught up, no matter what the event, or the dress. This time we've spent together, darling, it's made me understand the damage I have done. With two minutes to go until the party, perhaps it's not ideal timing to talk it all over, but maybe we can agree to find some time, lots of time. It's up to you.'

The years fell away, and I was five years old again, looking at my Mum as if she were the most wonderful thing in the entire world, wanting nothing more than her love and her acceptance. Bruised I may be, but I knew better than to throw away this chance. I squeezed her hand back.

'I'd like that. A lot.'

When Douglas put his head around the door to see if we were ready to go down, he found us hugging each other tightly, our glow coming not just from our golden dresses.

'I'll go now,' I said, breaking away. 'Give me another few

minutes and when you hear the gong, you can make your grand entrance down the stairs.'

As I passed Douglas, he caught at my arm and pulled me into a brief hug.

'So glad to have another daughter,' he said, his voice thick with emotion. I didn't dare reply, too worried that tears would start spilling out. Instead, I nodded, smiled and left the room, going downstairs with a new lightness in my heart.

I saw Sam almost immediately, standing near the front door. He was looking nervously at his watch, but his wrist dropped when he saw me.

'Fallon! Bloody hell, you look fantastic!'

'Thank you.' I smiled. 'Mum worked her magic on me.'

'Things a bit better between the two of you?'

'Yes. I didn't think Christmas miracles were a real thing, but one seems to have happened.'

'Do you think she's changed?'

'I'm not sure if changed is the right word. I think it's more that she's acknowledging a part of herself that was always there, but that she didn't dare let see the light.'

Sam arched an eyebrow at me and nodded towards Alexander, who was coming over. He was dressed in a simple black tuxedo with a crisp white shirt and looked incredibly handsome, if a little nervous.

'Maybe she's not the only one in need of an epiphany this festive season.'

I didn't have time to reply as Alexander came up, his face breaking into a smile.

'Fallon, you look so beautiful.'

'Thank you,' I replied, blushing. 'You look great too. Um, how are things going?'

'Nearly everyone is here. Are Dad and Jacqueline coming soon?'

'As soon as they hear the gong,' I replied. 'Come on, let's get this party started.'

Despite my misgivings, the party was a huge success. The band, who seemed barely out of school, were astonishingly good and played a crowd-pleasing mix of floor fillers and Christmas hits that had even the most curmudgeonly of guests tapping their toes, and the rest of us up and dancing. The food was utterly delectable, and I grabbed Coco as she swept past me with another tray laden with canapés.

'Thank you so much, you and Estelle have been incredible.'

'It's been fun,' she replied, her eyes sparkling. 'And Mum's enjoyed it too. She's even offered to help me start up my own catering business.'

'That's wonderful! You deserve it.'

I grabbed a tiny shortbread biscuit with Wensleydale and a sliver of pear balanced on it and let her continue doing her rounds. It was rare I had the opportunity to enjoy a party that I had organised, but I was loving this one, especially as Sam was taking the main responsibility for any behind-the-scenes hiccups. Of course, it was just as I was savouring another mouthful of cheese and biscuit when Annabel came gliding up.

'Hello there, Fallon. You're looking very... sparkly.'

The way she said it made it clear she thought I looked like I'd been dressed by a cheap supermarket, but the sneer in her voice couldn't get to me that evening. It helped that she had, unusually, missed the mark with her outfit and was looking twee in a red plaid printed dress in a 1950s style, high necked and belted with a red ribbon with white reindeer gambolling along it. We were standing near the fire and her flushed cheeks clashed terribly with the dress. She had had layers cut in since I last saw her, and with her hair in a girlish ponytail, I imagined she had been aiming for a sort of Bing Crosby Christmas cuteness. I decided to avoid any comment on what she was wearing.

'Thank you. Are you enjoying the party?'

'Very much. But I haven't seen Alexander yet, and I wanted to invite him – ah! There he is. Alex!'

She stood on tippy toes and waved at Alexander, who came over with a reluctant smile. Poor man! Which out of the two of us did he least want to see?

'Hello, Annabel,' he said, leaning down to kiss her cheek and being drawn into a warm embrace. When she eventually released him, she flicked her ponytail and went full Doris Day.

'Where is darling Theo? I have a little present for him, which I know he'll love, and I did so want to give it to him myself. It's so marvellous to see the joy in children's eyes when they open a gift, don't you agree, Fallon?'

I nodded and hmm-ed noncommittally, wondering how soon I could politely extricate myself. She tipped her head to one side and looked at me, her face a picture of pretty bewilderment.

'Oh! Maybe you don't think so. Anyway, Alexander, *do* you know where he is?'

'He's not one for big parties, so I think he's gone to his room with Runcible.'

'Runcible?'

'My dog,' I explained. 'They're great friends.'

'I see. Well, maybe I can find him later. But Alexander, I did want to pin you down about next Saturday. I can't invite *everyone*,' she added, glancing at me, 'it is very much a *soirée intime*, but having you there, Alex, would *make* it.'

'I'm so sorry, Annabel, but that is the day of the Christmas Fayre. I think I'll have far too much to sort out and I wouldn't want to turn up late and spoil things. I'll have to say no.'

She pouted.

'*What* a shame. I thought Fallon was helping with the Fayre – can't she finish things off there and free you up?'

I was tempted to remind her I was standing here, too, but deliberately drawing attention to oneself when wearing floor-length gold sequins seems a little *de trop*, so I stayed quiet, waiting to see what Alexander would say. He didn't know that I was seriously rethinking staying, after my conversation with Mum. Smart as ever, he stayed neutral and didn't give anything away. It would be nice if I thought that was because he was hoping I would stay, but I suspect he was just using me as some kind of human shield against Annabel's relentless advances.

'I couldn't possibly leave it all up to Fallon,' he said. 'Maybe next time. I'm so sorry, but I must go now, I have something important to do that can't wait.'

He nipped off before she could stop him and, with a final disparaging glance in my direction, she also went, leaving me standing alone and wishing I had some more cheese. I wandered over to find some, and another drink, and came across Constance, tapping her foot as the band played 'Rockin' Around the Christmas Tree'.

'Hi there,' I said. 'Not dancing?'

'I'm frankly torn between the dance floor and this food,' she said, holding up her plate. 'I can understand why you're so successful if this is the sort of bash you usually put on. Top notch.'

'Thank you. I can't take any credit for the food, Estelle and Coco did everything, but I'm pleased with the band.'

'Local lads, Alexander said? Excellent. They could probably even get some of my colleagues on the floor.'

I filled a plate, and we carried on chatting while we ate. We were just contemplating how many puddings we could sample without drawing attention to ourselves when Sam came over.

'Is everything okay?' I asked, immediately concerned, as always, that something had gone wrong.

'With the party, yes,' he said. 'It's going incredibly well, so maybe we should always plan things a week in advance rather than six months? Less time for problems. No, I just had a message from Alexander that something's up with the Citroën. He was sorry to drag you away from the party, but could you pop over and have a look?'

'Now? Um... all right, I suppose I can go and see. Do you mind, Constance? We were about to have a dance,' I added, for Sam's sake.

'Well, I'd love to dance,' he said. 'Everything's going smoothly, so I think I can join you for a boogie, if you'd like to?'

'Like to, young man? Just try and stop me!' Constance boomed, dragging him off.

Grinning, I put down my glass and started weaving through the partygoers and out of the Great Hall. It wasn't far to go, but the night was freezing, so I grabbed my coat and then headed over to the outbuildings, picking my way over the gravel in my heels and hoping I wouldn't be long: partly because it was so cold and partly because I wasn't sure how much time I wanted to spend alone with Alexander being polite and distant whilst resisting throwing my arms around him and admitting I'd made a horrible mistake.

TWENTY-SEVEN

I hobbled around to the outbuilding where the Citroën was kept and saw that the hatch was open and all the fairy lights were blazing merrily. What on earth was Alexander doing in the garage on the night of his father's engagement party: having some sort of pre-run? Why couldn't it have waited until the next day? It was true, of course, that I was meant to be going in the morning; maybe he had wanted to check everything was set up properly before he was on his own. As I got closer, thankfully now on solid concrete rather than gravel or grass, I saw that there were two wicker armchairs standing outside the van, draped in furry blankets, then I noticed Alexander emerging from the back door.

'Nice touch,' I called to him. 'Is this something you're thinking of for the Christmas Fayre? Nicer than the bistro tables and chairs, but you won't be able to fit many in.'

I saw now that he was holding two extremely pretty cock-tails, in crystal glasses. They were a soft amber colour, with little flecks of gold floating in them, and golden sugar around the rims. He handed one to me and gestured for me to sit down which I did, gratefully. He raised his glass.

'Cheers. Thank you for coming.'

'Cheers. That's fine! What's gone wrong, or did you just want to show me the new chair idea?'

'Neither of those. I'm afraid I got you here under false pretences – with some help from Sam. There's no problem with the van and these chairs are only for us. Are you warm enough, by the way?'

I nodded, confused.

'Good.'

He fell silent and I wasn't sure what I should do. The way he had set up the van, the chairs and the cocktails screamed romance, but I didn't want to second-guess him. I suppose I could have stayed silent myself, but I opted for small talk.

'These cocktails are delicious. Is there cinnamon in them?'

'Yes. I asked Coco to help me come up with something; they're good, aren't they? We were worried you wouldn't approve of cinnamon because it's not locally sourced, but they won't make it on to my regular list. Fallon – I didn't just ask you here to try a new cocktail either. The thing is...'

A whirl of emotion went through me as I tried to look relaxed, as if I found myself in this sort of situation all the time. I considered casually sipping my cocktail, but I didn't want to risk choking on it with nerves.

'The thing is, that, well... I wondered if you would reconsider... us. The truth is that I have fallen in love with you. I couldn't bear to see you leave tomorrow without telling you how I feel. And Theo loves you as well. Even if I was stupid enough to let you go without a fight, the thought of his fury if I didn't give it one more chance – well, I can't even think about it.'

My heart raced as I took in his words. *He loves me!* Then I smiled at the thought of Theo. 'I can see how terrifying that could be.'

'So... what do you think?'

Every fibre of my being was screaming yes, but my reply was pre-empted by a vigorous shiver.

'Oh, Fallon, I'm sorry, it's far too cold to be sitting out here. I thought the blankets would be warm enough, but I'm freezing too. Shall we go inside?'

'What, back to the party?'

'No – unless you want to? I meant inside the van. At least it'll be a bit warmer.'

'Good idea.'

He put the cocktails on the bar area, and we gathered up our furry blankets and hurried inside the van, where Alexander hurriedly shut up the flaps.

'Sorry, it wasn't meant to be like this,' he said, as we hunkered down on the floor on the blankets and he switched on a small electric heater. 'Hardly the grand gestures of *Mayfair Mews* – I should have realised.'

'I don't mind at all,' I said truthfully. 'It's better to be warm and it's very cosy in here with the fairy lights. Maybe you should hire it out for dates? Sorry, sorry, no work talk. Although it's not a bad idea.'

He laughed and wiggled his hand out from the folds of the blanket to reach for mine.

'Fallon, I promise I wouldn't expect you suddenly to be Theo's mother, or to commit to anything you aren't ready for. He adores you, but my reasons for wanting to be with you are entirely selfish.'

'So are mine,' I confessed, then realised that there was something very important I hadn't said. 'Alexander, I love you too. I was silly enough to look for reasons to stop all this happening, but none of them held up to the way I feel about you. And you know I love Theo as well.'

His eyes were glistening with unshed tears, and he cleared his throat before replying.

'I know.'

I edged a little closer to him, as he did the same, the hand that had held mine now moving up my arm. 'But no flowery aprons or pot roasts,' I said warningly.

'I hope not,' he replied. 'Being a mother – maybe even a wife – doesn't mean being anything other than you.'

Now it was I who had the lump in my throat, and I nodded vigorously while he continued.

'Fallon, you've made me feel so loved. You don't care, do you, that I'm not a surgeon anymore?' I shook my head. I hadn't even thought about it. 'See? I can't imagine you pressing me to do my physio so I can get working again, or suggesting a marvellous clinic in Switzerland where they can do wonders for both mind and body.'

'Is that where your ex-wife wanted you to go?'

'Yes. As soon as I came round from the accident, she was trying to get me back in the operating theatre and up in her estimation. I wasn't of any interest to her once I ceased having that role. But I wasn't going to play act for her benefit, just as I wouldn't ask you to do for mine. Just be Fallon.'

We had edged our way so close together now that all I had to do was tilt my head a tiny bit and it was the most natural thing in the world for our lips to meet. The kiss had a beautiful familiarity but also, now, an exciting promise of a future to look forward to.

When we finally broke apart, Alexander smiled at me with such warmth and love that the furry blankets were hardly necessary.

'I wish we could stay here forever,' I whispered.

'My love,' he said, his voice full of emotion. 'We can.' I snuggled closer to him and could suddenly feel him shaking with laughter. 'Well, maybe not on the floor of a mobile gin bar, but you know what I mean.'

I started giggling, too, with the ridiculousness of the joke but also purely because I was bubbling over with such happiness.

'I suppose we'd better get back to the party for now and raise a glass to our parents.'

'We should,' replied Alexander. 'But maybe they can wait just a few minutes more?'

TWENTY-EIGHT

The day of the Christmas Fayre dawned sunny but extremely cold, so taking Runcible out for her morning walk was brief but beautiful. We hurried back through the kitchen door to find Coco putting the final touches to breakfast.

'It looks lovely out there,' she said, piling hot, golden toast onto a plate. 'But it'll snow soon, I'm sure.'

I picked up a tray to carry through to the Buttery.

'Don't say that. The Citroën is good for driving around in decent weather, but it wouldn't make it through snow, especially on some of these roads.'

'You'll be all right,' said Constance, standing up to help as we entered the room. 'If I know this weather, snow won't come until later tonight. The Christmas Fayre finishes at eight, doesn't it?'

'That's right,' said Alexander, his hand brushing mine and sending off the usual fireworks as he took the tray from me. 'All we'll have to do is shut up shop and drive home – we should be fine.'

'I still don't see why I can't stay until the end,' said Theo. 'It's not that late.'

'I know,' replied Alexander, 'but you'll be bored silly by then, I promise. Far better to come chugging off with Fallon and me this morning and leave us with all the hard work later.'

'And anyway,' added Coco, 'I've got a special job for us to do later. That Christmas cake won't ice itself, you know.'

'Can we?' asked Theo, turning shining eyes to her, all thoughts of late nights forgotten. 'And can Runcible help?'

'Of course she can,' replied Coco. 'She can leave little paw prints across the icing, like one of Santa's reindeer.'

'Doesn't sound very hygienic,' said Mum, and we all swivelled our eyes towards her, disappointed, until a mischievous smile broke out on her face. 'But maybe I'll help you bath her first, and then it will be fine.'

'And I will take the photos!' added Estelle. 'You can't leave that one off your Instagram grid, Jacqueline, although Runcible in the bath will steal the limelight.'

Mum smiled.

'I'll concede to sharing it, just this once, and only because it's Runcible.'

I could hardly believe the work that Christmas magic had done. Mum finally falling in love with my quirky little dog was even more unlikely than me allowing my maternal side, previously assumed non-existent, to come out, but both had happened and both unfolded utterly naturally. Or maybe it was these Knight men, I thought, letting my gaze wander over Alexander before moving to Theo and then Douglas. They had such warmth, such acceptance, such clear-sightedness about life and it felt like finally coming home. I doubted that Mum and I would ever have repaired our relationship without them, let alone found our own happy endings.

After breakfast, Alexander and I headed to the outbuilding for our final checks on the Citroën and its contents. Slipping his arm around my shoulder and pulling me close to him, Alexander said, 'I could never have done this without you. Do you think the Christmas Fayre will go well?'

'It will be fantastic,' I said, with confidence. 'It's the perfect place to launch your brand, and remember, you were the one who came up with the idea originally.'

'I know, but even with Hetty's help, we'd never have been brave or innovative enough to do everything you have – buy the van, get all that publicity going.'

'It's my job,' I said simply. 'But I have to say that doing it here, with you, hasn't been much like work, and the perks are somewhat unexpected.'

He bent his head to kiss me, only interrupted by an amused young voice.

'Dad, Fallon, I'm going to have to cover Runcible's eyes.'

It was Theo, of course, carrying my little dog and beaming from ear to ear. Alexander and I held out our arms and they joined us in a warm embrace.

'Are we going soon?' asked Theo, wriggling free. 'Coco said it must be nearly time.'

'It is,' I said, reaching out for Runcible. 'I'll just go and make sure this one's comfortable and then we can be off. Why don't you meet me at the front of the house?'

Five minutes later, Runcible happily installed in her bed in the kitchen, the chugging of the Citroën's engine rose in the distance. As I stepped out of the front door, it came around the corner, Theo waving excitedly. The decals looked fresh and inviting, the paintwork and chrome gleamed, and with such a handsome proprietor and delicious product, I didn't see how the business could fail.

'Budge up,' I said, climbing into the front, and we were off, driving sedately through the beautiful, bleak countryside,

Christmas songs playing on the radio for us to sing along with loudly. Just over half an hour later, we pulled up outside the red brick Victorian town hall, its elegant, spired clock tower and arched windows making it look almost like a church. We were greeted warmly by one of the organisers and shown where to park: prime position by the wooden double doors to catch everyone coming in and out. Our set up was the easiest of all, as we only needed to check our water and electricity, turn on the fairy lights and drop the hatch.

'Let's go and see inside before the Christmas Fayre starts,' suggested Alexander. 'Then when the others come, Theo, you'll know exactly what you want to show them.'

I was surprised to find that the interior of the hall was imposing and had clearly been expensive to create. The floor was covered in small tiles, creating a geometric pattern in terracotta, green, yellow and white and at the far end stood a wide wooden stage, flanked by heavy red velvet curtains. The walls were oak panelled, and the magnificently carved ceiling was also oak. The large, latticed windows let the winter sun pour in, and the whole place was buzzing with people putting the finishing touches to their stalls. An array of goods was on offer, all locally made, and ranged from professional chutneys and jams to adorable hand-knitted dolls. Christmas carols played through speakers and delicious smells wafted through the air: baking from the kitchen, which was open and providing cream teas; festive spices from a nearby stall selling homemade candles; orange and clove from natural decorations covering a nearby tree; and fresh wood from a stall where a smiling man carved intricate Nativity figures and sweet animals. His wife, holding the hand of an adorable toddler with the same mop of curly dark hair as his father and the gentle face of his mother, watched as he worked. This, of course, was where Theo was immediately drawn. Alexander and I followed him.

'I like your animals,' he said to the man. 'Do you do birds as well?'

'Sometimes, although they're tricky. What sort of birds do you like?'

'All of them, but mostly birds of prey.'

'I take commissions,' said the man, looking up at Alexander and me.

'What does that mean?' asked Theo.

'It means I can carve whatever you want,' he replied.

'Oh! You could do Runcible!' exclaimed Theo. 'You'd like that, wouldn't you, Fallon?'

'Who or what is Runcible?' asked the woman. 'A runcible spoon? Lando's made a few of those.'

'She's a dog,' I explained, pulling out my phone to show her a photo. 'She's a bit of a mystery, like Lear's spoon, hence her name.'

'Oh, she's very sweet,' said the woman, then held out her hand. 'I'm Penny, by the way, this is my husband, Lando, and this' – she nodded at the little boy – 'is Billy.'

We introduced ourselves and explained that we would be selling gin outside in the Citroën.

'Maybe you'd bring us one later?' asked the man, grinning. 'This is the first time we've done something like this, so I think we might need it.'

'It would be my pleasure,' said Alexander. 'And you're welcome to come over one day and see where it's made. Are you local?'

'Only recently, and only for a while,' replied Lando. 'We live in Dorset, but I'm up here running a carpentry course – teaching youngsters the craft so that they can show it to others. There's a lot of tree work near here, so we only use offcuts.'

We spoke for a few moments more, and exchanged numbers, before heading back to the van, where we found the rest of the family, as well as Sam, waiting for us.

'Ah, there you are,' said Douglas. 'All ready for the off?'

'Definitely,' said Alexander, squeezing my hand.

'Good. Well, we wanted to do something to mark the opening of your business. I'm so proud of you, son.' He hugged Alexander, and then me. I hugged him back hard. Having never had a father, I could hardly believe that I was gaining such a lovely one. 'Now,' he continued. 'Champagne seemed a bit 'coals to Newcastle' given what you're selling, so we thought we'd keep it simple.'

On cue, they all pulled out what looked like large party poppers, held them up and pulled the strings. We were instantly standing in a glittering white storm of swirling flakes that floated around us before settling to the ground. Theo, who had screamed with delighted surprise, now looked disappointed.

'Oh, it's all melting already,' he said, looking at the floor.

'I'm afraid so,' said Douglas. 'It's all very eco-friendly and only lasts a moment, but wasn't it lovely while it did? And,' he added in a conspiratorial stage whisper, 'I've got plenty more at home so we can refill them and do it again whenever we like.'

There were a few minutes left for hugs and photos before Douglas and Mum took Theo's hands and led him inside, leaving Alexander, Sam and me to open up the Citroën and cross our fingers.

As it turned out, we didn't need any luck: the van was a huge success. From the moment the first customers started arriving at the Christmas Fayre, we were a knockout. Many of them had seen our advertisements and headed for us deliberately; others couldn't resist our festive van and stopped to see what we had on offer. Even if it was too early for many of them to drink alcohol, people were seduced by the flavoured syrups to drink then and there, or by the beautiful packaging to buy bottles for presents. By five o'clock, we had to ask Sam to drive back to the house to collect what we had left there, as we were in danger of running out. I came down to help him unpack the boxes from the car, and he put a hand on my arm.

'Fallon, you've made a huge success of this, it's amazing! But this is probably one of the busiest events we've ever done. I just wanted to check that you're all right? I'm sure Alexander and I can hold the fort if you need us to for a bit; I ran the others back to the house, but Constance said she'd be happy to come back and help. I can give her a ring?'

I hugged him.

'Thank you, but actually I feel fine. And don't worry, that's not my usual "fine" as in "I'm going to run myself into the ground and keep going on adrenaline and caffeine" fine. I'm enjoying myself.'

'Good. Well, just say if you need a break, deal?'

'Deal.'

We carried the boxes to the van, then carried on serving and smiling right until the very end.

'Phew!' I said, pulling the hatch shut before anyone else could plead with us for just one more. 'I think we can call that a success, don't you?'

'I can hardly believe it,' replied Alexander, who looked exhausted, but happy. 'I never dreamed it would go so well. And as well as all the sales, I've handed out hundreds of business cards and flyers to people who want to hire us for their weddings and birthdays. The organiser of that huge country fair even came along, said she'd seen our advertisement and now she'd seen us for real would love us to go to that. We'll be busy for a year. Thank you both so much for all your help.'

'None of that would have been worth anything without you,' I said. 'I think you could start thinking bigger – maybe in the New Year.'

'What do you mean?'

'We could get your gin stocked in local shops, even super-markets – quite easily, I would have thought. Then we can take it from there.'

Sam nodded.

'I agree. You'll be able to sell whatever you can make. It's sensational stuff.'

Alexander shook his head in disbelief.

'And to think this was going to be nothing more than a fun side-line. Come on, let's get home and then we'll finally be able to raise a glass ourselves.'

We secured everything, agreeing to deal with what was left of the washing up in the morning, then Sam returned to Constance's car, which was still here, and Alexander and I climbed back into the front of the Citroën, wending our way sedately back to Blakeney Hall to toast our successful day and then begin to prepare for Christmas, and whatever else the future may hold.

EPILOGUE

A YEAR LATER

The extravagant Christmas decorations bejewelling the York streets made the perfect backdrop to the wedding, as Mum and I once again travelled together in a smart car, sipping champagne. But this time, a year later, how different it was. This time, instead of feeling exhausted and defensive, waiting for the criticism I had come to expect from Mum, I was relaxed and happy and more than able to call her out if she slipped too much into old habits. My next task was to have her keep her opinions entirely to herself, on at least one of the following subjects: my hair, my nails, my make-up, my clothes, my shoes, my food choices... Ah well, Rome wasn't built in a day, and at least she approved of my boyfriend.

We had spent the morning getting ready in her suite at the Grand Hotel in York, with a vast flock of people around us. There was someone for everything: her hairdresser, Linda, three make-up artists, the outfit designer and her seamstress and two photographers and a journalist from *Hello!* magazine as well as Mum's PA and a representative from *Mayfair Mews* to make sure everything was in corporate colours, so to speak. But Mum had insisted that it should only be her and me in the car, so we gave our last smile to the camera out of the window, then sat back with relief.

'I wonder how Douglas and Alexander are getting on?' I said, smoothing my elegant cranberry silk dress over my knees.

'They're probably only just getting dressed,' said Mum, a smile rubbing off the edge in her voice. 'Those Knight men are ridiculously laid-back.'

'And very good for both of us,' I added. 'Who's with them? Not the army we had, I bet.'

'Not a bit of it,' she replied. 'They conceded to one photographer, but otherwise it's Alexander's PA Hetty making sure they look presentable. Mind you, Theo knows what's what, so he won't let anything go wrong; smart boy, that.'

I smiled. Thanks to Theo, Blakeney Hall was now not only home to Heathcliff the donkey but also a kitten that had been found sopping wet and lost on the riverbank, and named Moses, as well as – temporarily, Alexander assured me unconvincingly – an owl that needed regular attention and was spooked by the comings and goings at the sanctuary.

'Home is much more peaceful for her,' insisted Theo. 'She'll *definitely* go when she's better.'

Privately I thought she'd still be firmly in residence long after I moved in just before Christmas; that was an owl who knew a good thing when she saw it, and I related to her completely.

'Do you feel nervous?' I asked, slightly doubtful that Jacqueline Honeywood ever felt nervous about anything.

She turned from the window to look at me.

'I do and I don't. I think I'm more excited than nervous, and I can hardly believe that at my age – still undisclosed to anyone but you and the vicar, darling – I'm getting married.'

'I think most people are surprised it's wedding number one,' I said, grinning cheekily. 'They always expect you to have done the full Liz Taylor and for Douglas to be at least your eighth husband.'

'It's not for want of offers, as they well know,' she replied tartly. 'But I am extremely discerning.'

'I know, and Douglas was worth waiting for.'

'Exactly. And darling...'

She hesitated, unusually for her.

'What is it, Mum?'

Her words came out in a rush.

'I just wanted you to know that, however much I love Douglas, you will always, *always* be the most important person in my life. And you always have been. It was fun this morning, with all the fuss, but I so wanted it to be just the two of us in the car. There's something I want to ask you, and something I want to give you.'

She reached for my hand, and I took hers willingly – what on earth it could be?

'Firstly, I want to ask you if you would do me the honour of giving me away today.'

I gasped, tears springing to my eyes.

'Oh Mum, of course I will. I'd love to. Thank you.'

I saw her shoulders drop as the tension left them; she had been nervous about asking.

'Wonderful. I should have asked you sooner, but the vicar said it didn't matter, you just have to stand up when he gives you the nod and follow his instructions. And this is what I wanted to give you.'

She produced two small jewellers' boxes and handed me one. I opened it to find a ring, with two pink stones entwined in the delicate curves of the metal.

'It's stunning,' I said.

'I have the same one,' said Mum, opening her box to show me. 'They're made of white gold and the stones are pink sapphires. Two of them for you and for me. We love these

Knight men and I know we'll be with them for the rest of our lives, but I wanted to affirm at the same time my commitment to you, my darling daughter. I thought we could wear them on our right hands, as I'm sure your left ring finger won't be far behind mine.'

I was speechless now, grasping for a tissue as my eyes were filling so rapidly with tears that if I wasn't quick, my exquisitely applied make-up would soon be a mess. Mum grabbed one as well and we both dabbed frantically at our eyes as I stumbled out my thanks and love for her.

'I love it, I do, and I will always treasure it. Thank you.'

We hugged tightly, finally interrupted by a discreet cough from the driver who then said, 'We have arrived at the church.'

He stepped out of the car, but, to my surprise, the door at the pavement side did not open; instead, the opposite door opened and Jess, one of the make-up artists from *Mayfair Mews* who had been at the house, slid into the car.

'I thought we would probably both need a quick touch-up before we went in,' said Mum, 'so we're a few minutes early for Jess to do her magic.'

I laughed.

'Pure Jacqueline Honeywood, brilliant.'

As soon as we were declared both picture-perfect and suitably late, the chauffeur was given the nod and opened the door for us to get out. I went first, then stepped aside to let Mum pass as a bank of flashes popped to capture her at her most happy and her most beautiful. And she did look beautiful. She had shunned a traditional wedding dress – '*anyone* can dress up as a bride, darling' – in favour of a style and colour that suited her much better. She wore a knee length dusky rose shift dress with a stunning fitted cranberry velvet jacket which came to mid-thigh and was hand embroidered with spikes of rosebay willowherb for London and white roses for Yorkshire.

When she decided they had enough photos, she turned to take my hand and we walked together through the wooden lychgate of the church, then along the uneven path to where the vicar was waiting to greet us.

'How wonderful to see you!' he said, his face lit up with an enormous beam. 'I don't think Lingfoss has ever seen so many people, and St Josephine's' – he gestured up at the Norman stone church – 'hasn't had such a large congregation in all its thousand years.'

'Thank you for your warm welcome,' said Mum, surprising him with a hug. 'Douglas did so want the wedding to be here, and I know it hasn't been easy doing all the preparations with us coming and going to London all the time.'

Looking slightly starstruck, if vicars are allowed such whimsies, he smiled again.

'Well then, if you're ready?'

The ceremony was perfect and afterwards, when even more photos had been taken, we travelled the short distance down the road to Blakeney Hall, where the reception was being held. I would barely see Mum for the rest of the day, but the fact that she would be busy with everybody else no longer mattered; I knew, I thought, looking for the millionth time that day at the new ring shining on my finger, that no question marks remained over our relationship, or her love for me. As the arrangements for the day had been wholly handed over to an incredible team of wedding planners, there was nothing left for me to do but enjoy myself, and having walked in between Alexander and Theo, how could I do anything else?

The house was, once again, decorated to celebrate both love and the festive season and it looked spectacular. There was a tunnel made of entwined willow branches smothered in thousands of warm golden lights leading to the front door, with a deep red carpet to walk along. The door itself had been dressed with gigantic swathes of oversized baubles in the wedding colours of rose pink, cranberry and gold and in the entrance hall – clear now of its muddle of coats and shoes – stood no fewer than seven Christmas trees. They were covered in sparkling decorations and lights and had piles of wrapped presents underneath them. In the Great Hall, the fireplace was the focus. On the mantelpiece stood dozens of pillar candles with evergreens wound among them and cascading down on either side of the blazing fire. The tables were dressed with rose pink cloths, more candles and fragrant arrangements of white roses, red berries and rosebay willowherb, which was past flowering and swathed with gorgeous fluffy seeds that some enterprising florist must have found a way to preserve for the occasion. A string quartet up on the minstrels' gallery played Christmas music.

The first half hour passed in a whirlwind of hellos and congratulations as I hugged and shook hands with almost everyone at the wedding – or that was how it felt – but I took time to enjoy the rest of the evening. I was glad that I hadn't had to organise it, but the team had done an amazing job. The food was delicious, as I had expected, and also in the wedding colours, with a first course of baked beetroot and goat's cheese, a second of melt-in-the-mouth salmon with creamy potatoes and wild mushrooms, and a pudding of gold dust and rose petal sprinkled chocolate, cinnamon and pear mille feuille, followed by cheese. The string quartet played throughout the meal then, after a pause for the short but witty speeches – including one from Mum, I was surprised and delighted to see the young band who had played at the engagement party take their place on the minstrels' gallery once more and bring all their youthful energy and talent to the room, getting almost all the guests up and dancing. All the cast from *Mayfair Mews* had made the journey up north to be there, even Lucinda, the actor who had been none-too-subtly edged out of the show by Mum for daring to challenge her queendom.

'Fallon, you look *ravishing*,' she greeted me, bumping her cheekbone to mine to avoid any danger of lipstick transfer. 'You must take after your father. *Not* the handsome groom, one assumes?'

'Definitely not,' I said, stifling a laugh, then seizing my opportunity as I saw Coco and her mother nearby. 'But Lucinda, you *must* meet Estelle Knight and her daughter. They're huge fans of the show.'

'Skilfully done,' said a voice next to me, as I moved away.

'Constance!' I hugged her. 'It's been ages. I saw you in the church and I was so hoping we'd find each other here.'

'Quite a do my brother and your mother have put on,' she said, raising her glass to me and promptly having it topped up by a passing waiter in a sparkly rose-gold waistcoat. 'I must say, I could get used to this.'

'I don't believe it for a second,' I said. 'You'd miss your muddy fields too much. Is your son here, by the way? I'd love to meet him.'

'Seb? Yes, he's here, came over specially. He's been deep in conversation with your Sam every time I've seen him. I even spotted them holding hands, so who knows – maybe he'll be tempted back from Japan, and we'll have another wedding on our hands!'

'Oh, that would be lovely!'

'And talking of weddings, you and Alexander can't be too far behind your parents?'

I looked over to watch him as he chatted to Theo and Hetty. 'I don't know Constance – I hope so.'

She snorted.

'Of course you won't be. Good thing too. Good for both of you and for Theo. And how does it feel with Theo?'

'Incredible. I mean, I always liked him, which helped, and he liked me, but we've got something beyond that now. I've still been up and down to London a lot, and he still calls me "Fallon" – I don't know if that will ever change, and I don't mind – but there's a different *feel* to our relationship. Honestly, Constance, I am beginning to feel like his mum.'

'Of course you are. The times I've seen you together this past year it's been obvious, and it's done both of you the world of good. Nice to see him back in school and doing so well. You're moving up here for good soon, I hear?'

'That's right, in a week's time. The Yorkshire arm of the business I started has taken off, so Sam's going to take over most of London, with Talitha and a new hire. I'll be down every so often but mainly running the northern office – it's so exciting.'

'You've worked it out well. Not thinking of giving Theo a little brother or sister?'

I must have looked taken aback, because she quickly apologised.

'Sorry, none of my business.'

I laughed. 'It's okay. We've talked about it... Can I just say, "watch this space"?'

'You don't have to say anything at all. Oh, look, I think the bride and groom are about to head off. Do you have any duties to perform?'

'Only saying goodbye.'

Alexander came over and we walked together through the tunnel of lights to wave our parents off; not in an old banger with tin cans hanging from the back, of course, but in Douglas's vintage Aston Martin. Once the car had turned out of sight and the other guests had rushed back inside out of the cold, Alexander pulled me close to him for a kiss. Much as I enjoyed it, I shivered.

'We'd better get back inside,' he said, taking off his suit

jacket and draping it around my shoulders. 'It's only going to get colder out here.'

As he spoke, a snowflake spun gently past him, to land on the drive and disappear, but it was soon followed by another, and another. I held out my hands and laughed for pure joy.

'Oh, Alexander, it's beautiful! What a perfect end to the day!'

'Actually,' he said, reaching into the pocket of the jacket. 'I was hoping for an even better way to end it.'

And right there, in the middle of a snowstorm, he held out a small box.

'Fallon, you've made me happier than I ever dreamed I could be. The way you love me, and love my son, hardly feels real, and yet here you are. I love you, Fallon: will you marry me?'

A wave of shock and joy almost overwhelmed me as, for the second time that day, I gladly took an exquisite ring, this one for the fourth finger of my left hand, and gasped out my answer: yes!

'Three stones,' I said, looking at the diamonds and ruby. 'One for each of us in our new little family. It's perfect, Alexander, thank you.'

'I'm afraid I didn't ask your mother's permission, but I couldn't imagine her saying no,' he said with a grin.

'She'll be thrilled,' I said. 'Oh, Alexander, I'm so happy.'

He kissed me again, then said, 'There's just one person left, and I know how happy he'll be too.'

'Theo doesn't know?'

'Only that I was going to ask you, but not when, and we have his very enthusiastic blessing. Shall we go and tell him?'

A LETTER FROM THE AUTHOR

Dear Reader,

Huge thanks for reading *Christmas with the Knights*, I so hope you enjoyed Fallon and Alexander's journey to happiness, not to mention Jacqueline's *je ne sais quoi* and adorable Runcible! If you want to join other readers in hearing all about my new releases and bonus content, you can sign up here:

www.stormpublishing.co/hannah-langdon

If you enjoyed this book and could spare a few moments to leave a review, that would be hugely appreciated. Even a short review can make all the difference in encouraging a reader to discover my books for the first time. Thank you so much!

When I sat down, excited to write another Christmas book, it was the character of Jacqueline Honeywood who turned up first, demanding – as you would expect her to – that she appear centrally and fabulously. Joan Collins' Instagram feed provided perfect inspiration for creating her! Fallon is, in many ways, her mother's daughter, although of course she resents this fact – until she realises that it doesn't mean history has to repeat itself. I also enjoyed dreaming up the gorgeous Knight men, both of whom appreciate a strong woman as all heroes should, as well as Theo, who is struggling in the same way as so many children are post-Covid. Constance was a joy as she came striding onto the page, dispensing hearty wisdom and bucking everyone up. I'd gladly spend Christmas with all of them, just as long as I had little Runcible snuggled into my neck and one of Alexander and Fallon's festive gin cocktails in my hand!

Thanks again for being part of this amazing journey with me and I hope you'll stay in touch – I have so many more stories and ideas to entertain you with!

Hannah Langdon

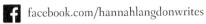 facebook.com/hannahlangdonwrites

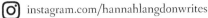 instagram.com/hannahlangdonwrites

ACKNOWLEDGEMENTS

Everyone at Storm Publishing has, again, been completely brilliant in guiding this book from its first draft to the finished copy you now read. Kathryn Taussig, my editor, has shown her usual unerring discretion and judgement in shaping the manuscript to be the best it could be. She also enjoyed my jokes! Thanks are also due to Alexandra Holmes, Amanda Rutter, Catherine Lenderi and Rose Cooper for her totally beautiful, sparkly cover design.

Thanks must go to Mum, Sarah and David for rallying around on the WhatsApp group and providing some suitably corny Christmas cocktail names on a hot day in August. Sarah also did an early edit for me and said lots of lovely, reassuring things – thank you.

Thanks to Alana for reading *Christmas with the Knights* and for all the bookish chat!

Emily was another early reader: thank you for all your encouragement and friendship, as ever.

My thanks as always to John for the kind of support that is understated but immensely valuable. Your generosity in listening to me and patience when I simply *must* scribble down a brilliant idea I had in the shower, before we can even think about supper, is invaluable.

And this time my biggest thanks go to Rose, who loved hearing about the Knights and Honeywoods, but particularly, of course, about adorable Runcible. And I hope she is pleased to see her Meg's/Greggs joke in print!

.

Printed in Great Britain
by Amazon